Forever Andrew

Forever Andrew

Robert J. Wetherall

Paradon Publishing

ISBN: 978-0-936750-24-8

Paradon Publishing Company
4370 Brookside Court
Suite 102
Edina, MN 55436-1438

Library of Congress Catalog Number: 201092 2070

Printed in the United States of America

Dedication

To Ronni, who gave me strength
under fire.

Other Novels by Robert Wetherall

THE MAKING OF BERNIE TRUMBLE

Bernie lives in a world run by women—who make the rules—while the men sit in their man-caves, drink beer and pass gas.

LAST FLIGHT HOME

Watch for publication in Summer 2010. The trials of a country girl from Nebraska who soars to become owner of the world's largest airline.

Chapter 1

My earliest recollected vision is of a brooding row of hills set back from towering rocky cliffs barely visible through a fine morning mist. I can still feel the strong arms of my father about my waist as we stood on the pitching deck of the splendid four-master that was rocking at anchor in the cold wind. I must have been four or five years old at the time. But even at that age I was charged with the excitement that coursed through the ship's crew and passengers who bustled about in seeming disarray as we prepared to step ashore upon this great new land.

"Father," I yelled into his scraggly grey beard, "is this our new home then?"

"That it is, Andy boy, that it is." He squeezed me extra hard and set my feet back upon the deck. "Stay here now 'til I fetch you," he said, and disappeared into a knot of men.

I could smell the salt in the air, mixed with the sweet aroma of cargo from the holds below and the sweat of the sailors whose glistening skin popped with muscles as they cranked winches, hauled lines and manhandled sails that flapped over my head.

It seemed that our trip across the great gray expanse of water had taken months—so much had happened. We had embarked from one shore a tidy little packet of a family: Mother, Father, my older sister, Ella, and myself. We had been battered by storms, blighted by disease, weakened by lack of adequate food and water, and embarrassed by the terrible lack of privacy. The other passengers, simple peasants and farmers for the most part, became surly and unruly as our vessel churned its way through the roiling seas. The same travelers who had been filled with happy anticipation at our embarka-tion soon were transformed into a sullen clutch of brooding malcontents. Then, just a few weeks before landfall, my own family had been reduced to just two of us. Mums and sister had gone to live with the angels, victims, I later learned, of a smallpox outbreak that spread throughout the ship. Although I recall feeling no discernible grief over their loss, my father would say many times later that it was a terrible price to pay for the privilege of traveling to this crude land of savages, op-portunity, and freedom. And even as we felt the English dock under our feet, my father scratched his head at the sight of so many other ships—these setting sail toward the land from which we had just come, America.

∽

That I was carried so far in my father's well-intended search for freedom makes my present circumstances all the more pitiful. My government-issue hospital room is barely large enough to contain a narrow bed, miniscule washbasin, and a toilet that gurgles constantly and makes sleep impossible. Overhead there is a ceiling fixture covered with a heavy gauge steel grate protecting one lonely light (bulb theft must be a real problem around here) which throws a weak glow that would be easily out shown by a sickly firefly's behind. But my guardians have not overlooked my need for mental stimulation and challenge. On the wall over my head, almost out of the reach of anyone but Magic Johnson, is a pathetic little bookshelf held fast to the concrete wall by solid inch-thick steel studs. Perched upon this lofty library of advanced learning is one copy of the Reader's Digest version of The Holy Bible, an old novel by Grace Metalious, a Treasury of Golf Tips, and a Betty Crocker Dessert Cookbook.

After almost sixty days in a place like this you get a bit stir crazy. Maybe that's why I've started thinking about Allison again.

Would it be uncharitable of me to blame my latest turn of luck on Allison? Yes, I suppose it would. After all, that sweet, sweet button of a girl, with her tinkling laugh and bent sense of humor, is unquestionably the high point of my existence. The best among many.

And now that I've had plenty of time to meditate, I realize that I have been taking her terribly for granted for a long time now. In fact, have I ever really paid her her just due—told her explicitly and sincerely how I felt about her? That I even love her? That I would walk over hot coals in flimsy sandals for her? How I truly miss her and how I am remorseful with guilt over how I have mistreated our fragile relationship? Even now, with the reek of the toilet assailing my nostrils, I can still see her, looming vividly in my mind's eye as she was on that day when we first met.

She was dressed in white with a little cap perched on her head, setting off a shiny thicket of blonde hair which fell to the top of her starched uniform collar. She was raising the window shade and looking at me with the palest blue eyes—saucy, impertinent eyes that reminded me of a ravishing vixen whom I had once romanced centuries ago in Barcelona. But that lass, now a wisp of dust in a long-abandoned hillside graveyard, paled in comparison to this young lady, whose perfectly pert nose wriggled and twitched, bunny-like, as if smelling dew-moistened lettuce in the air. She wrinkled her brow in thought, an endearing action that focused my attention on her high, wide cheekbones, set off by a fair and rosy complexion that radiated bountiful good health.

"Is this too much light for you, Mister Merriman?"

I raised myself up, squinting a bit to indicate mild discomfort.

"I can lower it a bit if you like."

"No, that's fine," I said, ever stalwart.

She stood with her back to the window, studying me intently. And, judging by the furrow on her brow and the slight shake of her head, she obviously wasn't too displeased with what she saw: A not unhandsome broad-shouldered youth. Almost twentyish, perhaps. Tousled mahogany mop of hair. Ruddy open face split by an honest well-used grin. Straight nose, wide-set intelligent brown eyes pleasantly distanced from each other. Strong cleft chin dotted with embarrassing adolescent stubble. Indeed, I'm sure I appeared to be so young, vital and nourished that she probably figured I didn't require any serious nursing.

She moved to my bedside, put a thermometer in my mouth and grasped my wrist. The touch of her hand felt deliciously cool and I looked up at the curve of her throat and her barely dimpled chin as she studied the moving second hand of her watch. Abruptly, she released my wrist and removed the slender glass tube from my mouth.

"Hmmmm."

"What is it?"

"No big deal," she said, placing the thermometer in a bedside tray. She moved toward the door, my alert eyes following the movements of her tidy little rear.

"Where's my regular nurse?" I inquired, recalling the image of the stout matron into whose muscular hands I had been first entrusted.

"Miss Lurch has been transferred to another floor. I'm taking her place." The door swung closed behind her as my heart soared. Perhaps my remaining time in that hallowed health care institution could be borne after all.

This particular hospital sojourn had begun four days before when my unconscious form was wheeled into the emergency room aboard a litter carried by two rushing ambulance drivers. They had scooped me off 5th Avenue a few minutes after a taxi, carrying an imprint of my body on its grillwork, had disappeared in traffic.

I had lain unconscious for two days before my eyes popped open in the Intensive Care Ward of Bethany Hospital, an aging pile of stained red bricks on the fringe of Manhattan. I felt bruised and battered but a babbling team of interns from various third world countries informed me that, aside from a few simple fractures, I had not been too ill-treated by the fleeing taxi. Indeed, they were amazed at my recuperative powers, which prompted them to remove me from the critical list and expedite my transfer to a regular bed on the medical floor.

"You one tough cookie, you better believe," said a young mahogany-skinned doctor.

If he only knew.

My run-in with the errant taxi certainly wasn't the first time I'd been in harm's way and survived. In fact, my memory of my very first confrontation with the hooded specter and his long-handled scythe still stands out in my mind. You see, it was also the very first time I began to suspect that maybe I was different from other people on this planet.

It happened on a blazing summer day in the year 1675. The sun burned a hellish hot hole through the blue sky, blistering the countryside around the little settlement of Caesaro, nestled on the Arno River in Central Italy a few days oxen ride from Florence. I remember it was early afternoon. Swirls of dust filled the air, burning my eyes. Oblivious of the heat, I was about my daily business, scouring the narrow streets of our village, collecting rich chunks of dung. Despite my father's work as a bootmaker, we were dirt poor. As a result, we were sure to freeze in the coming winter unless I spent the hot summer days gathering dung for the fires that would keep the chill from the miserable hut we called home.

So I persevered, knowing that I was helping my father, and ignored the taunts of idle village children who hurled epithets as I marched past through the streets, dragging my stinking sack behind me. I smoldered inside. And except for the fact that I was a small and frail eight-year old, I would have not taken their insults with such passive resignation.

"Hey-ho, dung-head," squeaked a ragged urchin. "Wash your hands before you eat your gruel," chanted a slovenly quartet of rough-housing oafs. "Here's a piece of foulness you missed," cried a huge slow-witted girl, setting down a load of wash to toss a brownish clod in my direction. I was not too proud to pick up the dung which ricocheted off my thin brown body.

I ignored the noisy riff-raff, looking neither right or left. And despite my brave silent front, I longed for an end to this daily persecution—and for the day when I could leave the squalid village.

You would think that I would have become accustomed

to such adversity. For in truth, I had known few happy moments since my father and I arrived in the community—the latest in a string of villages where we had stayed briefly and then, for one reason or another, soon left. It was a pattern that had continued ever since we had arrived in England three years before. We had traveled further south, seeking a home of permanence.

And so it was that, deep in thought, head bowed and ears closed, preoccupied with my musings, I failed to take notice of an immediate threat to my routine. A dark band of low clouds had moved in from the north, obscuring the sun and wetting the baked-clay streets with a sudden downpour. The rain increased in intensity and I heard rolling claps of thunder, interspersed with vivid, intense bursts of lightning.

Jolted out of my reveries, I quickly sought a place of shelter. But I was too late. From around a shack twenty meters distant, a rough snorting echoed briefly, followed by a shower of splattering mud thrown up by the hoofs of a huge charging bull, which apparently had torn loose from its tether in a nearby field. I raised my head just in time to see two blazing red eyes, foaming, slobbery lips, and an enormous fuzzy brown and white head, wider than my outstretched arms, charging down upon me. I felt a tremendous blow which simultaneously emptied my stomach and my bowels and, I learned later, flung my body high into the air where it fell to the ground in a broken, bloody heap. It was at this moment that fate stepped in. A terrible crackling rent the air, my body glowed incandescent as a jagged bolt from the sky coursed through me, filling my nostrils with the smell of burning flesh.

I awoke sometime later. Dimly, I could hear the sound of hymns. I squinted into the light of flickering candles and took in the flowered scent of incense. Low moans and anguished weeping flooded into my ears. I tried to grasp the meaning of this. Failing to find enlightenment, I groaned loudly, an act which was met by answering screams and exclamations in many pitches. Then I sighed and lapsed back into unconsciousness.

Some time later I awakened. My father and the village priest were bending over me. Tears flooded from their eyes. Rosaries were clutched in their fists.

"A joyous miracle," said the holy man. My father nodded in weepy silence.

"To survive two demons—the scorn of the bull and anger of the sky—is no small thing," the priest added.

In a matter of weeks, I had regained my strength and my body bore no signs of its tribulations. Of course, it was not lost on me that instead of resuming my life, I really should have been comfortably esconced in a wooden box under the clover in the shabby little cemetary a few leagues from the village. I felt no outpouring of gratitude, but I was absolutely certain that I must be destined for great things, otherwise God would not have spared me. Such is the arrogance of youth.

For the rest of our stay in Caesaro, I suffered no further insults from young villagers as I went about my daily dung collections. Instead, the riff-raff stood back respectfully, allowing me to collect my street treasure unmolested. I also lost my desire for revenge upon these poor souls. This was not due to any charitable feelings on my part but, rather, the practical realization that any vengeful efforts of mine would pale besides the terrible life-long torments already being meted out by Dame Fate upon these pitiful, ragged antagonists.

Eventually, a group of priests was dispatched from Rome to question me about my experience. I answered their questions as forthrightly as I could but they shuffled back to their marbled halls, hardly the richer for my observations. At odd times since my meeting with the bull and subsequent recovery, I would find my father studying me with a look of great wonderment in his eyes. He also began saying daily novenas in the tiny chapel near the edge of town, a habit he maintained for the remainder of our time in that depressing little hamlet.

"My name is Allison MacKenzie," she said, setting the tray on the table in front of me. "And your dinner's getting cold."

I gingerly removed the stainless steel rim to examine the steaming delectables hidden beneath.

"Ah, I can hardly contain my excitement," I cried. "I've been hoping against hope that we'd have these little dented frozen peas again tonight. How wonderful. And just feel this piece of bread. I like it crisp and hard like this—so good for the teeth."

"I'll take it away if you don't want it, Little Mister Smartpants," she said, reaching out for the tray.

"No," I said. "I was just kidding. This is a blessing, really. Imagine, all of this for just 375 dollars a day." I began eating with great gusto.

She frowned and busied herself about the bed.

"When am I going home?" I asked between bites.

"I haven't heard," she said. "Doctor's supposed to make up his mind tomorrow."

"Can't be soon enough for me," I said.

"That goes two ways."

I looked up. She was smiling. "We've treated you all that badly then?"

"No," I said. "It isn't that. It's just that I have a living to make—and I can't do that while medical science is experimenting on me here."

"What do you do?"

"I'm a musician."

"What kind of musician?"

"Hopeless Life."

"Why do you do it if it makes you feel bad?"

"That's the band I play with. Hopeless Life."

"Seriously? Why have I never heard of it?"

Arrogant nerd. "We're not exactly a household name yet. That takes time."

"Sounds like fun," she said. She brushed a loose strand of hair from her eyes. "I played piano once. Classical mostly."

"Why did you stop?"

"I wasn't very good at it, that's all. Seemed like a waste of time. And my father used to get stomach cramps when I'd practice."

"What do you play?"

"Guitar. Lead guitar, actually. I've gotten pretty good at it."

"Is that all?"

"Oh, I used to play a flute, some mandolin and violin. But that was a long time ago. A very long time ago, in fact."

She laughed. "You're not old enough to have done anything a very long time ago."

If she only knew.

"Has your band ever made a record?"

"Not yet. But we've got a great sound so it shouldn't be too long before we hit the big time."

"I'd like to hear you some time. Where do you play?"

"In Jersey," I said. "Place called Toddies." My God, she was an angel of beauty when she smiled.

"I used to live in Jersey," she said. "I moved a couple a months ago to be closer to the hospital. Got to be a real pain getting to work every morning."

"What days do you work?" I asked, angling for what I knew not.

"Monday through Friday twice a month, then Tuesday through Sunday the other two weeks. Nights mostly."

"Not much time for social action then?"

"I don't date patients."

"There's a first time for everything."

"Especially I don't date patients who think they're Darwin's gift to the species."

"Go out with me and maybe I'll show you my guitar."

"God, you think you're hot. Positively molten."

"Well, you can't blame a guy for trying, huh?"

"I can and I do."

She removed the tray from the table and left the room. Mouthy little wretch, that's for sure. I lay back on the bed, imagining how delicious it would be to humble this independent little Miss Nightingale.

Shortly before lights out she returned to the room and approached my bed, lips pursed and frowning in thought.

"Hey, Andrew," she said. "You're getting to be a real mystery man. What's with you, anyway?"

"How do you mean?"

"I overheard a little scuttlebutt in the smoking lounge. Seems the doctors are a bit puzzled by you."

"How so?"

"Oh, some of the things that turned up in your initial exams, plus a few things that have developed since."

"Such as?"

"Oh, something about your dental work. Seems you've got some stuff in your mouth that's really outrageous."

"Oh?"

"Like a bridge one doctor claims hasn't been made since

the turn of the century. In Russia of all places."

"Oh that," I laughed heartily. "I've been asked about that before."

"Another thing. You've got some kind of a brass pin in your femur that apparently was implanted by a technique that's straight out of ancient medical text books."

"Oh yes, that's right." I slapped my knee vigorously.

"What's so funny?"

I made a supreme effort to rein in my giddiness.

"Oh, I'm sorry," I said. "It's just that this has come up a couple of times in the past that's all—and the answers are awfully simple."

"Well, what are they?"

Here it comes again, I thought. God, I get so sick of plugging the dike with lies.

"Well, take the teeth," I said. "A while back, I think I was about twelve or thirteen or so, my folks took me to this old dentist. He was a Russian, and he still performed work like they did in the old country. He was really quite good at it." My chuckle had a hollow ring. "He said that modern dentistry left a lot to be desired. Wow, did it hurt. I do remember that. So much for the mystery, huh?"

I rubbed my jaw in memory.

"But this doctor says that even in Russia, they haven't done dentistry like that for over a hundred years."

"That may be true in the larger soviet cities," I said. "But out in the hinterlands, they're years behind the times."

"What about that work on your leg?"

"Same deal."

"Same deal," she repeated, sucking in her cheeks slightly. "You're not a teenage KGB agent then?"

"I'm not a teenager," I said. "Or anybody's agent for that matter."

"How old are you, anyway?"

I thought a moment—I didn't want to make a critical error.

"I'll be twenty on my next birthday."

"Then you're still a teenager."

She grimaced with triumph and left the room.

The next time I talked to her was about two weeks later, several days after I had been declared fit as a Samurai and was discharged from the hospital. I called her at her apartment one night.

"How did you get my phone number?"

"It's in the phone book, remember?"

"Well, I told you before; I don't go out with patients. Ex or otherwise."

"Well, ordinarily, I don't date nurses. But I'm willing to make an exception this time if you are."

I picked her up in a cab and we went to Fong's for some Chinese.

It was the first time I had seen Allison in something other than a white uniform. She was stunning. Blonde locks splashing over a thick pink sweater, carefully faded blue jeans and white running shoes. Freshly minted American womanhood—ready to be put into a display case. My display case.

"I'm sorry if I seem a little pushy," I said. "I just act that way some times." I sat back to see what effects could be reaped by this earnest display of humility.

"I take it you're not acting the part of an arrogant ass all of the time." She smiled sweetly. "Why don't you just back off a little and stop acting like God's great gift to poor people."

"Am I that bad?" I said.

"Listen, Merriman…"

"Call me Andrew."

"Andrew. You are that bad. You've been acting that way ever since I first talked to you in the hospital."

"I'm sorry then."

"Don't say you're sorry if you're not."

"What should I say then?"

"Don't say anything. Just, maybe quietly resolve to lower your guard a bit. Maybe knock it off with those fast comebacks. You act like you're a standup comedian or something."

"A strange thing happened to me on the way to the club tonight," I said.

She rolled her eyes heavenward. Maybe I'd have to tone down my approach.

A wizened little waiter appeared at our booth, took our orders and left.

"Enough of this gratuitous talk about me and my accomplishments," I said. "Let's talk about you."

She tapped her fingers on the countertop. "Are we through talking about you, then?"

"I certainly hope so," I said. "Over-dosed any unsuspecting patients lately?"

"Ha, Ha," she said. "Not funny. Anyway, I've decided to quit my job. I've been thinking about it for quite a while now."

"What are you going to do?"

"That's my problem. I don't know what I want to do. I'm 19 years old and I just haven't found myself. My Aunt Mary died last year and left me a small hunk of money. I think I'll use it to travel around a bit. Maybe pick up a few ideas."

The food arrived and we fell to eating silently. Just my luck. The first decent girl I've come across over a hundred years and she's decided to leave town.

"What's the matter?" she asked. "You look like your shoes are too tight."

"It's just that you're the first really swell girl I've come across in quite a while—and now you're taking off for parts unknown."

"Really swell, huh? You talk like a museum. Anyway, don't take it so hard. After all, we've only known each other for a total of, say about two hours."

"I get attached to people fast," I said. "A bad habit of mine."

"Well, don't get despondent on me," she said. "I couldn't handle the guilt."

"You gave me excellent care when I needed you."

"I'm a nurse. They pay me to do that."

After we ate we wandered up the avenue, bound for no particular destination, just people-watching and enjoying the cool autumn air. Then we caught a cab back to her apartment where I set about getting an invitation to accompany her inside.

"Thanks for chow mein," she said. "I'm going to have a Rolaids and hit the sack."

"Alone?"

"Alone," she said, shutting the door in my face.

"I'll call you sometime," I said to the thick slab of oak.

I remember returning to my apartment across town, the image of this marvelous, snooty maiden imprinted in my mind.

How could have I known that those simple times with Allison would constitute the last uncomplicated days of my life?

❧

The complications came thick and fast. One fine bright morning I was cleaning spilled beer off my Fender guitar, thinking New Age thoughts, and basking in a soft ray of morning sun shining through my apartment window. A sharp knocking roused me from my rapture.

I opened the door to see two men who looked like models from a Brooks Brothers ad. Grey pin-striped vested suits. Red silk ties. White button-down shirts. Tasseled loafers.

Jehovah's Witnesses, perhaps? I was immediately put on the alert when the one mannikin shoved his foot forward to prevent me closing the door.

"My name is Peters," he said. "We'd like to come in and talk to you for a few minutes."

"Sure, come on in," I said, feeling a fine sweat breaking out over my skin. They entered and I motioned them into a couple of chairs. "How can I help you?"

"I'm Fred Peters, Bureau of Immigration, and this is Reginald Hoskins, representing the United States Treasury Department. We'd like some information, if you don't mind."

"No, I don't mind." My body chemistry began preparing for immediate flight, unloading several cc's of adrenalin from my pancreas and preparing to dump it into my bloodstream.

"What is your date and place of birth?" Peters smiled at me beguilingly.

"Hmmm," I said thoughtfully. "That information isn't too easy to come by."

"How's that?"

"Well, the hospital and the orphanage I grew up in both burned to the ground. It was lightning, I think."

"Where and when did this occur?"

"Oh, let's see," I said, scratching my head. "In Smithville, Arkansas. Summer of '69."

Hoskins stroked his chin. "That's a bit of a coincidence, isn't it? Both the hospital and the orphanage burning down like that." He glanced at his partner, as if inviting him to share in this revelation.

I shrugged my shoulders. "I don't know. I never really thought about it. Why, do you think I committed arson when I was a baby?"

"Of course not," said Peters. "It just would make it awfully tough to track your background."

"Why on earth would you want to do a thing like that?"

"Oh," Peters said with studied nonchalance. "No particular reason. It's just that a few things have come to our attention and we've been asked to clear up some loose ends."

"How loose?"

"Well, according to our records, there are no documents available concerning your family members."

"I have no brothers or sisters."

"But there are no records of your parents, either. No birth records, school records, bank records, employment records. Nothing. We also have no records relating to your past. Employment, tax, school—you name it—you're a complete blank, as if you never existed." Peters looked at me expectantly.

"So?"

"So, it just makes us curious, that's all." The men nodded their head in unison.

"And I take it then that I've broken several laws by not having a background that's conveniently available."

"Let's just say that you're an enigma of sorts. And it's our responsibility in the interest of security to make certain that all of our citizens are properly accounted for."

"That's baloney. Whose security are we talking about any-way?"

"Call it what you like, Merriman. But it's a fact that we want to find out some things about you, with your help—or without."

"May I ask what's triggered this intense interest?"

"Sure you can ask. For one thing, you're a wage earner, are you not?"

"Yes, I am."

"There are no records, state or federal, that indicate that you've ever paid any income tax."

"But that's not correct. I am a stickler about paying taxes. I just use my stage name."

"And that is…?"

"Rod Stewart."

Both men began scribbling furiously. Then Hoskins raised the point of his pencil to his pursed lips.

"You were recently hospitalized?"

"That's correct."

"After you were discharged a hospital staff member con-tacted the local office of the Federal Bureau of Investigation. Seems the doctors found a few oddities about your case, or, I should say, about you. Thought you might be a Russian spy. A member of a special Russkie youth squad, actually."

I shook my head in disbelief.

"Are you?"

"Am I what?"

"A Russian agent?" Both men leaned forward.

This had gone far enough. "Yes, I am," I said. "I'm part of an elite strike force sent to this country to ferret out information regarding the fabrication and manufacture of Barbie Dolls."

Peters jumped to his feet and shook a finger at me. "Don't get smart with us, kid."

I got up and walked to the door, opening it wide. "Why don't you and your partner vacate the premises. I know my rights—and I don't have to put up with this cops and robbers crap any longer."

The men got up and moved slowly toward the door, puffing their chests out and straining the buttons on their wool vests.

"Can we assume we do not have your cooperation then?"

"Assume anything you want to, but I don't have anything to say to you guys. Spy, my rear end. You guys are hallucinating. Now get out of here before I call the cops."

"Don't think this is the end of this," Peters said as they walked out into the hall. "What ever it is you're up to, we'll find out one way or another."

"Give my very best to the spy who came in from the cold, will you?" I said, slamming the door.

"You'll be hearing from us, Merriman—maybe a lot sooner than you think."

So there was one incredible, inane complication. My first instinct was to clear out of town and start up a new life elsewhere. But instead I calmed myself and resolved to forget the episode. Which only proves that sometimes it pays to respect your instincts.

Two weeks later, I was treating Allison to a burger. The talk was a bit on the tense side.

"But what in the world could they want?" she asked. "They acted like you were some kind of criminal or something."

"I tell you, I don't know," I said. One of your doctor pals at the hospital shot off his mouth or something, the feds did some checking, and they're apparently still at it."

"But they said that they had tried to interview you and that you were being uncooperative."

"My buns."

"But why don't you just tell them what it is they want to know? You don't have anything to hide."

I smiled weakly.

"But come to think of it," she went on, "I really don't know anything about you. I mean, we've been out a dozen times, and I don't know much except that, A, you play rock guitar for a living. B, you're as cheap as they come. And C, you think you're the greatest thing to happen to girls since padded bras."

"What else is there to know except that I'm a terrific guy?"

She made a face as if she was going to be sick. But how on earth could I tell her anything substantial about myself—without spinning another ugly web of lies? I was sick and tired of lying to people. Especially her, since she had been open and candid about her own private life.

When she relaxed and talked about herself, her tone changed and her personality softened. Her eyes brightened with reflection and she scrunched up her face as she tried to sort out the past. Then words came faster and faster as she talked excitedly about her future in a rushing torrent of expectation.

She sat with both elbows propped up on the table, her chin cradled in her linked hands, those big beautiful eyes never wavering from my face.

She had been born in Kalamazoo, Michigan, the only daughter of a mother who never set foot out of the kitchen and a father who spent most of his waking hours with his face buried in the sports section.

"Oh, my parents were nice enough," she said. "But somehow, I never really felt connected with them." She reddened slightly. "Sounds horrible, doesn't it? Maybe I'm not being fair to them when I talk like that."

"No," I said. "I can see what you mean. You can have people close to you all the time and still feel kind of, you know, apart."

She nodded. "They're your parents and you love them—but there's kind of a detachment, somehow. Course, I even felt that way about my most of my friends, too. So I guess maybe if there's a fault to be found, I have to share it." She smiled grimly, as if facing up to bad news.

"I've been there," I said. If she only knew how much—

and how long—I had been there.

After high school graduation, she left home with a girl friend, Emmy Lou Anderson, climbing aboard a Greyhound bus that dropped her off a day later in New York City. Emmy Lou lasted one month before she fled the city and returned to Kalamazoo.

Allison stuck it out, attending nursing school on tuition money sent by her parents. Three years later, she got her first job at Bethany Hospital. It wasn't long before the nursing life started to pale—and the money left to her by her aunt was the escape hatch she needed to start a new life somewhere where there were no bedpans, doctors or sick people.

During all of this time, her life had been virtually bereft of companionship—outside of a brief temptation with an instructor at nursing school—and she chalked this up to her odd hospital hours. But she didn't dwell on this void and observed that "there is plenty of time for that and besides, when it happens, it happens."

It was clearly up to me to show her that she had finally met the man who could light a raging fire in her veins.

"Just your typical girl-grows-up type story," she told me. I thought I saw a certain wistfulness in her eyes.

My gaze drifted over her shoulder to a figure sitting in the shadows of a corner booth. There was something familiar about him but I couldn't place it. My concentration wavered as we talked. My eyes returning to the corner booth. Where had I seen that face before? The man was in his mid-fifties,

ebony hair, elegant high-boned face, bottomless eyes that
pierced and probed like the cherry tip of a hot poker. Looking
for all the world like a knight of regal bearing, except for the
casual sweater-and-slacks combo he was wearing. Where, oh
where, have I seen you before? The answer eluded me.

Then, as if the sheer intensity of my thoughts had bur-
rowed into his brain, the man's attention shifted from the view
through the window of the crowded street and he turned to
look about the restaurant. His eyes tracked the motley crowd
of burger eaters, then came to rest on mine. And then I knew.
The realization struck me with mighty force, a jarring, blinding bolt of recognition that flooded my senses, sent a cold chill
down my spine and weakened my bowels.

"My God," Allison said, looking behind her then back at
me, "what's the matter with you? You look like you're going to
throw up."

My mind froze and I could not answer. Instead, I got up
and headed for the door, my thought processes in a tumult of
confusion. I had to get out of that place. In my haste to get up
I knocked over our table, spilling Cokes and stray french fries
to the floor.

That face. It was impossible. Maybe it was just someone
who resembled him. No, that would be too easy. But it simply
could not be. But as I rushed out of the restaurant, oblivious of
the stares of customers whom I rudely brushed aside, I knew
in my heart of hearts the awful truth. The man in the corner
was exactly whom I feared him to be. Of course it had been

many years since I had seen him. And therefore I became aware
of two startling and awful facts:

First, I was not alone in my penchant for longevity. There
was another who was as I was.

And second, that he had steadfastly tracked me down
through the milky mists of time for over 200 years was frightening evidence that a heart bursting with rage and hate can
surmount any barrier in order to quench its thirst for bloody
vengeance.

Chapter 2

I was dumbstruck with conflicting emotions as I fled from the restaurant and disappeared into the crowded street, leaving Allison stranded and alone in a state of shock. My senses were blinded by confusion and unanswered questions. How could this person, this specter from my past, still exist? Why hadn't he died and rotted like everyone else, turning to dust to settle upon polished side boards and dining room tables? Was his hatred for me so strong that it galvanized his life force, enabling him to defy death? Was I then not alone in my long-living? Was he a me?

If so, were there others of us out there? This was not even credible! But then, was I credible? God, my soul cried out for answers. More than ever, I could see that my Gift was indeed a Curse, especially now that I was the prey in a pursuit that had endured down through the centuries.

This revelation stunned me. Throughout great chunks of passing time, I had almost succeeded in taking my situation for granted, as if it were an accepted law of humankind that I should be the Chosen One. That the powers on high would favor me with life unending. That while my fellow humans would live, die and rot, I, for whatever reason, would live on, and on, and on.

But wait. What could be more natural? Was I not superior and therefore deserving of Bonus Days? How smug and casual I had grown, normalizing my situation, as if perhaps I were the lucky winner of a grand and glorious Sweepstakes of the Universe. The lucky winner is Andrew Merriman! Grand Prize: Unending Life Span, complete with Deluxe Accommodations, Selected Meals and Sightseeing.

Now, I could see more clearly than ever that there was much more to this than I had ever dreamed possible. And that my existence, for the very first time, was finally being threatened. Thanks to the appearance of my adversary from out of the past, I could perspire, shake, sweat and seethe with anxiety—exactly like the rest of you ordinary mortals.

I returned to my apartment, slammed the door, grabbed a cold Coors from the refrigerator and threw myself onto the lumpy sofa. Here I was, up to my armpits in complications again: The government nosing into my business. An implacable enemy from the past hot on my trail. An innocent girl besieged with grave questions about me. I made a mental note to call her as soon as I had sorted things out.

So far as the government's pathetic trenchcoat boys were concerned, I wasn't too worried. I had aroused the suspicions of the high echelons more than a few times in my past, and I felt confident of my ability to put out any fires ignited by a curious bureaucracy.

But my other adversary was another matter entirely. Even now, I expected him to break down my apartment door, fall upon me, and begin tossing my body parts out the window to the streets below. Did I do anything to earn such enmity?

My dream of leaving the wretched little village on the Arno came true at long last—a few days before my fifteenth birthday when, following the death of my humble father, I struck out in search of a new life. As my talents to that date had been limited to the rather narrow activity of dung collecting, I was well aware that it might be difficult to elevate my station in life. But filled with the bountiful enthusiasm of youth, I looked to the future with great hope and excitement.

And so it was that my travels criss-crossed the continent as I tried my luck at sundry vocations: Blacksmithing in France; Oxcarting in Germany; I even tried to follow in my father's footsteps by taking up bootmaking. I gave this up when after I presented an English Earl with expensive boots I had been commissioned to cobble for his grand wedding. The boots were truly beautiful but, alas, they were both for the right foot. I was sentenced to receive thirty lashes—and I can still feel the sting of the leather thongs upon my bleeding back.

Bidding adieu the green countryside of England, I returned to the warmth of the south where I knew people to be more relaxed and tolerant—and where such a trifle as ill-fitting boots would not be viewed as an absolute calamity.

As I look back I can see that this period of my life was embryonic, a testing of the waters, as I struggled to fit my self into the scheme of things. This process was hastened one day by my chance street meeting with Rinaldo Arrivano, the layabout son of an officer of the court King James at Madrid. Rinaldo was effeminately beautiful with a mane of dark curly hair, flashing dark eyes, large white teeth, and a pencil-thin mustache, Taking a liking to my quaint peasant ways, Rinaldo took me into his employe and, as it developed, gave me the base from which I could bring order to a tenuous existence and begin to prosper. Several years at Rinaldo's side polished my manners and educated my senses. Through dint of discipline and a keen intellect, I left the lower classes behind and matriculated toward the higher echelons where I sampled life, love, and lechery. When poor Rinaldo died, racked by consumption and addled by syphilis, I was at last in a position to guide my own affairs—save for one confounding matter: My damnable youth. Here I was, a mature male in all intellectual respects—while physically I continued to look the part of a callow youth. How confusing!

By this time I had become a boy wunderkind—the owner of a counting house, and renegade banker of sorts, strictly legal mind you, whose services were required by wealthy patrons who wished to enshroud their delicate financial activities in secrecy. I was discreet. Despite my youthful appearance which stunned clients upon our first meeting, I was trusted. My fortunes were building. What more could a soul ask?

Now, you ask, how long did this total transformation take—this matriculation from dung-collecting village boy to young man of consequence? It took thirty years. And so it was that by the time I had reached this stage I was close to 50 years old, and therein lay the problem: My features were those of a young man of 20. Of course, this caused no problems initially. In fact, I had grown accustomed to my associate's jovial banter:

"Merriman, you rogue, you're positively ageless. How do you manage this boyish countenance?"

Such jibes were well-intended and playful but as time passed I detected a certain suspicious note rising in the midst of the choruses:

"Come, Merriman, what is your secret anyway? Have you unearthed the Fountain of Youth?"

I must confess that I had my own unspoken questions as well. My miraculous recovery from grievous wounds inflicted by El Toro remained fresh in my memory. And I couldn't help but notice that as my associates and friends began growing frail with age, I remained vigorous with ruddy good health.

And so it came to pass that the Prince of Death came into my life to chill my bones, like a cold midnight wind off a Scottish moor.

His real name was Prince Edwardo Scarlatti, and when I first saw him, sitting listlessly in front of a glass of cognac at a restaurant on the Boulevard Cirese, he looked much the same as he did when he materialized centuries later at the Burger Palace in New York. A tall, strapping tower of a man, bristling with strength, a glistening cap of dark hair, pasty white pallor, eyes that blazed like glowing embers when the light struck his pupils just right. His lips were a blood red slash across the silky smooth face under a large eagle's beak. A black cloak was draped over his shoulders and his hands, thrusting out of his sleeves on the table resembled talons: long thin shafts of fingers that curved, ending in shapely nails. One could almost imagine those talons clutched about a slender throat, squeezing hard, the nails, wetted by running blood, cutting deeply into helpless flesh. In short, he made Count Dracula look like a simpering wimp.

Unfortunately for me, I was paying less attention to the Prince than I was to the person sitting across from him—a young girl in the bloom of womanhood, with bronze tresses, flawless complexion of ripening peaches, green jeweled eyes that sparkled and caught the light like hanging crystal. She looked restive and bored, turning her pretty head this way and that, glancing about the room, testing the air like a chipmunk.

So taken with her was I that my bold eyes had wills of their own, refusing to remove their gaze from her loveliness. It was inevitable that her room-searching glance should at last link with mine. And so it was that my barely-contained lust spoke volumes to her from across the room and on the way out, as she and her companion took their leave, she dropped a shred of foolscap on my table as they passed by.

Late that night I entered her chambers in the Prince's magnificent home located across from the Gardens of the Palace of Arts. Buoyed by her assurances that the Prince was away with his young daughter and three sons, I showered her with compliments and attention, making it clear that, as a woman of shattering beauty, she deserved far more from life than the attentions of her aging husband. Swayed by my blandishments, it was only a matter of moments before she offered me her hand and led me toward the great circular bed in her room, a few paces from the Prince's own quarters. Imagine my astonishment when, just as I enfolded my beauty in an enraptured embrace, the door to the room swung wide and the imposing figure of the Prince strode into the room.

"What obtains?" he cried. I stumbled from the bed and snatched remnants of clothing off the cold tile.

In my haste I knocked over a large oil lamp and its liquid flashed a flaming path across the room. The terrified young woman, cowering over the Prince's thundering admonitions, struggled to clamber out of bed. Unfortunately, she lost her footing on the now slippery floor, skidded across the room and toppled out the large open window. Even as I heard her thin wail dashed into silence on the rocky ground many feet below, I could feel the exquisite tingle of a thin blade, skewering my chest. My eyes took in the vision of the Prince, standing over me, lancing and re-lancing my helpless unclothed body. Then I lapsed into sweet unconsciousness.

Of course, I should have died. Instead, like an old joke, I awakened. The smiling face of a Sister of Mercy looked down upon me and I could feel the soothing coolness of a damp cloth across my brow.

As I recovered, stealthy visits by a few friends kept me informed about the havoc wreaked by my evening tryst. They told me they had found my body lying near that of the girl outside the building where my aggressor had thrown me and had whisked me off in secrecy to a convent. Of course, the young woman had been killed in the fall. Worse still, the fire had consumed the beautiful residence, snuffing out the lives of the two of the Prince's three sons, his sister, mother, father, and three brothers.

The Prince was engulfed by such staggering grief and rage that he had gone berserk and had to be forcibly chained and dragged off to the lunatic asylum. There he lay in a filthy cell that reeked of sour straw and rat feces, his only seed of happiness sown by the knowledge that he had brutally stabbed the life out of my disgusting body.

But here I was: Perky. Resolute. Radiating improving health. Although run through to a fare-thee-well, my body, for whatever reason, had thrown off death's torpor and was busily mending itself, plugging unsightly blade slits and rebuilding broken arteries and bones.

My presence among the Sisters was kept a secret and I remained in their good care for several weeks. During that time, they treated me with the respect due a Lazarus.

Finally, I was able to leave the convent, healed and healthy. I closed my counting house, gathered up my assets and fled Madrid in the middle of a moonless night in a fast carriage, confident that my troubles were behind me and that I could start up a new life anywhere I pleased, with the Prince's enraged bloodshot eyes banished forever from my memory.

And now, centuries later, comes the knock at the door.

I shook off my haunted reverie, arose from the sofa and walked to the door, filled with trepidation and anxiety. Should I yank it open, fall on my knees and beg for mercy? Should I thrust out my chin with courage and sock him a few good ones? After all—I am not exactly a pipsqueak. But what if the Prince had brought along his trusty lance? Maybe I could throw Smudge, my feisty Siamese, at him and let him run the cat through while I expedite a strategic getaway.

I could feel a slight trembling along my spine and a queasy feeling in my stomach as I yanked open the door.

"You stupid jerk."

Allison brushed me aside and swept into the room where she stood glowering, hands on hip, tapping her foot in the classic pose of the disgusted.

"What do you mean, running off like that and leaving me stuck back there?"

"Huh?" I bleated, stalling for time.

She threw her purse onto the sofa, churning up a cloud of dust.

"Don't 'huh' me," she said. "You know what I'm talking about. You started acting weird, like you saw a ghost or something, then you run off to who knows where. What's going on anyway? You owe me an explanation, Merriman, and it'd better be good."

"Nothing big," I said. "I just happened to see a bass player that I owe a lot of money to. He said he'd break my legs if he ever got his hands on me."

"Bass player? Are you sure you're not caught up in some gambling mess or something? Answer me!"

"No I'm not caught up in any gambling mess. It's just too complicated to go into, really."

"This guy you refer to. You don't happen to mean that Bela Lugosi creep who followed you down the street, do you?"

I tried to remain cool but she saw my deep swallow.

"He followed me?"

"It sure looked like it. And he looked like a left-over from an old Frankenstein movie."

I sat down on the sofa and shook my head.

She sat down at my side and put her hand on my shoulder. "Now tell me, what's going on here." Her voice was several decibels softer. "If it's just money you need maybe I can help you."

"Thanks anyway," I said. "But you can't help me out of this one. Besides, I wasn't being quite honest. It isn't money he's interested in. It's me."

"But why would he be after you?"

"For something I did a long, long time ago." The memory made me shiver.

"Well, it couldn't be so serious as you're making it out to be. Maybe you're over-reacting. Maybe this thing—whatever it is—has been building up in your mind and you're making a big deal out of a little deal. Gee, maybe he wants to let bygones be bygones."

Her face was enshrined in hope. Such blessed naïveté.

"Fat chance," I said. "He'd like to rip my arms off and club me over the head with them."

She shrank back and covered her mouth with a hand. "But what could you have done that would get anyone so mad?"

I frowned and pursed my lips, like a small child kissing an ugly aunt.

"Well, what?"

"I'd rather not go into it."

"You'd rather not. Well, then I guess I can't help you after all." She picked up her purse and stood up. "If you're going to keep all of this to yourself, what ever happens is your own darn fault. I wash my hands of it. You can just go ahead and suffer for all I care."

She flounced toward the door.

"I murdered his family," I said.

She stopped and turned. Somewhere nearby, I heard a pin drop.

"You what?"

"I was responsible for the deaths of several people whom he loved. You could call it an accident, but still the fault was mine. All mine."

She returned to the sofa and sat down, hands tightly clenched in her lap. I could tell by her face that her brain was having a tough time believing this message from her ears.

"Tell me about it," she whispered.

I told her about it, hitting what I thought were only the highest of high spots, leaving out such nuances as dates, titles, places and building descriptions. When I finished she shook her head.

"That's incredible," she said. "But there's something I don't understand."

"What?"

"This lamp you accidentally knocked over. Why on earth would anyone have an old oil lamp in their bedroom? And why was this fellow carrying a sword of all things? Sounds right out of the Middle Ages to me. And who ever heard of someone carting off a wounded person on a horse of all things. I mean, that's what ambulances are for."

She looked at me steadily. I answered with a few silent blinks.

"Well?"

"It happened a long time ago."

"How long is long?"

"You wouldn't believe me if I told you."

"Try me."

"A coupla hundred years?"

"Go stuff it, jerk."

I could feel the sharp gust generated by the slamming door as she stomped out of my apartment.

Chapter 3

I didn't mind being called a jerk. In fact, I had been called much worse things by all manner of persons who, down through the years, had insisted that I "speak the truth" to them. My special brand of truth never did sit very well with them because it sounded so, so <u>un</u>truthful.

No, what bothered me was the sheer frustration of wanting to speak honestly, but knowing that however sincere I was, I would not be believed.

There were a few exceptions to this. In fact, several years after my flight from Madrid I found myself in the uncomfortable position of having to "speak the truth" to someone I cared about. In this case, it was dear Sofia, a kind woman of generous spirit whom I met while doing business with her father in Florence. By this time I had withdrawn completely from the world of high finance, since my success in that world of wise and mature practioners only served to accentuate my youthful image. Instead, I had taken up music as my new vocation and presently was established as a lute player. Sofia's father, Municifio Delarge, was a wealthy merchant who, having made his mark on life's business ledgers, now dabbled mostly in hot-blooded horses and women. I readily accepted his offer to provide the music at the wedding of Maria, his eldest daughter.

It was at that gala affair that I met Sofia, who had just turned fifteen, and who became my first wife. We lived together for more than four decades and, although she bore me no offspring, I remember those years as among my happiest. And we would have remained in this state of bliss had it not been for the advancing ravages of age—upon her, not me. One day she confronted me:

"How is it, Master, that you remain sprightly and vital, with skin like that of a baby's fine bottom—while I myself resemble a rotting prune?"

"Take heart, my dear one," I said. "I love you for your kind heart and beautiful soul—not your flesh. Although I do think you do yourself a grave injustice."

I hoped she would drop the subject but she pressed on, asking me to tell her my secret. And so she literally wore me down, and finally I told her the "truth." I told her that as of that date, I was almost one hundred years old—and that, so far as I knew, I would never look older than I did at that time. No sooner had my explanation escaped my lips than she uttered a shrill cry of disbelief.

"What madness is this you speak?" she cried.

Shrugging, I drew forth my pistol and thrust it toward her.

"Here, see for yourself, my love. Pray, take aim and shoot me."

She screamed again. "You have been taken by the devil, indeed."

"No," I smiled reassuringly. "Do as I say. Take aim and dispatch a ball into my heart and let me prove to you that I cannot be claimed by death."

She stood utterly transfixed so I reached out myself, pressed her finger to the trigger and squeezed.

The shock of the lead shattering my chest sent me sprawling into a corner. But, like Joe Louis in the first Schmeling fight, I slowly picked myself up from the floor.

"You're bleeding! I have killed you!"

"Not to worry," I said, pressing a lace handkerchief into the ugly hole in my vest. "Just kindly take me to the doctor so that he might remove the ball and stitch up the hole. I'll be right as rain, I promise you."

The doctor, as if in a trance, stitched up my chest. Then, scratching his head and muttering, he sent me home with a large packet of laudanum. True to my word, I recovered in a few days.

Sofia was never the same again. I had told her the truth—and she believed me. But she could not live with the knowledge. She told no one of the incident, but shrank from my presence and made excuses to avoid my company. Several years later, old and shrunken, she died. Under the suspicious eyes of her friends, I, the "young" husband, friendless and harried by rumors of every description, made plans once again to seek a new life elsewhere.

Now, here I was faced with the same situation—torn between telling all and losing Allison or telling nothing and losing Allison. I could see no clear way out of this predicament. As it developed, Dame Fate was about to stick her thumb into my plum pie. Ever since I had layed eyes on the Prince, I had been looking over my shoulder. A few days after Allison and I had our tête-à-tête at my apartment, I was driving away from the curb in front of Toddies where we Hopeless Lifers had just completed our nightly four-hour gig. I had just pulled out into the street when I noticed the appearance of a small circular hole in the side window of my VW, a few inches ahead of my face. At first I thought it was just some dumb kid's mischief with a slingshot. Then by the light of a street lamp I caught sight of a grinning figure in the doorway of a brownstone across the street. No mistake, it was the Prince. Obviously he was toying with me. For sure, if he had bothered to track me down through all these years, and if he knew anything about me at all, he wouldn't be counting on snuffing out my life with anything so clean as a bullet through the head. No, he had something else in store for me.

Trying to maintain a semblance of calm, I stopped at an all-night grocery store and filled a shopping basket with my nightly diet of Little Debbies and Fritos, my mind racing all the while. When I finally returned home, the jangling of the telephone greeted me.

"I guess we have to talk again."

It was Allison. And I could tell by her voice that something was up.

"What's wrong?"

"Those men were back here today," she said.

"What men?"

"Those government people. I've been trying to reach you all night. I think they're on their way over to see you. "

"What for?"

"I don't know," she said. "They're very vague but whatever it is, it sounds big. And very mysterious. That's why I want to talk to you again. It was something they said."

I heard a shuffling outside my door, then a loud knocking commenced.

"Whups," I said. "They're here now. You going to be around your place a while?"

"I guess so."

"See you later," I said, hanging up. I wasn't overly concerned as I went to the door. After all, what could these bozos want with me, anyway? Well, whatever it was, I could handle it, that's for sure.

I opened the door a few inches and saw the familiar faces of Heckel and Jeckel—the two guys who tried to waltz me around a few days before. Only now, their fists were filled with silver .38 Smith & Wessons.

"Open wide, Goldilocks, or we'll start huffin and a-puffin," one of them said. I backed away from the door, reaching for sky as they say. They followed me into the room.

"Don't you guys ever sleep?" I asked.

"We've got two warrants here, smartmouth," Heckel said, waving two pieces of paper in my face. "One for searching, the other for arresting. Now sit down and shut up."

For the next several minutes they rummaged through the apartment in a frenzy, pulling out drawers and dumping the contents onto the floor, prowling through cupboards, sticking their hands into coffee, flour and sugar tins, even frisking my clothes in the closets.

Finally I asked, "Is this really necessary? If you tell me what you're looking for, maybe I can help."

"Shut your face, wiseapple," was the response.

Finally, they emptied the contents of the drawers from my cherry wood desk onto the living room carpet and stuffed assorted papers into an official-looking briefcase—the heavy leather kind with the big buckle on the top that mafia attorneys lug into courtrooms.

That done, the shorter of the two men reached toward the back of his belt and drew forth a sparkling pair of chrome handcuffs.

"Give me your hands," he snarled.

"Now wait just a minute," I said, edging back onto the sofa. "You can't just cuff me and haul me out of here in the middle of the night. What's going on, anyway?"

"I'll tell you what's going on, sonny-boy. We've got a court order that says you're to be held in custody as a national security risk. I don't know what-all you've been up to, but the folks downtown say you must be somebody real sinister."

"Sinister?" I repeated, blinking rapidly. "That's ridiculous. You guys are making a big mistake, that's all I've got to say."

"I love it when these Trotskies quake in their boots," one of the men cackled. "It's the only fun I get out of this job."

"Come on," said the other. "Let's put these little cuffies on and you can tell your story downtown."

He reached over to snatch one of my arms and I went limp and fell to the floor. The sound of my head striking the oak planks made a delicious sound, like the cracking of a Christmas walnut.

"Damn-it-to-hell," I heard one of the men say. "He's fainted. Let's get the special squad with a stretcher and lug his buns out of here."

As I lay there, I considered the situation: First, I realized that the government watchdogs had continued probing into my background. And obviously what they found or didn't find was enough to convince them that something was flashing 'tilt'. Maybe they had picked up some scattered crumbs on the trail of my past lives—and realized that it was impossible for me to be who I claimed to be. That alone would convince them that I was certainly up to no good.

Well, no matter, I thought, I certainly had no intention of

playing the patsy. I would simply go along with this a few steps further, pray to the gods that there was at least one honest lawyer left who would agree to represent my interests, and see what happens. After all, I was secure in the knowledge that I had done no wrong and that justice was on my side.

With that realization ringing in my heart, I immediately ceased my play-acting fainting spell and sat up.

"Forget the stretcher," said one of the men. "He's coming to now." He looked at me and grinned. "Sensitive young fellow, aren't we? Now quit stalling and let's get a move on."

The shackles were clamped about my wrists and I was half shoved and dragged out the door and down to their blue Chevrolet Lumina on the street below. They pushed me into the back seat, clambered into the front and we were off in a chorus of screeching tires. I sat back and rubbed my wrists, trying to maintain circulation around the tight handcuffs.

"Are these shackles really necessary?" I said. "I certainly have no plans to engineer some kind of moonlight getaway." I held up my hands.

The two men looked at each other and one nodded.

"Okay, buster. But one false move and you make our bad-boy list, got it?"

He reached over and unlocked the cuffs. I smiled gratefully and tried to restore the circulation in my wrists.

"Will I be able to call my lawyer when we get downtown?" I asked.

"You got to be kidding," said the driver. "This is a security

matter, not a police case. We don't need any lawyers compli-
cating things."

"But that's not even legal," I exclaimed. "I know my rights."

"Yeah, you said that before, remember?" The driver winked
at his companion. "But I'll tell you something: Your rights ended
when you got into this car."

"Yuk-yuk," said his companion.

I couldn't believe my ears. Nor could I believe the sight of
that City of New York garbage truck speeding through the red
light at the darkened intersection ahead.

"Christ!" shouted one of the G-men. The car braked vio-
lently, swerved, and amid a cloud of flying glass and ear-pierc-
ing screaming steel was pushed up onto a sidewalk into a store
front.

I peeked over the front seat and saw the two blood-cov-
ered men slumped against each other, unconscious. The door
next to me popped open, beckoning me to take leave. I did so,
picking my way carefully through the twisted wreckage which
resembled the aftermath of an air raid. A few shocked onlook-
ers inspecting the havoc paid me scant attention as I dusted
myself off and, apparently none the worse for my knocking
about, took off down the street in a moderate jog.

Chapter 4

Sweating profusely and gasping for breath, I knocked on Allison's door less than an hour later.

"What's happened to you?" she asked, her eyes as big as coffee cups. She took me by the hand and led me into her kitchen. "You look like you've been in a terrible accident. Are you hurt?"

Trying to catch my breath, I managed a wan smile.

"What have you been running from?"

At last, my pulse slowed and I was able to squawk out a few answers. She listened silently, her face reflecting a variety of emotions: disbelief, shock, anger, fear—to name a few.

"But I don't understand," she said. "If you haven't really done anything, why would the government be after you? After all…"

"Where there are fumes there are flames," I said helpfully.

"Something like that," she said.

"Well, I tried to tell you before and you wouldn't listen. I know it's bizarre but it's the absolute truth."

"Oh, come off it," she said, rising and pacing the narrow limits of the room. "That bull about that man being after you for something you claim to have done at least two centuries ago. Get serious, Andrew. What do you take me for, some kind of chump? But it's not the blatant child-like lie that bothers me so much. It's the fact that this crazy charade of yours has brought these secret agent characters to my front door. I mean, if you want to insist on living a fairy tale, go ahead. But leave me out of it. I don't want to be involved—and I don't need to have the government bothering me because of some miserable stories you're spreading around. I don't know what your motives are but you can stop this nonsense right now."

She dropped onto a kitchen chair and stared bullets.

"I don't need it," she said, with emphasis.

I shrugged.

She frowned. "And now here you sit in my apartment in the middle of the night with probably the whole U.S. government after you. I'll probably be arrested for hiding a fugitive or something."

"The only reason I'm here is that you said you wanted to talk to me. Now what was all that about?"

"Oh," she said, a bit subdued. "I guess I did say that, didn't I? Well, it's just that the last time I talked to these two men from the government, they said something that got me wondering."

"What was it?"

"Well, the tall guy said their department had gotten permission to open some safe deposit boxes of yours. He said they found all kinds of interesting stuff. Valuable antiques, I guess."

"Talk about nosy."

I had to give them credit. Somehow they had traced me to various banks around town where I stashed my more valuable assets: Jewels from various periods, antiques of precious metals, letters penned by famous people who had long since turned to dust, and art objects created by simple craftsmen who had become revered and illustrious by the mere passage of time. The contents of the boxes were my emergency cache, consisting mainly of items which could be easily converted to cash when the occasion necessitated.

"They wondered how you could have come into possession of such things at your age, or if you were involved in art thefts or smuggling or something. He said some of the stuff had been reported stolen years ago and that it was a very common method of payment used by intelligence operations, spies and the like."

She looked at me with questioning eyes. "Are all those things really yours, Andrew?"

"Yes, they are. And government or no government, they had no right to get into those boxes, the contents of which have been confiscated I suppose."

"But how could you get ahold of these things? They said they were probably worth millions and millions of dollars, Andrew."

"Yes," I said. "That is an interesting question, isn't it?" A sigh of utter frustration escaped my lips. "How could anyone come into possession of such a treasure? Well, maybe now you'll listen to me. After all, no one could amass such a collection in just one lifetime. Certainly, not a person of average means, correct?"

She shrugged.

"No," I continued, "it would take years and years to collect such a horde. Years of living, buying, saving, and moving. Starting modestly, and, most important, being there when most of the items were worth only a fraction of what they are today. That would mean shortly after the painting was put on canvas, or the crystal was blown, or the jewelry designed. Because really, it has only been the passage of time that has increased the worth of much of what I own. Nothing more. What's that saying: 'Buy low, sell high'? When I acquired my assets, they indeed were cheap by today's standards."

Now I was pacing the floor and she was watching me closely. An inquiring wrinkle creased her brow.

"What's the matter?" I said.

"You're talking different now," she said. "Like you're playing Errol Flynn in a pirate role or something. I can't put my finger on it."

"Don't worry about it," I said. "It's just my past leaking

through. Sometimes, when I think of times past…" I was suddenly dreadfully weary. I sat down with my elbows on the table top, chin in my hands.

"You know what you're hinting at is impossible." she said.

"I'm not hinting at anything."

"Okay then, just for the record, how old do you claim to be?"

"I don't claim to be. I'm just a bit over three hundred years old—probably about 327 actually."

She blinked her eyes rapidly then smiled brightly as if she had been listening to a babbling patient in a lunatic asylum. Suddenly, I wanted to slap her silly patronizing face. It was all so predictable. I almost expected her to titter.

"327, huh. Why not six hundred, or even a thousand years, Andrew?"

Of course, if I smacked that look off her face, I'd probably face an assault charge.

"And why is it that you're living so long, yet you don't look a day over, say, twenty? And how can you alone go on living while the rest of us cave in at about seventy or so? Has God singled you out for special treatment or something? Don't make me laugh." She erupted in giddy laughter.

"I wish I knew the answer to that," I said. "But keep in mind, I'm not the only one."

"I suppose you mean that madman—the one who's supposedly after you for some dastardly deed of yours."

"That's right," I said. "In fact, he took at pot shot at me in the car."

"Okay," she said. "Have it your way. But prove it to me. Prove to me that you are what you say you are—whatever that is. Show me that I can believe one little shred of what you're claiming."

Here we go again, I thought. History repeats itself.

"Well, go ahead, prove it." She shouted the words at me, as if throwing a gauntlet at my feet.

"What do you want me to do?"

"That's your problem. Use some of the wisdom you've supposedly piled up through the ages."

I walked over to the kitchen drawers, pulled one open, then turned to face her.

"You're a nurse. Are you pretty good at stemming blood flow?"

"What are you talking about?" she said, taking a step toward me.

"This," I said. I pulled an eight inch kitchen knife from its nest and plunged it through my neck until the shiny steel blade protruded two inches out the other side.

Her screams echoed off the kitchen walls, causing me to put my hands over my ears, almost making me ignore the pain that boiled my senses, the cherry red poker I had plunged through my throat, shredding muscle, bone and tissue. Allison lurched to the sink and emptied her breakfast onto the clean white porcelain. Now the sight of her retching threatened to make me sick, a potentially life-threatening situation since my upchuck would probably be obstructed by the broad knife blade and I could conceivably choke. Exercising great will power, I withdrew the knife smoothly from its warm new home and dropped it onto the tile floor which by now was covered with my blood in a widening rosy pool.

"Now," I said, "how about putting some of your great nursing skills to work and stop this bleeding?"

She lifted her head from the sink and looked at me vacantly. Then she turned and ran from the room. I thought she had probably called the police or the nut squad but instead she returned, carrying tape and bandages.

"I tried to miss the most important parts," I said helpfully as I sat down on a blood-spattered chair to await her expertise.

She said nothing but worked at warp-speed, probing deep into the ugly wounds with shiny instruments, painting me with sharp-smelling liquids and stripping gauze strips and tape from rolls. Finally, my throat was nicely wrapped and I fancied I looked like a young King Tutankhamen.

"See," my wounded voice box squawked brightly, "I'll be fine in just a couple of days."

My pleased smile was promptly erased by a round-house Mike Tyson right hook that sent me sprawling over the kitchen table, crashing to the floor on the other side.

"You perfect, perfect ass," she cried and ran from the room. I heard the door to her bedroom slam as I reached for some paper towels to clean my precious bodily fluids from the kitchen floor.

❧

One of the advantages of my longevity is that fate, for whatever reason, has given me a lofty perch from which to view the foibles of my fellow human beings. And although social tides may ebb from generation to generation, I have discovered that there are enduring constants among our genders that are ageless and unchanging—and doubtless will remain so until the end of time, despite the efforts of some to bring about reform and change.

One of these constants is woman's traditional and unwavering methods of dealing with that special fear of the unknown that is generated by impending doom.

Allison's behavior, therefore, was quite predictable: First, the denial of having encountered a bizarre situation, manifested by refusing to believe a word I said. Then the anger, unleashed when my truthfulness was confirmed, and followed by her splendid right hook and abrupt departure to the bedroom. Now, confident in my knowledge of female behavior, I sat quietly watching television and bided my time, waiting for the moment when she would attain a state of calm, make an entrance, and of course, utter the usual apology.

Finally, just as the shadows outside were lengthening into dusk, I heard the door to the bedroom open. Precisely on time, I noted. She approached my chair and stood with her arms crossed over her chest. Not exactly an apologetic pose.

"Are you still here, you creep?"

I winced. "I'm sorry," I said, rising to face her.

"What are you sorry for? You can't help the way you are."

"So you believe me then?"

"Let's just say that I'm getting a good start."

"Well, I apologize for being so abrupt."

"And that theatrical grandstanding. You should be in a hospital, you know."

"Well, believe it or not," I said, "I'll probably do just as well with this bandage job."

"You realize that you're quite abnormal, don't you?"

"Please don't use that word," I said. "Besides, to tell the truth, I don't know quite what I am."

"Have you quit bleeding?" She edged toward the kitchen and peeked in at the floor.

"Oh, sure. No problem. I took the bloody towels and stuff down to the trash."

"No problem," she repeated. "Maybe we'll just take you down to the blood bank and have them top you off with a couple of quarts." She slumped onto a faded blue-flowered sofa. "What happens next?"

I sat down beside her and tried to take her hand but she pulled away from me.

"Don't do that, please."

"What's the matter?"

"Everything's the matter. And I can't just sit here and start holding hands with a person who has just risen from the crypt."

"I said I was sorry about that bit of melodrama. But I couldn't think of any other way to show you that everything I've said so far is the truth."

"So when do I get to hear your life story?"

"You've got to be kidding," I said. "Just like that? It would take days."

"Just give me thumbnail sketch then." Her voice rose in frustration. "I have to have some idea of who it is I'm talking to. Yikes, and to think I even fantasized once about letting you sleep with me." She shivered slightly, as people do when they are asked to handle a slimy reptile.

Saddened, I plunged into my story in dull tones, fighting down an urge to simply get up, leave the room and disappear like a noxious vapor. Perhaps I could become a fisherman on the Bay of Fundy. Or devote my life to counting frozen micro-organisms trapped within the icy wastes of Antarctica.

I told her about my meeting with the great bull that led to my discovery that somehow, for some reason, I was profoundly different than those around me. Taking pains not to overwhelm her with melodrama, I outlined my life—describing an exist-ence deeply scarred by a longevity that set me apart, causing twisted, broken relationships and a horrible ennui brought on by an endless parade of passing years and my shallow, passive identities and the knowledge that I was apparently forever doomed to live the life of an ancient boy-man.

By the time I had finished my story, dusk's shadows had long since deepened to black and the watchful eye of a cold full moon had risen over the city.

She had listened quietly, almost numbly, nodding occa-sionally as I painted my past in broad brush strokes that spanned

the centuries and touched the lives of so many beings now
long forgotten. Even as I talked, my own wonderment soared.
How could this be? I could not recall the last time I had told
anyone my story in a single sitting. The cumulative effect was
as stunning upon myself as it was upon Allison. The things I
knew firsthand, about which others could only read about, and
which I in casual self-centered arrogance had taken almost
entirely for granted. The unending stream of humanity, the
rich brocade of scenery, passing in review before my eyes. The
pages of history, torn cleanly from deep within my memory,
floating downward now into my consciousness. I was humbled
by the experience. And my humility deepened as old questions
reassembled in my mind, mocking me, trifling with my es-
teem and my sanity: Why me? For what earthly or unearthly
reason? Who made me this way? What does my future hold?
How will my end finally come? And now, how would this girl
fit into the scheme of things?

Allison went into the kitchen and made a pot of coffee. I
flicked on the television and half-watched a commercial for
Band-Aids as she bustled about. She returned carrying two
hot mugs and set one on the low table in front of me.

I sipped the near-boiling liquid and watched the flickering images on the screen.

She held her cup in both hands, gazing over the rim.

She nodded thoughtfully and, I thought, moved a
fraction of an inch closer to me.

I started to say something else but she cut me off, pointing to the screen.

"What's he saying?" she said, pointing her cup at the screen where the announcer was droning on.

"Federal authorities tonight are searching for a fugitive who escaped from custody on the streets of Brooklyn early this afternoon. According to officials, the man, who was being taken into custody to be held pending the filing of charges involving national security matters, fled on foot when the car he was riding in was involved in an accident at a busy intersection. A spokesman said two agents in the front seat of the car were injured when the vehicle was demolished by a runaway garbage truck and pushed across the sidewalk through a stone store front. A concentrated search is being conducted at this hour as authorities seek to track down the fugitive, whose identity is being withheld pending formal filing of charges."

"That's you they're looking for, isn't it?" she said.

"You got it."

"I'm sorry I called you a creep. What are you going to do?"

"I don't know. I doubt if I can go back to my place. They'll probably be looking for me to turn up there."

"Maybe you can stay with a friend or something for a few days."

"You're a friend, aren't you?"

"I'm not that good a friend, Andrew."

"I could sleep right here on the couch."

"What about your clothes and stuff? You only have the

clothes you're wearing."

"I won't need much. It's just for a day or two. Then I'll scram."

"You don't even have a toothbrush."

"I won't brush my teeth."

"Just promise you won't breathe on me, okay?"

During the next two days the sofa in Allison's living room began showing the effects of supporting my weight—a deep sunken crater that finally collapsed the front edge and threatened to spill me onto the threadbare fake Oriental rug. Allison had loosened up a bit, agreeing to go out and buy me a change of clothes, shaving gear, toothpaste and a toothbrush—a new high tech model with scientifically curved bristles. I made a mental note to pry loose some of my hidden cash to repay her for her kindness.

On the third afternoon of my R & R, Allison had gone to a nearby market to pick up some food for supper and I was in full repose on the couch, skimming the ladies bathing suit section of the Sear's summer catalog. The buzzer at the door sounded from the security phone in the lobby downstairs. It was Allison.

"There are three characters walking up the front stairs who look like ads for London Fog trench coats."

"See you in a flash," I said.

I hung up abruptly and dashed through the apartment, scooping up personal items and running into the hall to the elevator. I rang the call button and waited as the indicator followed the lift's ascension to the fifth floor. The door opened and there was Allison, beckoning me inward.

"Hurry," she said. "They're coming up the stairs."

The door closed and down we went to the street level where we cautiously peeked out into the hallway, then dashed out of the building to her car parked around the corner. She leaped into the driver's seat like a wheel man in a bank robbery and we tore off down the street.

"Great," she said over the engine roar and gear clanking. "This is just great. Now I suppose they'll be after me, too!"

"Relax," I said. "How do you know they were after me? They could have been going into the building for a card game or something." I hoped that explanation wasn't as lame as it sounded.

"Don't be a lame-brain," she cried shrilly, gunning the car to a faster pace. "Of course they're after you. Besides, I heard them checking the mailboxes. When they came to mine, one of them says 'here she is. They must be living together.'"

"Hmmmm." I rubbed my chin thoughtfully.

There is something about a chase that sets my blood afire, stokes my senses and heats my passions. Maybe it's because I've brushed up against so many situations in the past that have called for expeditious flight. Understand, it's not that I'm afraid to stay and face the music. It's just that I learned long ago that, although it may seem gallant and romantic, staying behind to fight has its distinct disadvantages—even for extraordinary mortals. Indeed, experience has taught me that it is usually best to show your adversary your fleeing backside, instead of the point of your onrushing sword.

A tragic event from the past supports my case: It was a crisp fall day in Paris when leaves of umber and mahogany were blown through the streets by a cold wind. The boulevards were warmed only slightly by the sunshine which beat down upon the cobblestones. The date was November 28, 1838. I was on holiday from my new home in England and was visiting friends in the great city. In those days I was still earning my keep as a storehouse of musical talent and had blossomed into a true flutist, mandolin and accomplished clavichord player. It was a way of life that fitted neatly into my desire to avoid noteriety and also eliminated the need to dally in one region for too long.

Unfortunately, I had long before stopped paying attention to local political upheavals and perhaps was not as attuned as I should have been to recent events that had inflamed the French countryside.

So it was that as I lingered before a colorful display of

scarfs in a shop window, my ears caught the sound of a restless crowd, surging up the street toward an open park a few meters distant. I turned to examine the motley glob of humanity as it brushed past me on the thoroughfare. Burly roughshod fellows with crude ugly faces, wild hair and unkempt common clothing. Screaming banshee women, wearing ill-fitting shawls and bonnets, brandishing sticks and shaking their fists in the air. The scent of unwashed bodies made my eyes water.

Then in the midst of the melee I could see oxen pulling a large wagon which had been made into a makeshift cage of sorts. Inside, fear-filled eyes stared out from between the wooden bars at the taunting humanity which parted in a wave as the squeaking oak wheels bore down the street. I could see at least a half a dozen persons inside the wagon, a civilized-looking lot in comparison with the shrill, mocking crowd which threw stones and spit at them. I wondered about the meaning of this bizarre scene and could not for the life of me guess what hideous crime could have been committed by these innocent-appearing captives to merit such scorn.

I tapped the arm of a portly businessman next to me.

"I say, Sir," I said. "What is happening here? Why are these innocent-appearing wretches being treated so?"

He looked at me archly through a monocle, as if I were a laboratory specimen.

"What have you been doing, boy—collecting cobwebs in a monastery somewhere?" He frowned. "These traitors are being taken to their just due, that's all."

"How so?" I ventured.

He laughed and made a slicing motion across his throat with a forefinger.

"I fear their apples will fill the basket."

"Apples?" I inquired blankly.

"Yes, you young ninny," he exclaimed. "And if you don't care enough for our revolution to keep abreast of it all, perhaps you should donate an apple as well!"

He turned and stomped off, striking the pavement with a heavy knotted cane.

Pulled along by curiosity, I allowed myself to be caught up by the crowd, sucked into the vortex of milling, marching bodies and the swelling cries of these noble constituents. Ignoring the fact that clumsy oafs were trodding upon my best boots, I became one with the mob and was carried along the cobbled roadway.

The air was filled with choking dust and reeked with the stench of tightly-packed perspiring bodies. Over the heads of those in front of me, I could see a thin white arm, stretching pitifully through the thick bars of the rolling prison. I was close enough to see it was arm of a young girl, it's smooth skin and curve dictating a lass yet to reach twenty. The slender fingers were reaching skyward, as if imploring God in heaven to reach down and pluck her upward. Then the lovely arm disappeared inside and the heaving cart distanced itself from me.

Soon the mass arrived at the park where the crowd spilled out across the vast lawn, toppling benches and trampling neatly planted rows of flowers. Many determined individuals shinnied up slender saplings and statuary for a better view of what was to come as the great cart lurched to a halt alongside a giant wooden platform. Upon the makeshift stage a group of men stood reading from papers and shouting to the people. I couldn't hear what they were saying but a strange machine caught my attention. I shielded my eyes from the sun to more closely study this strange contraption, an engine of sorts, consisting of two upright beams which towered over the platform by about fifteen meters or so. Although my view of the bottom of the machine was obstructed, I could see that every few minutes or so, a large block-like object would be raised to the top of the tower, from whence it would crash downward with a large thunk. Then the crowd would scream wildly, women would cry, tear at their hair and laugh hysterically. The brutish men pounded their knees, wiped spittle from their lips, clapped with approval and hugged their ladies in prolonged bear-like embraces.

I struggled forward, using my elbows to make headway, the better to see what was happening that could cause such a reaction from the assemblage. At last, I reached a vantage point, just as men in black were wrenching open the heavy door of the prison cart. They reached inside and pulled protesting occupants out into the sun where they rubbed their eyes with their fists and trembled uncontrollably. I could see now that the unfortunate prisoners were definitely of a decent class— that is, they were clean, their clothes were well-cut, and, despite their obvious fear, they held themselves straight with shoulders back and chins up. Plucky lot, I thought. My gaze fell upon the figure of a young girl with large brown eyes brimming with such sadness that my heart was stricken.

Obviously, since she was the only young person in the whole lot, she was the very same prisoner who had stretched her arm outside the cage. Now she staggered and uttered a small cry like a frightened kitten as her eyes took in the hungry crowd and the strange machine. She stumbled and leaned against the arm of a thin white haired man next to her for support. The old gent put his arm tightly about the girl.

Now for the first time I looked closely at the dreadful contrivance that towered over the platform. My knees turned to silk and almost buckled from under me as my dull brain at last understood what was happening.

At the base of the machine was a large basket, brimming with round objects. I could see crimson oozing from the basket, seeping across the platform toward the raving audience. Now a grim man upon the stage pushed the girl aside and grabbed the old man, yanking him forcibly toward the back of the metal tower. The man put up a pathetic struggle but the brute thrust him to his knees and placed his head down across a rough wooden block, locating his skinny neck in a centered groove. The old man turned his head toward the girl and spoke a few words, then the girl issued a pitiful whimper and looked about the stage with pleading eyes. Another piece of block was brought down across the back of the man's neck. Now the

audience could only see the thinning cap of silver hair on top
of his head. I felt my own body tremble as I watched in stupe-
faction as the scene played its course. The rough brute stepped
back momentarily and examined his handiwork. Then he nodded to a stout henchman who grinned and put a great fist around
a large piece of hemp. As a body of one, the faces of the audience tilted upward to the topmost section of the tower where
the sun glinted off a shiny oblique metal blade. Then, dream-
like, the blade drifted downward smoothly in its track, gaining
speed, silently, purposefully rushing toward its destiny.

In a blink, its work was done. The crowd gasped in appreciation as the head was neatly sliced from its mooring, reveal-
ing a raw spurting wound in its place. The head toppled onto
the platform and rolled a few feet. It's eyes blinked open and
its jutting tongue silently admonished the crowd.

I struck the ground in a faint, sprawling in a mess created
by my own heaving stomach. Then in a blur, I heard the clamor
of angry, taunting voices.

"Ho, this fellow doesn't care much for these proceedings.
Perhaps his apple should join the others."

"Up, you traitor. Your weak gut unmasks you as a stinking
sympathizer. Join the others where you belong."

"He's all got up like a traitor, isn't he now?"

"We'll see how much sympathy he has left after the blade
is finished with him." Rough hands jerked at me and I tried to
pull free.

"Let me loose," I cried in my rusty French tongue. "You

have no cause to take issue with me."

Despite my protests, powerful arms lifted me and passed me overhead through the crowd. Bobbing along on the sea of hands and shoulders, I soon reached the platform where I was rudely deposited at the foot of the man in black.

"Here's a green apple for your orchard," cried one man.

"He's no better than the rest. Give him his due," shouted a woman who spat a viscous string of fluid onto my cheek.

Suddenly I found myself on the stage, facing the horrible machine, the chanting of voices behind me urging the men in black to have their way with me. I glanced left and right, then spotted a rogue at the back of the stage, seated upon a huge gelding. In a flash I realized that I had only a split second to act. The crowd, whipped into a frenzy now, was almost in a swoon, lusting after my head. I quelled my desire to shout my innocence. Instead, I bolted across the stage and hurled myself feet first at the man on the horse. Startled, the man toppled off and I fell onto the saddle in his place. The horse reared magnificently and the crowd surged back as I snatched up the reins and bade the powerful animal to leap onto the stage itself. This it did and, without even a thought, I leaned downward from the saddle, grabbed the stunned girl around the waist and dug my heels into the sides of the whinnying beast. In a thrice, the animal, as if shot from a cannon, bounded off the stage and galloped through the shocked crowd, stamping slow movers into the turf. I felt hands grasping at my coat and beat them back as best I could, still clutching the girl who buried her tearful face in my bosom.

By now, the horse had streaked across the full length of the park and I was gratified to note that the crowd was now beginning to thin. Knowing full well that distance was my best defense, I urged the animal up a series of narrow streets and alleyways. Finally, the sound of the mob ebbed and I slowed the horse to a walk. Moments later, I dismounted and helped the girl to the ground. A slap on the rump sent the horse galloping off, perhaps in search of another poor soul in dire need.

It has long been my view that man has no greater joy than to have a beautiful woman in debt to him. And now, as I caught my breath, I realized that this was the happy predicament in which I found myself. I unclasped the girl's arms from around my neck and held her in front of me. She was indeed, a wonder to behold. Even the tears which stained her cheeks and mussed locks of her ebony hair could not hide her perfection. Nor could the torn gown camouflage her delightful figure. And even in sorrow, there was a precious, lively lilt in her voice that bespoke of a person blessed with intelligence and sensitivity.

"How can I thank you?" she asked.

Oh, such a provocative question.

As it developed, Adrianna Roux was daughter of the silver haired man whom I had seen lose his head to the guillotine. The old gentleman and his family, including Adrianna, her mother and brothers, had been rousted from their country estate by revolutionaries, stripped of their possessions and dispatched to hear the music of the descending blade. How the gods selected me to be this woman's humble rescuer I couldn't guess. But as fate would decree, it would be none other than myself who would volunteer to transport this young lady to the home of relatives in, where else, but merry old England. Happily, fate would also decree that Adrianne would not only become my cherished friend, but would marry a good compatriot of mine, bear him three handsome children and finally, at the age of 86, pass into that higher world where love, not revolution, rules.

Chapter 5

"Turn tail, run away, live to fight another day."

Allison shifted her attention from the road ahead and made a face at me.

"What are you muttering about?"

"Oh, nothing," I said, clearing my mind of the long ago past. "Where are we going?"

"So far as I'm concerned," she said, "I'm just looking for a place to drop you off. You can find some digs to hide out in for a few days and figure out your next move."

"And what will you do?"

"Me?" she said. "Heck, I'm going back to my apartment. I haven't done anything wrong, have I? Except perhaps harbor a fugitive."

"Well I haven't done anything wrong either," I said. "And look where it's gotten me."

I watched traffic whizzing by in both directions. The Bruckner Expressway was jammed as we headed north out of the city. We threaded our way onto U.S. 95 and joined commuters blasting homeward toward their colonial-style clapboard houses with neatly cut lawns in bedroom communities in Connecticut. A light rain began spattering the windshield and the sun was sinking lower on the horizon. Allison reached over and switched on the windshield wipers and the radio in a quick one-two motion. My stomach began growling.

"Let's pull over and get something to eat," I said. She nodded in agreement.

A few miles farther down the interstate we veered over to an exit and joined Highway 1 running parallel to 95 which linked a string of shopping strips and hamlets on the edge of Long Island Sound. Finally, we approached a tiny oasis in the dimming light, a combination restaurant and gas station, awash in garish red and purple neon, watched over by orange mercury vapor lamps perched high atop poles. Several unattended semi-trailer rigs, their throaty diesels idling, occupied most of the parking area.

Inside we found an empty high-back oak booth and ordered our food amid the backwash of a western ballad blaring from a jukebox and the expletive-punctuated conversations of truckers and locals. When our orders arrived, we ate quickly and silently, as if we hadn't eaten in days. At intervals, we looked at each other, saying nothing, then resumed eating ravenously, pausing only to catch our breaths. Allison looked pale and drawn but began perking up by the time our coffee arrived.

"I think terror increases the appetite," Allison said.

"It's supposed to have just the opposite effect."

"So what do we do now?"

"Well, drop me at a motel up the road and then you can head for home. Those guys were going up the stairs when I got into your car, remember? So I don't think they have any reason to think you've helped me out. If they question you about me, just say you were out shopping, which you were, and that when you got back to the apartment I wasn't around."

"What if one of them waited around after you left? Wouldn't they know I was gone for a long time?"

"Tell them you left the groceries in the car and went to see a movie."

"Alone?"

"People do go to the movies alone, you know."

"I guess so," she said. "But why don't I just tell them the truth, kind of."

"How do you mean, kind of?"

"I'll just tell them that when I pulled up to the building, you came outside and asked if I could give you a ride to a motel. Then I'll tell them that I dropped you off at some place other than where you'll actually be staying. After all, you are a fugitive. I could say that I had told you I didn't want you staying with me any more and that you agreed to leave and to consider turning yourself in."

"Turning myself in? Are you kidding?"

"No, I'm not kidding," she said, lowering her voice to a whisper. "Listen, Andrew, you really haven't done anything wrong. You should just go see the police and tell them everything right from the beginning. They'll understand. The police are very understanding people."

"Right from the beginning, huh. I can just see the look on the face of the desk sergeant. Besides, the police don't have anything to do with this. It's the feds that are getting all worked up about me."

"Call them, then."

"Maybe I'll just jump on a plane and head for Tanganyika or someplace," I said, rejecting the notion almost as soon as I uttered it.

"Oh sure, running would solve everything, wouldn't it? You seem to forget that you're not going to be able to disappear so easily anymore. The world has gotten a lot smaller. Every country has things like secret police and stuff."

I paid the check and we walked outside into the early evening. It was still raining lightly as we drove back up the Highway 1. She dropped me off at a small motel in Port Chester. It was no Holiday Inn, for sure. The single level building consisted of miniature units stuck together in the shape of a big U.

"Home sweet home," I said as we pulled up in front of the tiny office.

"Now I know where they filmed *Psycho*," Allison said.

I walked inside and after hammering the little chrome bell on the desk several times was greeted by a sullen clerk, a middle-aged balding man who was missing several teeth and was badly in need of a shave and shower. His huge gut jutted out over his wrinkled gray work pants and I could see his navel peeking seductively out of his bulging shirt. I was tempted to vacate the premises immediately but figured, aw, what the hell.

"I need a room for the night."

"Twenty bucks up front," said my gracious host.

I forked over a bill and he pushed a key across the counter.

"One-oh-nine. Checkout time is ten o'clock sharp."

I grabbed the key and headed back to the car.

"He didn't even have me sign the register," I said.

"I wonder how many presidents have stayed here," she said.

We parked in front of 109 and I unlocked the door, feeling around the corner of the wall for the light switch. Allison followed me into the room and did a fast inventory: one double bed with a concave mattress; chipped veneer nightstand with a lamp crowned by a dusty torn shade; Danish modern chair with orange plastic seat; yellow painted dresser with STP stickers plastered on the drawers.

Allison ran a finger over the dresser and mussed her nail with a thick coating of dust. "Sure you're going to be okay here?"

"I'm not looking for luxury. I'll figure out something more permanent for tomorrow."

"Okay," she said. "I'll call you when I get back to the apartment."

"Sure you don't want to spend the night?"

"In this crypt?"

"It's a long way back to town."

She disappeared out the door and as I tossed my bag onto the bed, I could hear the sound of her car starting and pulling out of the driveway.

"What to do, what to do," I said to the walls. First off, I wanted to take a shower. I stripped and walked cautiously into the bathroom, watching for little creepy-crawly things on the cold tile. A couple of threadbare towels hung from the loose rack on the wall. I got into the tub and cranked open the faucets, seeking that magical elusive blend of cold and hot. Amazingly, I found the perfect combination right away and the water was warm and friendly. I could feel my body relax as I stood under the spirited downpour.

Minutes later, I pushed open the bathroom door with my shoulder, rubbing my dripping face with a skimpy terry towel. I walked over to the foot of the bed and bent over to towel off my legs. My sudden downward movement at that precise moment reduced much of the velocity of the mass which struck my head, tearing my scalp, sending a splash of blood across the bed as I tumbled forward. My senses slipped momentarily into a black void, then returned as I lay on the bed, watching the spray of my own blood painting my chest and arms. There was a movement of shadow and a stocky man, now astraddle me, whipped a heavy instrument downward.

I rolled sideways and brought both my legs up. Fresh pain

erupted in my right shoulder. The man was flung to the edge of the bed but pulled himself upright just as my bare foot shot out, striking him full in the face.

I rolled off the bed and the man leaped at me, hands in front, clawing for prey. I reached for the bedside lamp and tossed the fixture at my assailant, who bulled his way through the splintered ceramics and grabbed me in a bear hug. I raised my knee sharply into his groin. He grunted loudly and dropped to the floor, then rose and grabbed me around the legs, trying to pull me onto the threadbare carpet. His efforts were cut short by the Danish modern chair which I sent crashing down upon his head. The chair cracked into several pieces and I snatched up a leg and began clubbing him over the head.

"I hope you've got insurance!" I cried. The chair leg, a perfectly suitable club, struck again and again, battering arms, ribs and legs as the man tried to ward off the blows. He made a beautiful tympani.

"Wait," the man groaned, holding up his hands. "You're making a big mistake." He pulled himself upright, stumbled to the door, yanked it open and disappeared.

The telephone on the nightstand jangled loudly. Should I answer? I picked up the receiver.

"Andrew, it's me, Allison."

"What's up?" I said, trying to catch my breath.

"Those men are watching my apartment. I drove by in the car and saw them parked outside. I'm afraid to go back there."

"Well," I said, "you can come back here if you want."

"Maybe I will."

"Except that I've had a spot of trouble since you left. I had a visitor."

"A visitor?"

"Yeah, some guy who tried to bash my head in."

"Are you all right?"

"I'll survive. Come on ahead."

I went into the bathroom and took another shower. The flow of blood on my scalp had stopped and I took care not to disturb the wound. Allison arrived nearly an hour later. She entered the room cautiously.

"It's okay," I said. "He's long gone."

"Do you know who he was?"

"Not the Avon Man, that's for sure."

"What did he want?"

"I haven't the vaguest."

I walked over to the door as she entered and looked outside, up and down the small driveway. Everything was quiet. The parking area was empty except for Allison's car in front of my room door and a maroon Chevrolet parked several doors down.

"I wonder if that's his car parked down there?" I said. I spied a glint of metal on the pavement. It was two keys on a ring. "Looks like he lost his car keys. Must have taken off on foot."

Allison peeked around the edge of the door.

"So?"

"So, I'm going to see if they fit that car."

I opened the door and walked across the parking area to the Chevrolet. Peering in through the driver's window, I could see nothing unusual. I walked back to the trunk, took out a key, placed it in the lock and the trunk sprung open. Inside was a spare tire and brown leather briefcase. I took the case, closed the trunk lid and returned to the room.

Allison sat silently on the bed while I sorted through the case. There was a thick file containing all kinds of official-looking documents. Some were stamped TOP SECRET in red stencil, just like in spy movies. Several glossy pictures spilled out onto the floor. I scooped them up and went through them. Then I tossed them onto the bed to Allison.

"Recognize this handsome lug?"

Her jaw dropped as she riffled through the pictures.

"What would he be doing with pictures of you?" she asked.

Exactly what I wanted to know. There were pictures of me getting into my car, standing in front of Allison's apartment building, in front of my own building—assorted shots that indicated I had been under constant surveillance for several weeks.

But my discoveries were just beginning. One stapled sheaf of papers looked more official that the rest so I read it first. My pulse quickened and my breath came faster as I absorbed the information.

"I can't believe this," I said. "This is the most stupid thing I've ever read."

"What's it say?"

"According to this document, some people in our government think I'm responsible for the theft of some top secret formula nearly a year ago.

"What kind of formula?"

"It was taken from a safe in a Central Intelligence Agency laboratory in Virginia. Papers that spelled out the details of some cell regeneration project. They called it METHUSALA."

"Whoopee."

"Methusala. That's biblical," I said, "right?"

"Yes," Allison said. "He's the guy who supposedly lived to be over nine hundred years old. It's an ancient legend."

Sure. Just like I'm an ancient legend."

"Oh boy. How do you suppose they ever made a connection between you and that project, whatever they call it."

"The hospital. It must have been when I was being treated after that accident with the car."

"Remember how that one doctor kept asking me questions?"

"Yes," I said. "I remember you mentioned that to me."

"He must have done something with a sample of your blood."

"Maybe turned it over to someone he knew in the CIA?"

"Something like that."

"And of course, when they check my blood, they must have found something in there that had to do with this drippy project of theirs. But I've had my blood checked lots of times.

Nothing like this has ever come up before."

"Sure. But maybe this is the first time your blood's been examined by someone who's actually been suspicious of you and who has the technology at hand to look deeper than anyone has in the past. There must be something in your system that's different from the rest of us."

"And that same something obviously is involved in the Methusala operation, too."

The room fell silent, except for the rumble of traffic outside. I got up and started pacing.

"Neat, huh?" I said. "They probably think I've filled up my veins with whatever joy juice they're experimenting with in that lab of theirs."

"So they think you've discovered the Fountain of Youth or something. Where does that leave you?"

"No problem," I said. "I'll just take off."

"Great. And I suppose you'll just keep running every time something like this happens."

"What else can I do?"

"Stick around and try to get to the bottom of this. If I were you, I'd be darn curious as to why I am what I am. What if it was something simple—like something in your blood? Wouldn't you like to know?"

"Of course—but you've got to understand, I've been through the 'darn curious' stage a thousand times. When you've been looking for answers for as long as I have—and don't find them, you start losing interest."

Would I really like to know? Come of think of it, I really wasn't sure...now. Of course, my search for answers was back in the days when even a hot candle was considered high technology. Now, what if a science was available that could solve the riddle? Would I want to hear the answer? I wasn't sure.

"You don't seem very positive about the whole thing."

"I'm not negative, either. Let's just say I'm ambivalent. Except that, I'd rather be like I am than terminally ill with the black plague or something."

"You don't want to be like other people."

"Maybe not," I said.

She shrugged. "At least you're honest about it."

I felt a distinct need to change the subject and deal with problems at hand.

"Now," I said, "I get attacked by this bozo. I wonder why he jumped me like that? No warning whatsoever. He obviously works for someone in the government."

"Maybe he just wanted to talk to you."

"Talk to me? He hit me over the head with something without even saying hello." I felt my head gingerly.

"He must of really meant business."

"He did say one thing to me. He said I was making a big mistake."

"One thing doesn't make a whole lot of sense," she said. "If these guys were after you because you supposedly stole some kind of formula, why wouldn't they try to capture you, instead of just bashing the daylights out of you? I mean, what good would you be to them dead if you had something that belonged to them?"

"I don't know."

"Incidentally," she said, "remember when I called to tell you that those men were sitting in a car watching my building?"

"What about it?"

"And you know that weird guy from the restaurant—your pal, the Phantom of the Opera?"

My heart skipped a beat. "The Prince," I squawked. "What about him?"

"Well, I forgot to tell you that I saw him, too. He was in another car watching those three guys in their car. Real cozy."

"How could you forget to tell me something like that?"

She ran a hand through her hair. "I don't know. I just did. Anyway, what's the big deal?"

"The big deal," I said patiently, "is that this Phantom as you call him is obviously still hot on my trail. My God, he could even know that we're in this room, at this very moment."

I went to the window, cautiously drew aside the curtain and looked out. Nothing unusual.

"Let's get out of here," I said.

"But you paid for the night. You might as well stay."

"No, I won't have you sleeping in this pig pen. Anyway, we can't stay here. That hit man's going to be coming back with reinforcements."

She slumped onto the bed. "So now there are two of us on

the run, huh?"

"Looks like that. I'm sorry." I managed what I hoped was a heroic smile and picked up the briefcase. We left the room, jumped into the car and headed up the highway again. As she drove, I tried to determine if we were being followed. The coast looked clear.

"You know," I said, "maybe we should turn around and drive back to tinsel town. It'll be a lot easier to lose ourselves there than trying to hole up out here in the boondocks."

"Sounds okay to me," she said.

We turned off on a service road and peeled back onto the highway, pointing the car toward the glow on the horizon in the distance. On the way into the city, our conversation was sparse. Both of us were alone with our thoughts, nervously wondering what new surprises the future would bring.

The Shaughnessy House Hotel was a collection of small suites, bound together by a teetering framework of aging timber, dusty leaded glass windows and quaint turrets, wedged between new apartment towers a few blocks off the Deegan Expressway in the Bronx. Staying at the hotel was Allison's idea. She remembered that her elderly aunt had once lived in the Shaughnessy, years before its Victorian elegance had faded and its shrinking clientele had died off. Now the building catered to aging pensioners and welfare families.

We needed a place to catch our breath, regroup and sort out our predicament, which now fully involved Allison as much as it did myself. I was fully aware that my situation, like a sticky spider's web, had also entrapped her. But I was at a loss at the moment to think of a way to extricate her. Perhaps given time and a night's rest, I could come up with some options.

After parking the car in a ramp across the street, we checked in at the Shaughnessy's front desk and were greeted by a tiny grey haired lady carrying a key ring as big around as her waist. She handed us a room key, directed us up the stairs to the third floor, and winked broadly.

So it was that Allison and I spent our first night together. She was reluctant at first, but my charm won her over. There was also the fact that our room had but one bed. And with no sofa or deep chair about, there remained only the cold oak floor as an alternative. Therefore, as I prepared to stretch myself out onto the dusty planking, she succumbed to my sad eyes and invited me under the covers.

Unfortunately, that's as far as the invitation went. Once in bed, I waited patiently for my eyes to adjust to the darkness. Soon, I could make out the outline of her bare shoulders, seductively framed by the gold of her hair. She was lying with her back to me. Excellent. The element of surprise had always stood me in good stead. I stole a hand under the sheets in her direction. My fingers reached her ribcage, moved forward a few more inches and, at last, clasped themselves greedily over a soft bare mound. Abruptly I felt her teeth sinking into my index finger.

"Try that again Buster Brown and you'll sleep on the floor."

Much of the remainder of the night was agony. Not from my damaged hand but, rather, my injured spirit. I could feel the warmth of her precious body just inches from mine, but dared not touch her again.

"Don't even think about it," came the whispered threat.

I decided to try another tack. "Women have cried out in anguish and begged me for my attentions."

"Must have been some real bimbos," she replied.

At last, my frustrations were quieted by deep and welcome sleep.

Chapter 6

"I've been thinking."

I stirred at the sound of Allison's voice, struggled to turn over, and finally freed myself from the tentacles of twisted sheets. She was sitting on a straight backed chair at the foot of the bed. The sun streaming through the small window cast a glowing halo over her shoulders and she looked like one of God's messengers, even in her wrinkled shirt, jeans and dirty tennis shoes.

"I've been thinking," she repeated. "We're not getting any-where hanging out like this. We need some input from other people."

"Such as?"

"There's an old friend of my father's who might be able to help us. He's a neat person, very smart, and very open-minded."

"How could he help us?"

"He's the kind of person we could talk to without him becoming terrifically judgmental or thinking you're half crazy. Besides, he's involved in weird stuff all the time and I don't think he'd be fazed by any of this."

"What is he—a scientist of some kind?"

"Not exactly. His name is Prescott Atkinson. He's a doctor of something but I don't know exactly what. I do know he investigates parapsychological events—strange phenomena like haunted houses and stuff."

"You think I might be haunted?"

She took a deep breath. "No, of course not. But let's just say that although you may look normal, you're anything but. Okay? And I think we can trust Prescott to help us get a handle on just what is going on with you."

I must have looked unconvinced.

"Do you have a better idea?"

"No." I admitted.

I got dressed and we walked down the creaking steps to the lobby.

"Oh, young man—I have a message for you."

Allison and I looked at each other, then at the little old lady behind the front desk who was holding a scrap of paper in her outstretched hand. I took it and we walked outside to the street. Allison pursed her lips and looked over my shoulder for a better view as I unfolded the paper and read the scrawl that snaked across the sheet.

"What kind of writing do you call that?" she asked.

I scanned the paper quickly. It was written in ancient Italian—a particularly rustic form that hadn't been in use for a couple of centuries.

"Greetings Andrew Merriman: To have found you at last makes my aching heart sing. The past never forgives or forgets our misdeeds. And so it is that yours, too, have not been forgotten. Although you may be blessed with long life, those around you may not be as fortunate. Therefore, look about you with great care and diligence. I intend to set matters right. I toast the future, Merriman!"

The note was signed, "SCARLATTI"—a slashing signature in black that oozed malevolence.

"What does it say?" Allison asked.

I tossed her the piece of paper in a crumpled ball. "It's a little love note from my friend, Prince Ugly."

"What's he say?" She tried to smooth out the wrinkled paper and decipher the contents.

"No big deal," I said.

"I'll bet. You get mysterious notes in foreign languages all the time."

We walked across the street into the parking ramp to her car. "Darn it, wait a sec," she said, tossing me the keys. "I left my purse in the room."

She took off on a run, her blonde hair bouncing. As I watched her fleeing figure, I was struck hard in the gut by the sudden realization that, because of me, she was now in harm's way. It was a physical reaction that took my breath away as the full meaning of the situation sank in. For the first time in my memory, an innocent person—a spectator to my passing parade—could come to grief by merely associating with me. There was no question about it: Scarlatti's note meant business. If he couldn't harm me personally, he would harm someone close to me. Allison would be that someone, unless I could protect her.

Now the knowledge that she could be harmed—and that I might be affected even a trifle by this—unnerved me. Because this was a confounding new experience for me: Caring so much as a whit about the welfare of another person. It made me feel less in control—and vulnerable. My discomfort scale was heightened by a lack of easy alternatives. If I sent Allison away and struck out on my own, her safety would still be in doubt. Scarlatti would know precisely what I was doing and would not be sidetracked. And in that event, I wouldn't even be around to shield her. On the other hand, I could quit playing the role of sitting duck and go after Scarlatti myself. How I would accomplish this I wasn't sure. After all, although I didn't think I was exactly stupid, the qualities of subterfuge, deceit and cunning were foreign to me. But I knew I would have to find a solution to this dilemma—and fast.

Oh, for those simpler days long past when the curtain could be promptly rung down on a dicey situation by leaping onto the back of a fast horse and pounding down a lonely road at full gallop on a moonless night. But I knew those days were gone forever. This was a complicated new age. An age which demanded that I use my ingenuity to the fullest. Thankfully, there was one thing I was exceedingly good at: Survival. At least the survival of MYSELF. And I resolved that, when this bizarre episode was over, I would never, ever burden myself with the unnecessary complexities created by becoming "involved" with anyone again. Especially someone as willful and stubborn as Allison MacKenzie. When all of this was over, I would become cold and sterile. An island of independence. An isolated being who would be responsible for no one except myself.

I got into her parked car, found the right key and put it into the ignition. Even as I did so, a bright red neon flickered in my mind's eye. Dumb, dumb, dumb.

The force of the explosion blasted my body upward at an angle, through the convenient moon roof where I careened off the concrete garage roof and fell to the floor in the midst of a firestorm of flaming car parts. The concussion deafened me and the effect was like watching a silent reenactment of the eruption of Krakatau. I could smell my singed hair and my body felt as if it had been tenderized by the pounding of a hundred hammers and shoved into a broiler. Then I was lying on the refreshingly cold concrete, watching the burning chunks of Chrysler around me. I saw Allison running toward me, followed by a mob of people.

"Andrew," she screamed. "Was that an explosion? Are you hurt?"

"Of course I'm hurt," I snarled, trying to get to my feet.

Several of the people in the growing crowd put their hands to their faces and shrank back as I began walking about. I must have looked like one of Dr. Frankenstein's failures.

"Let's get out of here," I said, taking Allison by the arm and steering her toward an exit.

"But you're burned," she said. "You need to see a doctor."

"You're telling me," I said. We hit the street in a fast walk and returned to the hotel.

Thankfully the little old lady behind the desk was absent from her post and we climbed the stairs to our room without being seen.

"My God," Allison said, "you were almost killed." She was breathing hard and her words spilled out in little clumps. "And what about my car? Will my insurance cover something like that? How am I going to get around? It only had a little over twenty thousand miles on it. Damn!"

"So sorry about your car," I said. "Now just let me glue myself back together." I went into the bathroom and checked the damage in the mirror.

"I didn't mean that like it sounded," she said. "I'm more concerned about you than the car."

"Oh, sure. You bet."

"Then don't believe me." She sat down with her arms tightly crossed, gripping her elbows, frowning.

The mirror reported that my wounds looked worse than they actually were. A few superficial burns, ugly soot streaks—

but no bad leaks or broken bones. I cleaned myself up and picked another pair of pants and a shirt from the pitiful supply in my bag. I took several deep breaths, trying to quell the rising fear within me. Then I called a cab and we headed downstairs again to the street.

The cab arrived and we sat tensely in the back seat. Several minutes passed before Allison broke her silence.

"Why do you think my car exploded like that? Maybe you started it wrong."

"I didn't start it wrong," I said. "Somebody wired a little surprise into the ignition system."

"Who would do a thing like that?"

"Well, I can think of one 'who' right off," I said.

"Your pal, Scarlatti."

"Right."

"This note he sent you," she said, patting her purse, "it's a threat, isn't it?"

"Yes, it's a threat."

"But since you're Captain Indestructible, he couldn't do you much damage, could he?"

I busied myself looking at the passing stores.

"So, if he can't hurt you, what's the next best thing? It's the people you know, right?" Her eyes brimmed with suspicion.

"Well, isn't that the case?"

I smiled weakly.

"Great," she said, slumping back into her seat. "That's just great. So I'm the pigeon now. You don't have to worry, do you? That bomb was meant to kill me—and you were just supposed to witness the event, right? He just wants to make you feel bad with an eye for an eye."

She bit her lip and looked out the window. I tried to take her hand but she pulled it away.

"Listen," I said. "I know how you feel, but I didn't do any of this on purpose. I feel terrible about it. But I promise I won't let anything happen to you. Trust me."

"Trust me," she said. "That's what brokers say."

"I'll figure something out. After all, I haven't lasted this long without being somewhat resourceful. And who knows, maybe this friend of yours will help." She looked at me and I smiled with a confidence I did not really feel.

"Old Mister Resourceful," she said, then turned back to the scene outside her window.

Professor Atkinson lived in a fifth floor co-op on the west side, just off Columbus Avenue on 87th street. As our cab turned up 87th, we could see the number "One-Fifty" elegantly inscribed on a faded green canvas awning in front of a gray stone building wedged into a row of weather-stained brownstones. Across the street sat a row of white-washed brick buildings laced in climbing ivy with bulging first floor bay windows. Where had I encountered this scene before? Phalanxes of brick rooftop chimneys watching the street like sentinels. Bands of black wrought iron tracing the perimeters of window ledges, front steps and doorways. Tidy rows of uniformly fat mulberry trees rising to precisely even heights from tiny squares of green. A sign reading THIS STREET PATROLLED BY UNIFORMED GUARDS. Another advertising LUXURY RENTALS. Plump-wheeled perambulators and dogs of all sizes, pushed and towed by stylish men and women casually sure of their place and substance, showing off their loose bright sweaters, streaked blue jeans, sagging wool sox and white running shoes with speed stripes. A tight chain of compact cars hugging the curb, breaking their ranks only for an occasional fire plug. The high noon sun splashing down upon the entire scene, which, I now realized, reminded me of a Woody Allen movie.

The taxi pulled up in front the building with the green awning. I paid the driver and we went into the building where Allison studied the names on rows of brass mail boxes, then pushed a button under a slot. A weak buzzer sounded and she pulled open the door to the first floor hall where we caught a creaky elevator to the fifth floor.

"He lives in five-eleven" she said, walking ahead of me down the dim hallway. We arrived at the last door on the end and she knocked softly on the heavy oak. After a short wait, we heard rustling sounds inside and the door was opened slowly by a slight, elderly man who resembled a scaled down version of what Ichabod Crane might have looked like.

Prescott Atkinson was well under five feet tall and couldn't have weighed more than 95 pounds. I judged him to be in his seventies or eighties, although aside from his stooped carriage, it was difficult to tell because his face was virtually unlined. His head was bald and glossy with a monkish fringe of gray hair on the side. His ears were quite large for his skull and looked as if they had been stuck on in a hurry. I reached down to shake his tiny hand.

"Ah, dear Allison," he said. "And this is young Merriman I presume," he said, leading us into his living room. His wide mouth smiled widely, showing a complete set of even white teeth. I liked him immediately, maybe because of the honesty and good humor that radiated from his eyes— qualities which I expected we would be much in need of. He motioned us to be seated and climbed up into a huge recliner.

"Now," he said, clapping his hands together, as if commencing a party game, "tell me about your little problems." He smiled at me over his Ben Franklin glasses.

"Little problems? I'm not sure I understand," I said.

"Well, I'm given to understand by this beautiful young lady that you're concerned that, in the first instance, you believe you are being pursued and endangered by evil forces and, in the second, you are convinced that you're—immortal, shall we say."

"No, not immortal. Let's just say that I've been around for an awfully long time and so far, I don't show any signs of kicking the bucket. That, and the fact that Allison and I are being chased by some goons who are convinced that I've stolen one of their priceless state secrets."

The old man scratched his head and puckered his cheeks. "Let's take this one step at a time. Now, when were you born?"

"Near as I can determine, in the 1660's."

Atkinson turned to look at Allison. She shrugged.

"I suppose that's A.D.——not B.C.?" he said.

"That's correct."

"So you claim to be, let's see——over 300 years old, correct?"

"Right. 327, to be precise."

He grimaced terribly and blinked, as if I had just passed gas.

"You are aware, of course, that that is entirely impossible."

"Yes, I'm aware that it is entirely impossible——for most people."

"And the exceptions?"

"Apparently me——and one of the guys who are after me…who tried to blow us into eternity less than an hour ago. That's two people I can think of."

"You believe that others exist who are also, shall we say, long-lived?"

"I wouldn't know. I only sure about this one person."

"And that person is…?" The old man looked at me expectantly.

"Maybe I should start at the beginning."

Allison got up. "Maybe I'll put on some coffee. This'll probably take a while."

Two pots of coffee later, my tale drew to a close. I was exhausted—and almost bored. Allison had fallen asleep on a small day bed at the end of the room. Prescott Atkinson looked pale and drawn, as if he were coming down with a severe case of catarrh. During my discourse, I had led my host on a long journey, starting with my earliest childhood memories, through my adolescent years, my maturing days on the continent and, finally, my recent years in America. He was strangely silent through much of my ramblings, as if he were letting the sheer incredulousness of my tale wash over him like a warm sea. From time to time, he would raise a hand and stop me, then ask questions in great detail. I knew what he was doing—trying to see if life during my times matched the words of the musty history and research books lining the walls of his apartment. In some cases, my recollection of events clashed mightily with his secondhand knowledge—a situation I found quite amusing. He also asked pointed questions about my medical history and at one point asked me to show him scars from ancient wounds. Of course, most of the scars had long since disappeared, although the circumstances surrounding their infliction remained vivid to me. He studied these faint blemishes and then looked me long in the eye, probing deeply, as if willing that signs of my veracity would pop out upon my forehead like beads of sweat.

From time to time, exclamations would burst forth from

his lips, spraying spittle onto his lap in a fine mist.

"Totally fantastic!" he would cry. "My colleagues would not give credence to this for even an instant."

At one point he struggled to climb out of the grasp of his huge reclining chair. He brushed off my efforts to help him and, instead, collapsed back into the deep cushions in silent defeat and contemplation.

Finally, I began pacing the floor, then stopped and put it to him straight.

"Do you believe me or don't you?"

"Your story is positively surreal in its implications," he whispered. "Your mere existence forces a whole new conception of life and death—the pinnacles of our universal world." He sighed, removed his glasses and cleaned them furiously with a wrinkled grey handkerchief. "The whole of it pretty much scotches the precepts which men have lived by since time began."

He paused and a sorrowful expression came over him. "Can the world even stand such a revelation?"

Ever the sensitive one, I shrugged. "You still haven't answered my question."

He groaned and, with great effort, literally threw his shrunken body out of its upholstered prison. He tried a few tentative steps across the room, like a two-year old on a slippery tile.

"I want desperately to believe you," he said, eyeing me warily and stroking his chin. "But you must understand this from my point of view: You are not supposed to have happened."

"But I have happened."

"Yes, my boy, you have indeed. And now what on earth are we supposed to do with you? Send you off on the lecture circuit? And if your own circumstances don't offer enough pause for thought, we have this Scarlatti character to deal with as well. Very extraordinary, to say the least."

I looked over at Allison's sleeping form. "It's her I'm concerned about. I can take care of myself. But my old nemesis is opening up his gunsights now—and she's in jeopardy, unless I help her."

"Yes," he said. "I understand that."

"I could even be putting you in danger—by just being here."

He nodded in silence.

One thing is for certain," I said. "She can't go back to her apartment, or to any of the places she hangs out at. She needs money and clothes and things—which I can provide. But she also needs a place to lay low until I figure a way out of this."

"She's welcome to stay here for the nonce," he said. "Her father and I were great and good friends. I certainly owe him that. But what about you?"

"I don't know," I said. "But it'll be easier to figure my alternatives if I know she's okay."

Atkinson's eyes sparkled. "Your feelings do you honor."

"It isn't what you think it is," I said. "It's just a practical concern for another human being."

"Yes," he said. "To be sure." He winked and a sly grin creased his face. I was tempted to erase his humor with a well-aimed remark but decided not to when I saw that Allison was stirring from her sleep. She stretched, then yawned, sat up and gingerly put her feet on the floor. A sharp crack of thunder startled us and the apartment windows began rattling under the impact of sheets of rain. Then the lights flickered and I almost shivered as my memories drifted back to another place, and another storm-lashed night.

I was resting snugly in my cabin deep beneath the decks of the HMS Richardson, sipping brandy and reading Chaucer, unmindful of a gathering storm outside my porthole. The Richardson was a decrepit, leaky four-master which had been carrying cargo and passengers up the English coast for decades. Most of my belongings were safe in the ship's storage and I was looking forward to the end of this, the final leg of my journey from the Mediterranean to London where I was planning to embark on another in a succession of my "new" lives—this time as the principal cellist with the newly-established City Symphony Orchestra.

Now, my appreciation of a particularly beautiful couplet

was rudely interrupted as my lamp flickered and the ship was caught in the grip of a giant fist. The heavens split open with thunder and torrents of water poured down upon the vessel as it pitched in the wind and tried to maintain headway. We were off Cape Barbara, a few miles off the English Coast and hell-bent for port when nature's elements unleashed their fury.

Now, as the freshening storm battered the ship, I could hear its ancient bones scream as the rough sea twisted its planking, shaking its innards like an old dog with a panicked squirrel.

From my cabin in the bowels of the vessel I could hear the shouts of the crew and frantic cries of the other passengers. It was evident things were getting out of hand. My lamp crashed to the decking and darkness claimed my compartment. I was knocked to and fro, and finally tossed bodily off my couch onto the floor. The porthole over my cot blew open and the wind shrieked as the storm poured into the cabin, soaking my belongings.

There I was, scrambling around in the darkness, trying to find my shoes and thankful that, at about half-past ten, it was well past dinner and my plain meal of mutton and potatoes had been digested long ago.

With much travail, I made my way in the darkness through the door into the hall beyond and began climbing ladder rungs to the decks above. Claustrophobia gripped my soul. I was pushed and shoved by screaming passengers and thought for a moment I would be crushed by the growing stampede. At last,

I reached the top deck where I breathed deeply of the cold night air, unmindful of the wind that tore at my shirt and the salt spray that stung my eyes.

Now, free of the terrors below, I could assess the situation. The night was black as tar and, although I could hear its snarl, I could barely make out the roiling sea. In which direction lay the coastline, I had not the slightest notion, as the ship was being tossed about hither and yon, first steering headlong into the gale, then being blown broadside far off course. Suddenly a loud tearing sound rent the air and the entire boat shuddered as its decks were struck by its falling masts. I could hear the screams of people trapped under the huge poles and the swearing of others trying in vain to pull the victims free.

"Lower all boats!" came the cry and gangs of stout crewmen rushed about, pulling thick hemp lines and cranking giant ratchet-like devices. Then, with the deck crammed with milling people, lifeboats jammed in their races, and seamen pulling at their hair in frustration, the ship groaned in pain and gave up the ghost. I hung on for dear life to a rail as the tired vessel rolled over like a dying whale. Bodies flew over my head into the water, many engulfed and sucked into the black depths by swirling eddies created by the vessel's death throes. Finally I was forced to let go of my grip on the rail, lest I too be drawn beneath the water. I heaved myself into the sea and paddled furiously away from the hull until at last, I turned to watch the boat's keel arch upward. Then, accompanied by a chorus of screams from those tossed overboard and wreathed in a cloak of drenching rain, the Richardson slid gracefully into the depths to its burial place on the bottom thousands of fathoms below.

Now I turned my attention to an immediate matter: How to prevent myself from following the Richardson. Through the murk I saw a lifeboat bobbing in the waves. I swam furiously toward it, being careful not to lose sight of it as it disappeared between the rolling waves. At last, I was at its side and, grabbing an oar extended by an occupant, I heaved myself on board and collapsed in a freezing puddle of water collecting in the bottom. The next hours were the most miserable of my life. And dawn arrived to reveal our huddled mass of survivors—eight of us, including two women, one small boy, a slightly older girl and three men of varying ages. We were a wretched lot to behold: Cold to the bone, half-dressed, bruised, bleeding, shocked to the core. I had been aboard for less than an hour when my attention rested on one of the girls. She was not yet twenty, a very pretty brunette who, although shivering and obviously stunned by fright, was wearing a brave face and kept a protective arm about a young girl at her side. I judged them to be sisters and smiled back at them weakly when they saw that I was looking at them. Suddenly, our boat was buffeted by a huge wave and we pitched upward, actually leaving the surface of the water for a moment. The girls screamed and when we at last had steadied, I saw with horror that the older girl had been thrown overboard. Looking over my shoulder, I saw her, a few feet from the boat, trying to keep herself afloat.

"I can't swim!" she shouted, flailing about furiously and

gulping seawater. Her younger sister screamed at the rest of us to do something. I looked about frantically, for a lifeline or something with which to span the growing gulf between the boat and the girl. Finally, seeing no other way, I plunged into the water and began swimming toward the girl. Unfortunately, my bodily resources did not match my pluck. My progress slowed and my muscles became moribund. Exhausted, I watched helplessly as the girl's eyes beseeched me to come to her rescue.

"Please," she cried out to me. "Please."

Try as I might, I could not be her savior. Instead, barely afloat myself, I watched as the water quelled the girl's screams of terror and Neptune enveloped her in his cold arms. I watched in fascination as her head came forward and she began descending almost calmly into her new home, as if having received a message that all was serene and peaceful. It was happening in terrible slow motion, draining every nuance of horror and pity from a stricken audience. Finally, her upstretched arm, fingers spread in farewell, disappeared from view.

I floated in the water for a time, then, with leaden arms and legs, made my way back to the boat. No one helped me back on board. The victim's younger sister turned her back to me. The gloom was palpable.

We rode the waves for several hours until, I imagine it was about mid-afternoon, the clouds lifted, the rains eased, and we could see what looked like the English coast lying far off in the distance. Our mood lifted even as the sun reappeared in the sky, painting the water with silvery flashes. We cheered hopefully and noted with rising spirits that our little boat was actually closing the distance to the beckoning shore. The wind, now trying to make up for its evil of the awful night, was now pushing us directly landward. We hugged each other and screamed with delight, forgetting the fact that each of us was probably near death from exposure. The mere sight of land warmed our bodies and our souls.

Presently, our boat struck the rocks strewn along an empty shoreline and we dragged ourselves up onto dry land. In short order, we made our way to a road where a tradesman stowed us aboard his rickety cart for a short ride into a hamlet a few miles distant. The friendly citizens of that community warmed and fed us and, a few days later, we were all well enough to resume our journey to London via land.

From that episode onward, I swore that I would never, ever set foot upon a boat deck again. As happens, it was a vow that I was, out of sheer necessity, forced to break many times, but not without feeling each time that I was indeed tempting the gods.

And many times, when rains come outside my window, I remember that vision, the slim pretty hand, slipping beneath the surface. And I remember that I, with all my useless immortality, could not save an innocent girl.

Chapter 7

I am always amazed that whenever my life becomes tumultuous, I tend to recall with great fondness those same days that used to bore me to stone because of their unrelenting predictability. Now as I returned to Atkinson's apartment carrying a sack full of sandwich fixings from the corner deli, I realized that I would pay handsomely if it were in my power to buy a few moments of boredom and bliss. But except for the nagging feeling of being under surveillance, I did not feel that either Allison or myself were in any immediate danger. That morning, after Atkinson had driven off to his class at nearby Thesfield Junior College, I took a cab to the Lower East Side and withdrew a tidy sum of cash from a little bank where I

kept funds stashed for just such an emergency. I knew that
much of my assets were under federal lock and key, but I figured that my account in this bank would remain secure. That I
had figured right was borne out by the roll of cash in my right
pants pocket.

I entered the apartment building and used Atkinson's spare
key to gain entrance to the hallway. When I got to the fifth
floor, I was stunned to see the door to his apartment a few
inches ajar. I had made a big issue of telling Allison not to open
the door for any reason. How could she have ignored my warn-
ings. I cautiously pushed open the door and peeked inside.

"Allison?" I called. No answer.

My heart beat picked up a few paces and I walked into the
room and looked around. Setting the bag down, I cased the
bedroom, the bath, even a small store room in the back. No
Allison. Nothing was disturbed. Nothing seemed amiss. Except that Allison was not there.

I stood for a moment in the center of the living room. It
was quiet. I could hear the rattle of an elevated train far off in
the distance and the chatter of birds darting in the elms just
beyond the windows.

Something was very much amiss. I slammed my fist into a
palm, wincing, and sat down. Where could she be? I had dis-
tinctly told her not to leave—for any reason. My God, I couldn't
have been gone for more than an hour. I drummed my fingers
on my leg. Maybe she was in the basement doing laundry. Ab-
surd.

The jangle of the telephone made me jump. I could feel my heart knocking against my breastbone as I lifted the receiver. A roofing and siding salesman perhaps? Or maybe Sears was calling to tell Atkinson his Craftsman cordless drill had arrived.

"Hello?" I said. There was a breathy silence.

"Hello?" I repeated.

"Is this Andrew Merriman?"

How could anyone have known I was standing in Atkinson's living room at that precise moment?

"Who is this?" I said.

"We have Allison."

"What?"

"We have Miss Mackenzie with us, Andrew. And she is going to remain with us unless you agree to start cooperating."

"Who is this and what do you want?" I sputtered.

"We would like to spend some time with you—it's as simple as that. Do us this one trifling courtesy and your little lady here will be released, right as rain. And you will be free to resume your life as well."

"Let me talk to Allison," I said.

"Can do."

The phone was set down and few muttered exclamations later, picked up again.

"It's me," she said.

"Are you all right?"

"So far, sure. But I think you'd better do what they say."

"Don't worry," I said. "Put that gangster back on the line."
The phone exchanged hands again.

"You listening?" said a strange voice.

"What do you want me to do?"

"Be down in front of your building in five minutes. We'll pick you up. Don't talk to anyone. Just keep quiet and follow instructions."

A sharp click terminated the conversation and I sat back on the sofa.

❦

It was a silent and sullen ride through rolling stretches of back woods real estate a few miles from Rye on Long Island Sound. This time, they apparently weren't taking any chances. I sat in the back seat wedged between two strapping men. Another man and a driver occupied the front. They all stared straight ahead, looking crisply menacing and efficient, ignoring my questions.

Although I saw no weapons, I could feel the presence of lethal hardware. Actually, it wasn't needed. They knew—and I knew—that I was a willing, if reluctant, passenger.

They had picked me up in front of Atkinson's apartment building in the space of a few seconds, the big black car gliding to the curb, pausing to scoop me up, then leaving. A passerby wouldn't have noticed a thing.

"Just sit still and don't give us any more problems," one of the men said.

By 'more' problems—I assumed he was referring to the nasty traffic accident that occurred the last time the government took me on a little ride.

After an hour's drive, we pulled off the main highway onto a rutted country road, bounced for a few miles, then wheeled into a driveway in front of an ancient stuccoed house, with sagging shutters, heavily curtained windows, rising out of a doily of flaking paint. The building was steeped in gloom and could have been a retirement home for bats.

I was hustled out of the car, up the creaky front steps and into the house where we were met by a large graying woman who scowled at me. Her hair was drawn back into a severe bun and she wore sturdy black shoes and a dark dress with tiny roses imprinted on it. With the sweep of a fat arm, she motioned us all into a large musty room containing a few empty bookshelves, a large desk and several old leather chairs. A fire burned dimly in a huge fireplace in a futile attempt to displace the chill in the room.

The woman pointed me to a chair and I sat down. Everyone else followed suit, except the woman, who stalked out of the room.

We sat for a few minutes in complete silence.

"When time does the movie start?" I asked, showing them I could still be of good cheer.

This brought forth no response at all. Presently, clicking

footsteps announced the arrival of a tall elegantly-dressed man who entered the room and sat down at the desk. He looked prim and purposeful, with well-coiffed silver hair, crisp blue pinstripe suit, Harvard silk tie, and starched cuffs that extended beyond his suit coat by almost two inches. His thin face was neatly subdivided by a patrician nose, intelligent slate-gray eyes and a wide thin-lipped mouth that showed two full rows of expensively-capped teeth.

"Andrew Merriman, I presume," he said, looking at me gaily.

"Why have I been brought here and where is Miss MacKenzie?"

"All in due time," he said, raising a hand. "Perhaps the rest of you gentlemen will leave us to ourselves for awhile. I'll call if the need arises."

The men rose and trooped single file out of the room like a squad of boy scouts in a flag-raising ceremony.

"Have you eaten?"

"I'm not hungry. Let's get down to business."

"Excellent. Then let me introduce myself. My name is Jonathan Rogers. I represent an obscure branch of the United States government and I've taken the liberty of having you brought to our little home on the prairie so that I might ask you to help us."

"Ask me?" I said. "Those pals of yours who called were telling, not asking me. And what about Allison? You have no right to hold her, no matter what business you think you might have with me."

"Mister Merriman," the man sniffed. "I would be exceedingly grateful if you would do me this favor: Just sit quietly in your chair and listen to me. I think I can answer most if not all of your questions. Does that sound satisfactory?"

I said nothing.

"All right then. Let me start at the beginning. You're probably wondering why we, that is, my associates and I, became interested in you in the first place. What is there about you that could pique our curiosity so? Why should a young, innocent-appearing person such as yourself suddenly find himself undergoing very careful scrutiny by government agents? Has he been evading his tax responsibilities? Participating in the evils of the drug trade? Or perhaps engaged in other pursuits: smuggling, terroristic activities, child pornography, to name a few."

"It's a living," I said.

Rogers rose from his chair, put an unlighted pipe in his mouth and began pacing the room, eyes studying the dusty oak floor at his feet.

"It was that accident of yours, Andrew. When you were bounced off that taxi in midtown Manhattan. Remember?" He turned to look at me, then resumed his pacing.

"I was very lucky," I said.

"Luck? Oh, yes, I suppose you could call it luck. After all, you took quite a jolt, I'm told. Enough to put an average man away for good. Yet you were rushed to the hospital and lo and

behold, a few days later your condition had improved remarkably. In fact many of the attending staff, including Miss
MacKenzie I believe, were simply amazed at your recuperative powers. And so, too, was one of the more perceptive staff
doctors. In fact, this man was so intrigued that he mentioned
your case to one of our associates and even took the liberty of
providing us with your medical records and blood samples.

"Now normally we wouldn't be interested in such a
miniscule happenstance but, as it occurred, one of our newest
technicians with time on her hands decided to have a look at
your blood samples just in the sheer one-in-a-million chance
that something was going on that perhaps we should be keeping abreast of. And guess what? This lowly technician discovered that your blood is subtlety different from that of the average man. Moreover, so is your cell construction. Something to
do with DNA molecules and healing processes. This is terribly
coincidental—and not a little suspicious—because it seems
that one of our most secret lab projects concerns cell regeneration and the like. In any case, that in and of itself could have
been construed as some aberration of some sort, that is, until
we began taking other issues into consideration.

"For example, by all accounts, you're living the life of a
law-abiding citizen. A nicely sub-average income gleaned from
strumming some electronic musical instrument in a rodent-
infested disco—with a correspondingly modest living situation: No fancy cars, outrageous houses or other accoutrements
of your typical big spending lawbreaker. Just a modest apart-

ment. No special friends, with the exception of Allison MacKenzie of course. Oh, and dear me. Let's not forget these items."

He picked up a slip of paper and waved it at me.

"This, Andrew, is a list of safety deposit boxes which we have stumbled onto. They were opened in your name at various institutions both here in the New York area, Washington, D.C., and a few other cities in this country and even in Europe. My, you are well-traveled."

He paused for dramatic effect, pursing his lips and raising his eyebrows in a very good William Buckley impersonation. "Do you know anything about these, Andrew?"

I said nothing.

"No matter," he said. "But you can just imagine how curious we were when we obtained court orders to have these deposit boxes opened up. And do you know what we found? Nearly two hundred items—a vast treasury is the best description I think, of worthy collectibles with a value according to our own experts of several million dollars."

He looked at me and smiled. "That, as the plain-spoken might say, is definitely not chickenfeed. Especially for a person of such tender years."

I started to say something but he went on.

"Now, we asked ourselves: How could a young man of such obviously modest means accumulate such wealth—and in so short a time? Well naturally, giving you the benefit of the doubt, we conjectured that an inheritance was undoubtedly the answer. So we began diligently tracing your past to ascertain which of your ancestors so generously bequeathed these riches to you. And do you know what we came up with? Nothing. No ancestors. Not a single soul. Well, we thought, it's obviously our Andrew is an orphan—whose past went up in smoke when perhaps an errant hot coal ignited a fire in the basement of St. Joesph's Home or some such place. But try as we might, we could not make headway in this direction, either. And, as for school, birth, work, insurance, tax, and social security records, the same story: One impressive goose egg. Needless to say, we were exceedingly frustrated. It was almost as if some great God had deemed that you should be birthed from a Golden Egg, without benefit of mother or father.

"Now, what are we to do with this situation? Well, clarification is certainly in order—so that we can drop this entire case and get on to more substantive issues. So we try to obtain more information. We invite you to participate in some easy give and take with our representatives. You do not get into the spirit of this and tell us to go fly a kite. We talk to your friends. We interview Miss MacKenzie. Our agents keep track of your activities but turn up nothing.

"Now, just put yourself in our shoes. We were convinced that you are an individual with something to hide. But what is there to hide? Your treasures? Your background? What is there in your past that you have hidden away with such diabolical thoroughness? Indeed, Merriman, what simple explanation do you have for this needless mystery? If you are not a foreign agent, criminal, or terrorist, what are you? More to the point, exactly <u>who</u> are you? It is the lack of answers to such ordinary questions that increases our determination to insist on your cooperation in giving us answers.

"So what is there for us to do but react as we have? At this juncture you have left us no choice. You have refused our earlier invitations to discuss your situation with us in honesty and candor. So with great reluctance, we make an effort to motivate you in the right direction."

"You kidnap Allison."

"No. We invite Miss MacKenzie to accompany us out here, in hopes that we can convince you to see the light."

"Since when is the government into kidnapping and extortion?"

Rogers smiled primly. "As you say—we are minions of the government. Thus, we can take whatever steps are deemed necessary to conduct our operations."

"Very convenient for policy-makers, isn't it?"

"Now, let's cease this verbal sparring and get on with it. Who are you, Andrew?"

"You know who I am. Andrew Merriman."

"How old are you, Andrew?" His eyes became small shiny beads with the cold gaze of a giant anaconda slithering through a glade toward an unwary wart hog.

I decided my immediate refuge lay in silence—which didn't prevent him from shooting a full quiver of questions at me.

"Can you give me the name of your parents? Where are they buried? Do you speak any foreign languages—and if so, how many? Are you a United States citizen? Have you ever been a citizen of another country—and if so, which countries and when? Have you ever been in the employe of a foreign power?"

He paused for breath. Another smile and his eyes became friendly again.

"Of course you can't answer these questions, can you, Andrew? Because you know full well that if you did answer them—truthfully, that is—you'd be opening a Pandora 's Box that you'd probably never be able to slam shut again. Am I right, Andrew?

"But let me move on to other issues," he said. "Now, does the name Methuselah mean anything to you?"

"Not particularly."

His eyes narrowed into a squint.

"Well, let me explain a few things and perhaps you'll appreciate the quandary we're in. Three years ago, my colleagues in the Special Sciences Unit were given the task of proving or disproving a rather unique theory concerning cell growth in the human species. Some work had been carried out in this area for many years, but nothing concrete had ever been developed that would hold water. We were given the task—with an unlimited budget—to answer once and for all this question: Is it possible to isolate the chemistry responsible for cell growth and maintenance—and formulate a method of using this material selectively to prolong cell life?

"We called the project by the code name Methuselah, after that biblical gentleman who managed to eke out a life span of more than nine-hundred years—so the legends say.

"Now then, through dint of discipline, dedication and dour threats, the personnel assigned to this task finally triumphed and developed a scenario that proved the viability of such a process. It was a physiological and genetic breakthrough that confirmed at least the plausibility of inducing cell revitalization and regrowth through DNA manipulation. Further, our scientific team even discovered what blood and cell characteristics would have to be present in order to stimulate this process.

"Can I get you something to drink?" he said.

I declined.

"Well, now, imagine our surprise when, less than six months ago, we discover that the Methuselah Project has been compromised. By whom and for what intents, we haven't the foggiest. But we are terribly concerned that someone else will be in a position to hitch-hike off our hard-won labors and pull off this whole stunt.

"And that frightens us. Because, you can just imagine the turmoil created by a country with the technological prowess to promote rapid healing and significantly extend life. You see, a country whose citizens are limited to a life span of, say, seventy-five years, would hardly be a match for a nation whose citizens can enjoy a span of, say, one hundred years or more.

"Or, it needn't be an effort put forth by one country. One single person or group of persons could perfect our work to the point where they could cause untold harm. Imagine if you will the ramifications of one tidy little clique of terrorists who possessed the ability to outlive their pursuers. But I digress: Because, Andrew, this is where you come into the picture."

A bright smile lighted up his face and he nodded at me like a benevolent uncle.

"Imagine our great surprise when one of our technicians puts a bit of your blood and cell shavings under an electron microscope and sees the sum composition of all the characteristics we had been searching for in the Methuselah Project. What joy!

"The problem is of course, how in heavens name did all of this come about in your system? I mean, here we are, spending millions and millions of taxpayer dollars trying to achieve what someone, namely you, has apparently already achieved. Why you, Andrew Merriman? And of course, that leads us to the supposition that perhaps you, or someone you know, had something to do with compromising our pet project.

"Now, with that as a background, perhaps you'll understand our position and, more important, see fit to tell us why you are walking around with your system positively bursting with the very latest in micro-bionetic technology."

He looked at me earnestly, and my mind was racing. Had the moment arrived when I should come clean and spread my cards out on the table? I considered my options: few. But could

I trust this glib government servant, whose interest in my—and Allison's welfare—probably went no further than earning him a bonus, a hearty slap on the back from his superior, and a kick up the bureaucratic ladder? Would they view me as a threat to them—to their whole system—and decide the one sure way to remove the threat was to eliminate it?

His eyes probed deeply into mine. "I know what you're thinking," he said. "And I can't say I blame you. But, I can tell you this, I won't let anything happen to you or your friend if you're honest with me. But it is essential that you provide us with enough factual information so that we can determine what—or who—is behind what amounts to an untenable threat to this country. We need you, Andrew, and I promise you that if you trust me, I will respect that trust."

I thought a few moments longer. What did I have to lose? After all, I was already in their custody. The room was quiet. I could hear the faint ticking of a large clock somewhere. I thought of Allison. Yes, it was clear: Common sense dictated that the time had come to surrender my independence. So much for common sense.

"All right," I said, "now let me say a few words."

His face brimmed with renewed good cheer as I rose from the chair.

"First of all," I said, "I have to congratulate you. I'm always amazed at how sanctimonious you civil servants can become even while you're shredding the rights of your constituents, trampling on our personal freedoms and seeing to it that, where government interests are concerned, the end justifies the means."

Rogers opened his mouth to object but I didn't give him the opportunity.

"Just look at yourself: Sitting there smugly in your Hart Shaffer & Marx suit, warm and secure in the knowledge that you're doing your duty—no matter the cost. And let's take a look at the cost. For one thing, somewhere in this house you're holding a woman—a United States citizen—prisoner, incommunicado and against her will. So much for her rights and her freedom—the same freedom that you're supposed to be safeguarding. And what has she done to deserve this? Her sin is that she knows someone that you're curious about.

"And what of my rights? With no other justification than your own vague suspicions, you check out my medical records, analyze my blood, subject me to extortion, search my private bank facilities, confiscate my possessions, assault me, abduct me, and subject me to illegal interrogation. And you have the guts to say you're committing this entire outrage on behalf of the citizenry with great reluctance—to motivate my cooperation.

"What a load of deceitful bull. At least those two goons of yours—the ones who got smacked by the garbage truck— told it like it was. They told me 'we can do anything we want— we're the government.' Not pretty, huh? But at least they layed it right out there for me.

"And you ask me about this 'Methuselah' operation of

yours. I mean, do you really think for one minute that I believe that stuff about this crumby experiment? Cell regeneration. DNA molecules. You'd better tell those thumb-sucking scientists of yours they'd make a terrific living writing fairy tales. If it's cooperation you're looking for, you can look to somebody else. You can keep me in this hole until doomsday for all I care. You won't get another word out of me."

I sat back in my chair and folded my arms across my chest.

For a long time Rogers directed his attention to the high ceiling above, as if searching for an errant spider. Finally he spoke.

"You speak of goons. Exactly what goons are you referring to?"

"Don't look saintly for my benefit," I said. I'm talking about all those busy little speedball operatives of yours: That bozo who tried to put out my lights in that motel room. And those two space cadets who dragged me out of my place in handcuffs before they were cornered by that garbage truck."

"Those men were not my operatives."

"Come off it."

"No, Andrew. You come off it. You may not have much respect for your government, but give us some credit. We wouldn't be talking here right now if we wanted to harm you. Maybe you should consider the possibility that we're not such the tawdry gang of blackguards you would suppose us to be."

"Then whose men were they?" I said.

"Ah, and that's precisely why we're together here today,

Andrew," he said, smiling brightly. "Perhaps you can enlighten me about that."

Oh boy. I could tell by his display of Colgate dentures that he truly was waiting for enlightenment. Could it be that I'd been wrong? Had I been a bit too cynical, perhaps—too eager and ready to blame my difficulties on higher authorities? In my mind there flashed an image of Scarlatti's waxen face. Had these goofballs been working for him—and not for men like Rogers? Could I be that wrong? Not a chance.

Rogers smile turned to a grimace of disdain. He spoke a few words into a telephone on his desk. Presently, one of his strongarms entered the room.

"Take our Mister Merriman down to one of our cozy basement suites. Give him some time to think things through a bit."

Rogers walked passed me out of the room, his heels clicking on the hardwood floor. I could hear him whistling as he disappeared down the hall.

Chapter 8

There is nothing like a dose of solitary reflection to clear your mind and distill your thoughts. And in my drafty cell in the damp basement, I had plenty solitude and time in which to noodle over my prospects.

The room itself must have been a pantry at one time. It was a cement block affair, lined with shelves and swing-out bins, which I could easily envision filled with potatoes, rutabaga, apples and other staples in cool long-term storage.

Rogers' associate had tossed me headlong into my new quarters after leading me down several flights of stairs. Thankfully, he switched on an overhead light so I wouldn't have to conduct my reflections in absolute darkness.

Once a day, they would lead me out of the room to re-lieve myself. They would also use the occasion to take me be-fore Jonathan Rogers—who would detect my unbroken re-solve and consign me to the depths again for additional medi-tation. My daily food intake was minimal. A pitcher of water and stale roll in the morning—which I suspected was a refu-gee from Rogers' own breakfast tray. In the afternoon, a goose liver sandwich. At night, a Snickers bar and an apple.

One day passed into two, then three, four, and five. Each day I expected to be dragged out of my cell, taken to another chamber and put upon a rack for some indelicate stretching exercises. Or possibly carried into a laboratory, held down by thick leather straps, and subjected to a diabolical truth serum. But nothing bizarre occurred, except for my face-to-face meet-ings with Rogers who would look at me sternly like a disap-pointed school master.

Aside from being terribly bored, I was very concerned about Allison's welfare. I also felt guilty, realizing that if it weren't for me, she wouldn't be mixed up in this mess. Was she safe? How was she being treated? Perhaps Rogers and his henchmen were torturing her. Or maybe that greying ox of a house lady had layed hands on her. Even now, I conjectured, she could be lying in a cell much like mine, wracked with fear and sobbing her eyes out.

One saving thought occurred to me: As long as Allison was in custody within the hallowed walls of this building, she was out of evil reach of my old friend, the Prince. That thought somewhat assuaged my concerns.

In the meantime, I used my time to set some order to recent events. Rogers babblings about his Methuselah project intrigued me for a couple of reasons. First, I had to admit my curiosity was piqued by the possibility that the answers concerning my personal condition could be discovered under a microscope by some lab technician. In a way, it was a blow to my pride that my 'omnipotence' might be explained in such casual terms as 'cell regeneration' and DNA tidbits. In a way, it was dehumanizing, despite the fact that I never considered myself god-like in any way.

Or had I? Had I indeed become some kind of an immortal snob, superior to those lesser members of my species—those poor unfortunates who were doomed to crumble and crack with old age, like cheap pottery? Yes, the truth of this dawned on me: For lo these years, I had been telling myself that I longed to know exactly why I was different. And now that there was even a possibility of the answers being found—I was flinching. Of course, Rogers' little army of lab folks could be wrong. Although, I had to admit it was interesting, if true, that the blood coursing through my veins contained the Right Stuff ordained by Methuselah hypothesizers.

And what of Rogers' declaration that the project had been compromised? How and by whom? It seemed oddly coincidental that this would occur while I was in such close proximity. And, assuming the project ever reached fruition—for what purpose was it to be used? To transform the Earth into a planet of ancients? Or perhaps to pass out Methuselah's gifts to just a chosen few?

How did Scarlatti fit into all of this? Or did he at all?

On the sixth day of my incarceration, I noticed a change in daily routine. I awoke, took a sip of fetid water out of yesterday's pitcher and awaited the morning visit from one of my jailers. The hours passed by, and I could measure the passage of time by my swelling bladder. Still, no one came to the door of my pantry. Finally, for no reason except that I was growing impatient, I pushed on the door.

Voila! It opened wide. I smiled. Someone would probably pay dearly for this incompetence! I poked my head into the dark corridor. All was silent. How could this be? At this instant it occurred to me that the house had been inordinately silent for several hours—minus the usual bumps, slams, and sounds of running water generated by a houseful of people arising and getting on with their day. Then too, I recalled being awakened briefly before dark and hearing the roaring of car engines.

I made my way cautiously down the hall, then suddenly halted at the approach of footsteps. Zounds! One of my jailers on his rounds. How foolish of me to think my freedom could be had so easily. I crouched beside a heavy table, removing an empty vase which I gripped in my right hand. A nicely balanced club with which to stun the unsuspecting jailer who even now was just a few feet away in the gloom. In one superb leap, I sprang forward, raised the vase high overhead and brought it down toward the skull of my craven victim.

"Andrew!" a familiar voice screamed. Allison leaped nimbly aside and I followed the vase to the oak floor in a miserable heap. "What in the world are you doing?" she said, looking down at me. "You could have killed me."

I got up. "Nice reflexes," I said. "I thought you were a guard or something." I came forward and gathered her up in my arms, hopeful that my manliness would give her courage.

"Leggo," she said, pushing me off her. "Where have you been? I've been looking for you for an hour."

"I've been resting in my basement apartment," I said. "Where is everybody?"

"They must have left during the night. I found my door open a couple of hours ago. I've been up one hallway after another trying to find you."

We went up to the first floor and into the front rooms. It was obvious we were alone in the big old house.

"Why would they leave us here like this?" Allison wondered aloud.

"Maybe they figured they were digging a dry well," I said.

Allison walked over to the desk Rogers had occupied during our long discussion nearly a week before. She picked up an envelope and opened it.

"It's from that Rogers character," she said, handing it to me.

"Dear Mr. Merriman and Ms. MacKenzie," I read aloud. "Your release from custody should not be perceived as an indication that we have terminated our investigation of you (and most especially you, Merriman). Rather, we want to provide you with a brief respite while we pursue other facets of the situation. Our paths will cross again. In the meantime, in the face of your reluctance to cooperate, it serves us no good purpose to continue holding you indefinitely. Despite your outspoken opinion of me and my colleagues, you'll be gratified to learn that we have no interest in prolonging your discomfort. Perhaps after you have the opportunity to think this situation through together, you will come to the conclusion that you both will be better off working with us, instead of against us. In the meantime, we have called off the dogs, so to speak. Your bank holdings have been returned to you, Mr. Merriman and, so far as we are concerned, you are free to resume your normal lives, if you still can. Accept the enclosed stipend as partial payment for the inconvenience we have caused you. Use the car in the garage for your immediate transportation needs, just leave it on any city street and it will surely find its way back home to us. Enjoy your freedom. Should you change your mind and wish to talk to me, please call the number on the attached card."

"Swell guy, huh," said Allison. "Inconvenience, my foot," she sniffed.

Somewhere in the house, a clock bonged eight times and we went into the kitchen, ransacked the cupboards and made ourselves coffee. It tasted good after our caffeine-free diets. We sat there, kind of dazed.

"How have you been?" I said.

"I've been better," she said. We exchanged stories of what had happened to us since we had last seen each other. For her, it meant being snatched out of Atkinson's apartment and being deposited at the government hide-away. She said she had been treated well, questioned only briefly, and guarded most of the time by Mrs. Sotheby—the stolid matron.

"Do you think those people are really who they say they are?" she said.

I told her about my little interrogation sessions with Rogers.

"Maybe this Rogers is telling the truth," she said. "Maybe he hasn't had anything to do with those other men who've been after you."

I refused to accept that possibility.

"You figure they really have found out what makes you tick?" she said.

"I don't know. Sounds like they're on the right track. And for some reason, I really don't find myself liking it."

"Don't want to be like the rest of us—is that it?"

"Could be. To tell you the truth, it's just a little bit frightening. Maybe I've seen so many people bite the dust, it's hard for me to think about doing the same thing."

"Hard to lose your immortality, huh?"

"I don't know. I really can't say exactly how I feel."

"Well, however you feel, I like you a whole lot better this way."

"Mortal, you mean?"

"No, not that," she said. "I like you sharing with me how you really feel about something."

"Is that such a change?"

"For you, yes," she said. "Another thing: I'm glad you told that Rogers guy to buzz off. The old maid told me about it."

"Did you think I'd cave in to those guys?"

"No, not exactly. It's just that you're never that serious about things. And I never knew the point at which you'd actually make a stand about something."

"Well, now you know."

"Yes. Now I know."

She got up from the table and kissed me on the cheek. So acute was my delight that the soft touch of her lips sent a shiver of red hot pain through my system. At last, I was making progress with this wench. It was inevitable: Soon, I would have my way with her.

∾⑤

"Okay, shall we take off?" She looked about her nervously, as if the walls were closing in.

"Where to?"

"How about home? Rogers says he'll lay off."

"Great. But that doesn't help us so far as the Creature from the Black Lagoon is concerned."

"Right. How could I forget about him?"

"One thing is sure—we have to call old Atkinson."

"Yipes," she exclaimed. "He's probably got the police out looking for us. I wonder if the telephones in this mausoleum still work."

She ran off and left me in the kitchen. I could see that time was what we really needed. Time to just catch our breath and relax and, of course, work out a suitable offensive against the Prince. That he would still be in hot pursuit I had not the slightest doubt. It occurred to me that it was too bad I couldn't have told Rogers about this little problem—but he would have insisted on knowing everything and I could not see how that would be possible.

Allison returned and plopped onto the chair across from me.

"Well, to say he was glad to hear from me is the understatement of the century. He discovered we were missing when he got home from class. Didn't want to call the cops because he figured this whole thing would be too bizarre for them to handle. So he's just been sitting tight, chewing on his fingernails—and cleaning up his place."

"What do you mean?"

"Somebody ransacked it real good. And he doesn't think it was the usual neighborhood scum—no money or anything important was taken. "Rogers and his little Circus maybe."

"I wouldn't be so sure. Anyway, he said he's been thinking about us—you especially. Wants to talk to you as soon as you're able."

"Well, I don't dare clutter up his life again until we get some of these folks off our trail. No sense endangering him any more than we have already."

"Why don't we leave here now—before your friend comes to greet us?" Allison shivered and we got up from the table.

We found the car out back, as promised. It was a tired-looking, ancient Mercedes.

"Is this what well-wheeled government agents are driving these days?" Allison asked.

"No," I said, pulling up the hood. "This is what government suspects are driving."

"It's probably wired for sound," Allison said.

I looked under the hood. It looked like a storage compartment for old electrical and greasy engine parts.

"Looks like the Little Engine That Couldn't," Allison said.

I slammed the hood down and we got in. The keys were in the ignition and it started right up.

"At least it runs," I said, pulling out of the drive.

"I hope it stops, too," Allison said, handing me the emergency brake handle which had come detached from between the seats.

⚛

We drove upstate for over an hour, then pulled off into a small shopping center and bought a supply of clothes and food with the money Rogers had left for us. As we were leaving a small general store, we spotted a note on a bulletin board near the exit.

FOR RENT: LAKESIDE CABIN. FULLY-FURNISHED. BY THE WEEK, BY THE MONTH.

Not needing to be conked over the head with a board to get my attention, I recognize this as an opportunity and trooped off to a nearby pay phone to call the number on the notice.

By noon, we were unloading the car and carrying our supplies into a tidy two-room cabin, surrounded by a stand of pines near a small pike lake. The furnishings were simple but adequate: A small metal fireplace in one corner, sink and counter in another corner. A sofa, lounge chair, reading lamp and a small table took up the rest of the room. A pair of windows overlooked the lake which lapped the shore less than fifty yards from the cabin. I peeked discreetly into the small bedroom. There, against one wall, was a double bed.

The year was 1910 and New York was a great gray yawning city awakening and beginning to feel the power of what
she was to become. Veiled in a mist of smoke and haze, the
metropolis wedged between the Atlantic Ocean and Long Island Sound was criss-crossed by dusty streets where crowds of
bustling citizenry surged toward their destinies amid the chatter of foreign tongues that befitted the melting pot of the western world. Reddish steel skeletons of office buildings that would
soon tower twenty stories and higher, dotted the island of
Manhattan under the sooty sky.

I walked down the gangplank extending from an ancient,
creaking freighter (even now leaning heavily against the dock
in its death-throes) with one suitcase under each arm and hope
in my heart, relieved to be setting my feet once again upon dry
land. Ever since that ill-fated voyage on the Richardson so long
before, my feelings about over-the-water travel had been fragile at best. If I had know then that such a miracle as commercial air travel would soon be changing the face of the world, I
would have been incredulous and overjoyed.

As it was, I was filled with happiness and curiosity to be
back in the homeland of my father—whose misguided wan-
derlust had resulted in my departure from this great land in
the first place. Now a prodigal son returned, I was determined
to seek my rightful place and to make up for lost opportunity.
Seven sea-days before, I had emigrated from the rolling
greenscape of Ireland—one of thousands seeking to escape the
misery and poverty of the old country. And with my own pros-

pects at their lowest ebb in decades, I had decided to strike out from the continent to find out whether the country of my fore-bears could present me with a brighter horizon.

So there I was, standing in the mob of people on the wharf—without friends or family—a perspicacious, curly-haired young man wearing the worn coat and trousers of a down-and-out tradesman, but with an ear-to-ear smile, a sparkle in his eye and a battered music case under his arm. Onward and upward—there'll always be a Merriman.

A long walk on dusty streets brought me to a narrow rooming house where I found accommodations. The widow, Abigail Pittman, operated the establishment with the help of her daughter, Rebecca, a rambunctious and shapely girl who, when she wasn't cleaning floors and seeing after the kitchen, flirted with the boarders.

Rebecca and her mother were opposites. Rebecca, laugh-ing, eyes flashing, long hair the color of deep caramel, pre-cious Michelangelo curves, sweet disposition. Abigail, dour, downcast, barrel-waisted, red-faced with unvoiced anger.

I obtained work unloading merchandise at a department store by day and plucking guitar in a bistro at night. From my very first pay envelope, I put a few coins aside with which to purchase a nosegay for sweet Rebecca. She was thrilled with the little clutch of daisies and squeezed my hand with thanks. The next week, it was a small bag of chocolate covered pea-nuts. She thanked me profusely and kissed me briefly on the lips. The third week, I took my lunch money and bought her a pretty white blouse and a fashionable skirt, which earned me an opportunity to slip my trembling hands inside her new garments. On the fourth week, I presented her with stockings and a pair of elegant red slippers. I had hoped that this explosion of generosity (I hadn't eaten in so long I was nearly starving) would gain me my entrance to Valhalla.

In this instance I was mistaken. But I still believe that relationships with females are like good investments. And that a gentleman who shares his largesse with a lady friend will be repaid many times over.

∽

"How about a chocolate cookie?" I said. "There's just one left."

"That's all right," Allison said, "you can have it."

We had been in bed for just a few minutes. It was dark outside. We had talked for hours, exploring our alternatives. I had yawned with great drama and made a display of checking my watch. Yes indeed, it had been an exhausting day. How nice it would be to sleep in a bed for a change. No, I didn't care which side I slept on. I knew that I would be masterful from either side.

She turned over abruptly and faced me. "You know," she said. "I think you've just scored a first."

"How's that?" I said, comfortable with my traits of leadership.

"You're the first guy to every try to bribe me by offering me an Oreo."

"It wasn't a bribe," I said.

"Listen, Andrew, if just once you'd kick that Rudolph Valentino act of yours and try to be human, maybe you'd score once in a great while."

"I don't know what you're talking about."

"Yes, you do. That God's-gift-to-girls act you put on. Why don't you just stop apologizing for your natural human drives and try to act like normal men act with women. You try to be so cunning and clever you end up acting stupid. All that yawning in there and those dumb hints about 'early to bed, early to rise'."

The room was filled with my silence.

"Now, Andrew, I'm tired, I'm cold, and I'm tense. So why don't you just put your arms around me like a human being and try to comfort me. If something happens, then okay, it happens. But you don't have to try to engineer it like some drippy knight at the roundtable. God knows how long we're going to be around anyway, so let's try to get something out of it while we can."

As I slid across the sheets and put my arms about her, I couldn't help but wonder what it was about the simple mention of chocolate that always made a maiden so passionate.

The days that followed were pure escapism: Mornings for talking of love; afternoons for walking through the pine forest, strolling the lakeshore, and skipping stones; evenings for blushing, tremulous embraces. My mask of Victorian male ego fell away and, with Allison's help, I was able to see myself as I was: A lone survivor of ancient wars, not victorious, but instead bearing half-healed psychic wounds created by years of building defenses for my emotions, shielding my one-ness, protecting myself from the prying eyes of passersby whose trips along this trail would be much shorter than my own. This girl, who once nursed my physical self in the sterile confines of a hospital room, now cared for me in a more telling manner, within the warm shield of her patience, trust, and common sense.

She was good to me, yes, and I must have been good for her, despite my flagging penchant for self importance. The more we were together, the less reactive we were with each other. Her jibes became more good-natured. She was no longer so quick to point out my gross frailties. Perhaps in discovering why I was how I was, she was discovering important truths about herself as well.

We were a couple on holiday, without care or concern— an illusion we created in an unspoken compact and managed to hold in place for nearly a week. Then, it was back to reality.

"I wish things could be normal with us," she said the night before we left our cabin hideaway. "I wish you were like everyone else, that we weren't involved in what's going on around us. That we weren't afraid all the time."

"It shows?"

"It does," she said. "You're afraid—probably more for me than yourself. And I'm scared, too. The mere fact we've been here a whole week without so much as talking about it shows how we feel. I wish we could just disappear somewhere and start over."

"I've done that dozens of times, all over the world, for all kinds of reasons. And look where its gotten me."

"You've survived, haven't you?"

"There's got to be more to this whole charade than mere survival."

"Yes. You're right."

A certain look flickered across her face. There was something familiar about it—a mind a continent away, reflecting about some other time, some other place, perhaps almost forgotten, but not entirely.

"A drachma for your thoughts," I said.

"Oh, nothing. I was just remembering something. I must have been sixteen or seventeen or something. Mom and Dad were going away on a winter vacation. Florida, I think. Anyway, I was supposed to stay home by myself. In a way, I wanted to. You know, teenager gets a chance to show she's all grown up and ready to accept the responsibility of watching over the house without having pals over to trash it out while the folks are away. Except for one thing. I wanted to go with them. To be with them. But I wasn't going to beg. I asked why it was that I couldn't go along. Mom said it was because they needed time alone, too. And now that I was a big girl, I shouldn't need them. Dad didn't look directly at me, but I could tell he agreed. They didn't want me along, period. I think that crushed me. Because I really never felt that I had ever had them, alone to myself, in the first place."

"So did you and your pals trash up the house?"

"No, nothing like that. I behaved like a regular fairy princess. But by the time my folks came back a couple of weeks later, I discovered that I wasn't really missing them any more. Oh, maybe I felt like I was living out on a deserted island some place—maybe I was even lonely. But I didn't need them any more. I didn't feel bad toward them—I didn't sulk or pout or anything like that. I didn't feel put upon—like I had been given a raw deal. I was even happy that they had enjoyed themselves together—they both looked great. But I just felt kind of disconnected from then on. And I guess I realized that I didn't miss them any more and that kind scared me. Does that make any sense at all?"

"To me it does, sure."

She took my hand and squeezed.

"I don't feel lonely right now," she said. "I like that."

We were sitting sideways on the sofa, looking at each other. Her face was soft and glowing in the dimming light and her eyes had that far-away look in them again. I felt a powerful stab of concern, for I wanted in the worst way for her to be thinking those safe, sane, hopeful thoughts that would make her smile and fill her with happiness. Sitting sweater and jeaned with legs crossed under her and barefoot, she looked totally vulnerable. What had I done to this girl? How could I ever make it up?

"Maybe if I could ditch this forever-and-ever existence of mine for just one normal life with someone like you, I would." Even as the words tumbled from my lips, I was shocked. This was not the Andrew Merriman I knew and loved.

A strange look came into her eyes. In the silence I could hear the chirp of crickets and a chill night wind playing about the windows. A burning log in the fireplace gave up its sweet incense of ancient bark and bubbling sap.

"Would you, really?" she said. "A lot of people would sign a pact with the devil to be in your shoes." She sighed. "Anyway, I wouldn't let you if you had the chance."

"Why not?"

"Because, it's too much to ask of anyone." She looked down at her hands in her lap. "I mean, giving up a chance to maybe live forever—just to spend twenty or thirty years with someone like me. That's not a very good exchange, is it?"

"I would give up forever for you—I think I would. In fact, I'm sure I would."

"You're sweet to say that. But you don't have to."

"Yes, I have to. Because I mean it."

"I think maybe this country air is getting to you."

She laughed. Then a tear trickled down her cheek. I felt as if my pounding heart would break out of my chest. In that instance, my being exploded with a blend of emotions I had never experienced: profound sadness and ecstatic joy. Was this what love was all about? And if so, why did it hurt so terribly?

From that moment on, we became one. And, I knew that if fate ever came to claim Allison, I could not, would not, go on without her.

We left the cabin the next morning, leaving the back country solitude to weave our way back to see Professor Atkinson. Although we were uncertain that he would be able to help us, we both felt had nothing to lose and that, if anything, our week of seclusion would leave any pursuers with a very cold trail.

I pulled the reluctant Mercedes out onto the two-lane blacktop that would take us to the southbound interstate into the city and, in the rear view mirror, saw a black dot getting larger. It was a big car, perhaps a Lincoln Town Car or a Cadillac, and it was closing on us fast. As the image grew I could see a lone driver behind the wheel. I gave Allison a warning pat on the knee.

"Don't look now but we have a visitor."

She turned around and gasped, just as the Caddy crashed into our car's rear bumper.

"Yipes, he's trying to kill us," she exclaimed. Our old

clunker careened across the highway, out of control, but I managed to regain the upper hand just in time. I pushed the accelerator pedal to the floor and pulled the car back into the right lane, knowing as I did so that I was just asking for another bashing. It wasn't long in coming. Allison screamed as the shock of the second strike slammed our heads against the seat-backs. The big car pulled alongside and I got a glimpse of a smiling face. Scarlatti's.

"He's enjoying this," Allison said. "Look at the jerk."

The big car closed the gap between us and struck the Mercedes broadside, knocking us nearly six feet sideways.

"Wow, one more like that and this car'll split open like a Crackerjack box."

"Can't you go any faster?"

"Are you kidding," I said. "The rubber band is already wound up as tight as it can go."

It was almost impossible to turn off the road and there was very little room for maneuvering. We were a few miles east of a little town called Codding in an area of rolling hills, stone fences and heavily-wooded terrain, all of which provided a natural barrier that sloped down to the highway.

I could see Scarlatti poised for another run, probably the coup de grace. And then I spotted an opening at the side of the road and a clearing beyond.

"Hang on," I said. "Time for a little cross-country maneuvering."

I waited until the car was nearly eating our tailpipe then

swerved abruptly off the highway. The car bounded down an embankment, nearly tipping over, then began mushing across a narrow strip of open field bounded on two sides by thick woods.

"That got him," Allison yelled, looking back to the high-way. Scarlatti had screeched to a halt, backed up, paused to study the situation, then roared off after us, his big car up to its gunnels in soft dirt but making pretty good headway. It was clearly time for some good power management. I down-shifted in hopes of squeezing the most efficient blend of power and traction, trying to pick out the firm ground which would hold our weight without bogging down. The tired old engine roared pitifully as we zigged and zagged our way over the crest of a hill, bouncing up and down, with only our seatbelts prevent-ing our heads from banging on the ceiling. All the while, the big black car gradually narrowed the distance between us. We bounded over the top of the rise toward a clump of trees about one hundred yards away. Suddenly, the ground turned to slime. The car slipped and slided, then, after spending its last reserves of energy pulling itself out of the muck onto dry ground, gave up its ghost. There we were, sitting in the car with its nose pointing down the steep grade toward the trees, when our pursuer pulled up alongside, that smile still plastered on his face. Could we run for it? The issue was settled when the prince leaped from his car and was upon us before we could even get unbelted.

I could actually feel his hot breath upon my face and taste

the faint odor of garlic as his eyes bored into mine through the window. Those Scarlatti eyes, raging with hate, the pristine, icy cold face, the coal black hair—he looked now just as he had in his wife's bedroom that night so long ago. And yet, there was something different. My left foot pressed the baby clutch peddle to the floor and I slipped the car out of gear.

"Get out of the car, both of you." He motioned with a very efficient looking pistol. We did as he ordered, slowly, as if reenacting a dream. We walked a ways down the hill, Allison gripping my arm.

"That's far enough," he said.

"Why are you doing this?" Allison shouted.

"Be quiet, Miss MacKenzie," he said. "It is my turn to speak."

"You've waited a long time for this," I said.

"In a manner of speaking, yes. But then, you have nothing but time, isn't that true?"

"Speak for yourself," I said. "You're not exactly getting any older."

I tried to think. When last we met, Scarlatti must have been about twenty years older than myself. That would make him...what difference did it make anyway?

"Oh, but I am," he said. "I get older every day, just as your lady friend does."

I was puzzled. What did he mean?

"Who do you suppose me to be?" he asked.

I wasn't really up to parlor games.

"I am Scarlatti, am I not?"

"So you are. So what?"

"So, I am not THAT Scarlatti whom you suppose me to be," he said, defiance flashing in his eyes.

His meaning escaped me.

"The day you saw me in the restaurant," he said. "I could tell by the frightened rabbit look on your face that you believed that I was the Prince, the very prince whose life you ravaged many generations ago, whose honor was sworn to be avenged by his heirs, myself among them."

My memory flashed back. There was a Scarlatti son that had not died in the fire that night.

Our inquisitor turned to Allison.

"Did you know, then, that your pompous friend here is a murderer and a rapist, whose evil deeds snuffed out the lives of seven Scarlatti's in one horrible evening?" His voice rose in pitch as he recited my alleged misdeeds.

"But how can you know this?" she cried.

"Because I am a Scarlatti, the direct descendant of the one son who escaped the clutches of this…this monster who should but cannot die."

He glowered at me and spit on the ground. "He is the devil incarnate, for who but a devil could wreak such evil and have the power to live many lifetimes?"

His glower turned to a smirk. "And through each of his lifetimes, there has been a Scarlatti son, proudly taking up the chase, tracking this, this vermin. But now the chase takes a different turn." Another smirk.

"You see, I have taken steps so that, perhaps, I can join this devil in his workshop. I have taken great pains to acquire certain information. Perhaps, sooner than you think, there will soon be not one, but two persons on this small planet for whom time means nothing. And after that, perhaps more."

A light went off in my head. "The Methuselah Project," I said. "You're the one they're looking for."

"Perhaps. In any case, be assured that soon your secret will be my secret and then I will have all the time I need to deal with you as I might."

"And I suppose those have been your goon squads who've been rattling my cage lately."

"Oh, are you referring to my associates? Well, I do enlist the aid of others when necessary. Sometimes one must turn up the flame under the watched pot."

"So what was the point of trying to cave my head in—and the rest of those charades?"

"Simple," he said. "Information gathering, expedience and sheer pique. Satisfied?"

He beamed at us almost benevolently. "In the meantime," he said, "your immortality presented myself, and the Scarlatti's that have gone before me, with a few problems. To be sure, how can you kill a person who will not pass on to be judged in the other world? But the answer is quite simple."

I could feel Allison's grip tighten on my arm, which already was feeling numb.

"The solution of course, is to slay someone close by, to separate you forever from some precious being, even as you did to my family so long ago."

The horror of what he planned suddenly dawned on me. Allison's awful prediction, made days ago after the car bomb explosion, was coming true. He was going to kill her. Now.

"That is what I bring you, sir," he said. "Vengeance supreme, a just eye for an evil eye. You may live on, but this lady shall not. And you shall have an eternity in which to grieve."

"I don't suppose it would do any good to tell you that what happened on that night was an accident. I make no excuses for being in Scarlatti's bedroom. But I can swear to you that everything that occurred, the fire, everything, was an accident."

"No, as you say, it doesn't do you any good. I have made a vow—and vows are beyond contrite confessions."

He pointed the pistol at Allison and I could see his finger tighten on the trigger. Her shoulders sagged for an instant and I feared she would swoon.

I glanced back to Scarlatti and a movement behind him caught my eye. Eureka—the old Mercedes was moving! Crapped out and worthless, the decrepit relic was taking one more step for mankind before saying goodbye. I remembered the broken emergency brake handle. Now, pure physics was in play as gravity tugged the machine down the hill. Slowly at first, then gaining speed. The car glided silently forward, taking dead aim at Scarlatti's proud back. Would it cover the distance in time?

"Pray to your Devil for your Miss MacKenzie," Scarlatti chortled.

That was the delay we needed. Just as he squeezed the trigger, the sturdy rusted bumper on the Mercedes cracked into the back of his legs, pitching him forward. The shot went awry and Allison fell to the ground in a faint. Scarlatti screamed in pain as the car rolled up his back and stopped, pinning him to the ground like a giant insect in a collection.

Knees shaking, I bent down, scooped Allison off the ground and carried her to Scarlatti's waiting Cadillac. I layed her down on the sofa-like front seat and slammed the door. I could hear Scarlatti yelling as I started the engine.

"You won't get away with this," he gurgled, his voice distorted by pain. "I'll follow you to the ends of the earth!"

The big tires spun in their tracks then bit into the dirt and the car carried us back to the highway in style and comfort.

Chapter 9

Allison sat in shocked silence as we sped down the highway, putting as much distance as possible between us and Scarlatti. She stared straight ahead with her arms crossed in front of her, as if waiting for a bus. I could see specs of straw on her sweater. Her face was smudged with dirt. If there had been any doubt in my mind before, I now was clearly convinced that our crisis had deepened to depths that were no longer tenable. We had to seek help, from whatever quarter.

In one way, the meeting with the descendant of Prince Scarlatti's son had relieved me of one concern: Now I knew that our pursuer with the cold smiling face was not the original Scarlatti. Maybe I should have been able to figure this out by myself, but because of my own situation, it had not seemed entirely without reason that someone else had also acquired the mysterious gift of longevity. And by extension, if one other person could do this—why not ten, a hundred, or a thousand? But now I knew that I was indeed, for better or worse, a one of a kind. And I was relieved. For I knew that life was complicated enough with just one of me. God knows what events could transpire if there was a whole gaggle of Andrews roaming around.

But my relief could be short-lived because now, here was this new Scarlatti, claiming to have stuck his finger in the Methuselah pie. I could just imagine what would happen if this guy somehow managed to finagle a life extension. Maybe the God in charge of living knew what he was doing when he gave me a lifetime pass. After all, I had been a pussy cat for most of my life, flitting about harmlessly, really not taking advantage of my situation. I had not become power-hungry or a ruler of nations, and I could have. I had not used my accumulated knowledge for evil purposes, and I could have. And the few assets that I had accumulated, although quite a treasury by common standards, was actually a pittance compared with what I could have acquired, had I a mind to.

But what would happen now if Scarlatti was to use his acquired information to crack the secret of Methuselah? God only knows. And I was struck forcefully by two thoughts: First, Scarlatti's attempt to use the formula posed a threat of such proportions to the world at large that my own stake in the entire situation paled in comparison. And second, maybe Rogers had been telling me the truth after all. Although he did have a strange way of operating—maybe he represented the good guys. It would be very interesting to get Professor Atkinson's perspective on all of this.

After several minutes, Allison finally began stirring from her torpor. She still looked dazed and bewildered, as if she had just awakened from a long sleep.

"Where are we?" she said.

I patted her knee. "Just a few blocks from Atkinson's."

"Why do you suppose that car started rolling all of a sudden?" She was looking at me with one eyebrow nicely arched and a lock of blonde hair partially obscuring her vision, ala Madonna.

"Providence," I said.

I glanced nervously at the rear view mirror. How long would it take Scarlatti to pry himself out of his predicament? That he would survive his bout with the Mercedes I had no doubt. I was certain that it was just a matter of when and where he would strike again.

The little professor welcomed us with open arms when we arrived at his apartment.

"I've been at my wit's end," he said, putting his arm around Allison and steering her into the front room.

He left us alone for a few moments and returned with a tray of donuts and hot coffee.

"All right, children," he said. "I assume life has not been exactly dull for you."

We briefed him as well as we could about events that had

transpired since we had last seen him. Allison's kidnapping, our confinement in the hideaway, and our latest brush with Scarlatti.

"My, we've been active, haven't we?" he said, scratching the bald spot atop his head. "Well, let us see if we can sort through this a bit. First off, it's quite evident that you can't continue being used as the cue ball in the game of life. Although you, Mister Merriman, might have nine lives, our friend, Allison is limited to just one. And if we are to conserve that one, we're going to have to get help.

"Now, let's talk about this Rogers person for a moment. I want you to know straight off that he has been in contact with me."

This brought me up sharply, but Atkinson waved aside my interruption.

"Oh, I didn't have to tell you that," the old man said, "but I think a little real honesty wouldn't hurt anyone. Frankly, Rogers asked me to entertain the idea of convincing you to throw in with him. He admitted that you were reluctant to do this on your own—and he thought perhaps that I might be able to coax you."

Atkinson paused to light up a small pipe. "Now," he said, blowing a plume of blue smoke toward the ceiling, "it seems that this Scarlatti fellow has done the coaxing for me. Not that I wouldn't have told you about Rogers' pleas—I would certainly have. But I do think Scarlatti's actions have put a certain patina of urgency on the matter which perhaps, did not exist in your mind before."

   That was true. I remembered Rogers telling me about his fears of what could happen should the Methuselah information fall into the wrong hands.

"I was more concerned about the way they had treated Allison and myself," I said. "I didn't take this Methuselah mumbo-jumbo very seriously."

"Well, I can't blame you for that," Atkinson said. "They really botched up their end of the matter—and Rogers pretty much admitted that. I think any future dealings you'd have with them would have a much more salutary effect. But the fact is, they are not aware of just who is responsible for siphoning off information about this little scientific endeavor of theirs. You do know. I would say that, because of that, Rogers needs you."

"But we don't need Rogers," I said.

"Oh, come off it Andrew," he said. "You can be stubborn on your own time, but not on Allison's. The fact is, Rogers has the resources at his disposal to provide a very effective shield against this Scarlatti character. Can you say the same?"

"Can you?" Allison chimed in.

"No," I admitted. "I can't. But how do we know we can trust him?"

"Maybe you can't," Allison said. "But what have we got to lose?"

"The girl's right," Atkinson said through a smoky haze. "How many more run-ins with this man do you expect to survive?"

I got up and paced the floor. They were right of course. How dare I let my damnable stubborn pride get in the way of things. How could I expect to protect Allison?

"Okay," I said. "What do you want me to do?"

Chapter 10

"Well, hello there, Andrew. So nice to hear from you."

Despite Atkinson's advice, it made me uncomfortable being in the same universe with Rogers, let alone having to talk to him again. But out of consideration for Allison's welfare and respect for Atkinson, I had gritted my teeth, dug out the card Roger had left behind, and dialed his number from the privacy of Atkinson's small study.

"I've got some information about your Methuselah project," I said.

"Oh, have you now? Well then, why don't you come down and see me and make a clean breast of it?"

"Listen, Rogers, knock off the smart attitude or you'll be listening to a dial tone."

"Oh, let's not be hasty, Andrew. I'm just trying to keep it light."

"Do you want to talk or don't you?"

"What's convenient for you? Would you like to come by my office?"

"I'll pass on that, thanks. I'd rather make it on neutral grounds. You know where Gardner Park is—two miles west of Atkinson's place off the freeway?"

"We'll find it."

"Not 'we'—just you."

"How's nine tomorrow morning sound?"

"See you then."

❦

Gardner Park was a block square chunk of fenced concrete bordering FDR Drive consisting of a miniscule playground, a few scattered wooden benches and a basketball net under which several neighborhood kids were scrambling about. I arrived early in order to give the place a good scan before Rogers' arrival and took a seat on a bench that unleashed a quiver of slivers into my backside but provided a good view of the colorful graffiti sprayed on the walls bordering the enclave.

A light fog was beginning to break up over the East River and the sun was just beginning to burn through, waking small flocks of sparrows who were chattering among themselves high in the scraggly elms on the boulevard across the drive.

A small black Dodge Neon pulled into a driveway on the

side street behind my bench. A gray-haired man struggled to free himself from the cramped front seat, then slammed the door and began walking toward me. It was Rogers, wearing a trench coat with the collar turned up, in true master spy fashion.

"Is that the kind of car you guys drive these days?" I said.

"Waste not, want not," he said, sitting down beside me. "You know how the government abhors waste. Now, what can we do for you?"

He still wore that smug patrician grin. I wished I could belt it off his face. "It's not what can you do for me—it's what can we do for each other."

"As you will," he said. "Now, I must say, your telephone call came much sooner than I expected. Tell me what has happened to merit such a fast response."

"I know who's been messing with Methuselah."

Rogers smile disappeared. "Oh. Who?"

"You expect me to tell you just like that?"

"If you don't wish to tell me, then why on earth are we sitting here?"

"I need assurances."

"I gave you assurances during our last chat. You weren't too impressed with them."

"They didn't go far enough."

"How far do you need them to go?"

"I want an iron-clad guarantee that you'll offer protection to Allison MacKenzie. Me, too, if there's room."

"You have my word on it."

"Your word isn't good enough."

"It's going to have to be good enough. I certainly can't give you a contract signed by myself, the Director of the CIA—or anyone else for that matter. That's not the way things are done."

"Tell me how things are done."

"Just as you said earlier: You help us, we'll help you. No more, no less. You give us the information we need to help put matters to rest, and I'll see to it that no one lays a hand on fair Allison's head, or yours either—within reason."

"What's this 'within reason'—an escape clause?"

"Not at all. It simply recognizes that some things occur for which we can't be held responsible. But we'll protect your interests as best we can."

It was time to put up or shut up. I could see no way out but to accept his deal. I could not have cared less about my own future—after all, I was the impregnable fortress, right? But Allison was another story—and with Scarlatti probably popping blood vessels in his forehead at that very moment, I knew it was time to toss in the towel.

"Okay," I said. "Let's go for a walk. A long one."

We took off along the cracked narrow sidewalk unwinding around the perimeter of the park. I jammed both hands into the pockets of my windbreaker. Rogers walked carefully, as if on a tightrope, head down, studying the rise and fall of the substandard cement work. The tap-tap-tap of a basketball hitting concrete provided a background for me.

"My name is Andrew Merriman," I began. "I was born in the year 1675 in Louisiana—north of New Orleans, I believe. My father, George, was a blacksmith and of French extraction. My mother, Martha, bore him two children. I was the youngest. My older sister, Ella, died at age ten on board the Southern Yankee, a ship my father had booked passage on for our immigration to England."

"Your father took you from North America back across the Atlantic to England?"

"I'm afraid so."

"So you are in fact, an American citizen?"

"Yes, I am. But there were no United States of America then. I didn't get my citizenship until after I had returned to this continent in the 19th century. Of course, my citizenship is probably invalid since I obviously lied about my age."

"I should imagine you did."

Except for similar questions illuminating some point of fact, Rogers showed remarkable self-control, considering the unique aspects of my tale. In fact, his reaction was such a non-event that I began to wonder how much of my story he had guessed for himself—or had ferreted out by other means. In any case, we circled that little park many times while I unraveled my life's tale, yard by yard. After the passage of an hour, we got into his car and bounced over to a nearby restaurant where I continued my recital over coffee and raspberry Danish.

When I had finished, Rogers simply shook his head.

"Not your everyday bedtime story, is it?" I said.

"Nothing surprises me anymore, Andrew. Absolutely nothing. Although this does come remarkably close."

We drank our coffee in silence for a few moments, then the questions came.

"This condition of yours—I'm surprised that someone, somewhere in the medical or scientific field hasn't caught on to you until now."

"I've have never been concerned about these brainy types," I said. "It was my neighbors, people I lived and worked with, that always became suspicious. I mean, if someone knows you for thirty or forty years and you still look like a teenager, they start asking some tough questions. Sooner or later, if I stayed in one place long enough, people noticed there was something unusual going on. When that happened, it was time to go. But it hasn't been the length of life that raised the suspicions in a lot of cases. It's the fact that when I do something dumb and get hurt—or get knocked down like I did by that taxicab, that's when the trouble starts. I mean, you don't have to be a genius to figure out that something weird is happening when the guy in the next hospital bed with the broken legs, ruptured spleen, and punctured lung suddenly is all healed and goes home whistling Secret Agent Man. And now, when someone gets curious, they've got the technical equipment and the know-how to start looking into things. It wasn't like that a century ago when people would just scratch their head. Or, in the more ridiculous cases, hang garlic over their doors so you wouldn't come back to their house. I mean, in some societies, I could have been burned at the stake."

"All right Andrew, now let's talk about our little Methuselah Project. Who is our villain?"

I told Rogers everything I knew about Scarlatti and his relentless search for me, including the episode in the field on the steep hill.

Rogers puckered his lips and wrinkled his brows.

"One thing puzzles me," I said. "Just how would a man like Scarlatti get away with classified information of yours— and how could he hope to make use of it?"

"We discovered someone had been hacking our computer system."

"But, aren't those systems supposed to be secure—impossible to tap into?"

Rogers sighed. "In theory, yes. In reality, no. It's like this: Once upon a time, the National Security Agency, our government's version of The Godfather, discovered that many of the hack-proof computer systems operated by individual agencies and large private corporations were, in fact, not secure at all. Geeks, vandals and foreign governments were busily tapping telephone lines, collecting classified data. So the NSA got busy and promoted the private production of encryption technology which the agency had designed—and would control. The idea was that all top security information could be encrypted before it was transmitted, and thus be shielded by eavesdropping eyes and ears. Unfortunately, although this sounded like an excellent idea on paper, it took too long to be put into effect. My agency, which is nothing more than a blemish on the NSA's backside, was last in line for such technology. And we're paying the price."

"Well, if someone got a look at your Methuselah Project information by breaking your computer security, how can you trace them?"

"Well, oddly enough, the mere fact that this person had the capability to do what he or she did narrows the possibilities. And, of course, with you delivering us a name—it shouldn't be impossible to track the culprit down."

"Then there's no problem, is there?"

"Yes and no. It depends on whether or not Scarlatti is working alone, strictly in his own behalf, or whether he has shared this information with others. I doubt very much that one man could possess the ability to not only steal the information in the first place, but also act upon it. Remember, we had not actually found the pot of gold at the end of the rainbow. All we have done is to make a judgment that the pot is actually there."

Rogers sat quietly for a moment, deep in thought. Then he looked up at me across the plastic table top. His eyes brightened with revelation.

"But we do have a distinct advantage now."

"What's that?"

"We have you, Andrew."

"What's that supposed to mean?"

"Don't get alarmed. It's just that you're very likely the key to the entire Methuselah theory. And that being so, I'd like to propose a course of action."

"Oh, oh, here it comes."

"I want my associates to get on with the job of tracing this Scarlatti person. But at the same time, I'd like you to allow us to examine you."

"Forget it, Rogers. You and your pals aren't going to be using me for a guinea pig."

Rogers waved his hand and laughed softly. "Nothing so dramatic, I assure you. But you'd be giving us an incredible opportunity to check our theories against a real-life situation. We'll draw some fluids, collect a few cells—things like that."

I must have looked unconvinced.

"I think we're going to have to view this entire situation from a wider perspective, Andrew. Bear with me for a moment. Now, let's assume for a moment that this Scarlatti does have resources at his disposal that would enable him to make more out of the Methuselah information that we have. Let's say he and his associates actually, through dint of hard work, brilliance, or just plain luck, manage to come up with some formula, some elixir—call it what you will—that enables them to duplicate the essence of your unique physiology in the bodies of other men and women. And let us assume for a moment that these other men and women are hostile to the free world.

"What then, Andrew? Do you want a whole army of

Andrews running amuck about the earth? And do you think for one moment that these Andrews would be like you—or would they be a bunch of little Bin Laden's, bent on destruction of life as we know it today?

"Think of Allison. Would you want her—or any woman—to raise her children in a world run by zombies who don't die?"

"Thanks for the compliment."

" Within your body, Andrew, you may well be carrying the seeds of immortality. They are far too precious to be entrusted to anyone but those sworn to uphold those precepts and values which we all cherish. Put another way, those same seeds of immortality can become seeds of destruction, should their secret fall into the wrong hands.

Rogers' usually placid face was beginning to glow red now and his voice was rising in pitch. His words sounded unreal and melodramatic.

"But even if you could isolate those magic somethings that make me different," I said, "what makes you think that our government is any more capable of seeing that they're used for good? I've been around too long in too many places to think that any group of people and any government operates in the name of the public good all the time."

Rogers sighed but said nothing.

"Even you and your pals are a good example of that," I said. "It didn't bother you at all to drag Allison and me off to that house of horrors of yours when it served your purpose.

You mumbled something then about me forgiving your actions because they were being carried out in behalf of the public good. So how can you can be entrusted with these so-called seeds of mine? You're not beyond evil, when it justifies your objectives."

Rogers nodded and ran a hand through his hair.

"Well, I certainly can't blame you for feeling the way you do," he said. "But please remember that when we took you into custody, we had reason to believe that you could have been involved in the theft of the Methuselah data—all the more so because we knew enough about you to believe that your body contained properties that closely resembled Methuselah characteristics. The specimens obtained by that ambitious hospital intern started us thinking. For all we knew, Andrew, you could have been the very first guinea pig. We had what appeared to be a very real emergency on our hands."

We left the restaurant and stood on the street watching passing traffic.

"Well," Rogers said. "Which is it to be? Continue on your own and take your chances—or throw in with us and take your chances?"

I remembered last Scarlatti's threat. 'To the ends of the earth' he had screamed.

It was an easy decision.

The year 1917 stands out clearly in my mind. Not only did my newly-adopted country become involved in World War I, but it was also the year I saw my first airplane up close. The two events are linked together, because the one led to the other.

I had been in this country for more than ten years and was well settled into a hum-drum job playing third violin in the pit band at the Roxy. Since fiddle players weren't exactly vital to the war effort, my job certainly did not shield me from the prospect of becoming a doughboy once the country went to war.

So it was that, still looking indecently boyish, healthy and handsome, I decided to escape the boredom of my current existence and answer the call of an Army Air Corps poster attached to the brick facade of our local post office building. The colorful sheet seethed with patriotism and trigged a spasm of guilt within my chest. I could do nothing but answer my country's call to duty immediately.

I arrived at Fort Bragg, North Carolina on the morning of June 13th after an all-night train ride from Grand Central Station. There were no airplanes on this military field. Several thousand naive and trusting recruits, myself included, were there to commence five weeks of basic training. I managed to complete this grueling course with sufficient ease, then took a battery of tests. Finally, I was admitted into the august ranks of the Air Corps.

Another train ride, this time northwest to Omaha, Nebraska, brought me to the Sanford Aerodrome, located a few miles south of the little plains community. The land was pancake flat, baked rock hard by the sun, like one giant landing field.

It was a windless summer morning when I came face to face with my first airplane. The sun had risen a quarter ways across the sky and we nervous but hopeful birdmen could already feel its rays hot upon our backs as we trudged through green clover toward the center of the field. Captain Raymond Burger brought us up to one of the aircraft and made us stand around the strange beast in a ragged circle, as if preventing its escape should it decide to make a run for it. Thus cornered, the winged creature squatted in the grass quietly as the Captain introduced it to us.

"This is an aeroplane," he announced. "It is used only for flying. During the next few months, it is hoped that at least a few of you gentlemen will learn to fly one of these. Your government is sparing no expense toward this end. And I can assure you that my fellow officers and I will also do our small part toward achieving that objective."

As the captain looked on, we walked around and examined this strange and wonderful flying machine. It looked like a giant grasshopper in its speckled green camouflage. It had two cockpits, one twisted wooden propeller on its nose, one huge lovely tail, and two big barn door wings trussed together with a mad crisscross of poles and wires. My noise wrinkled at the smells of cotton, leather, grease, oil and varnish that enveloped the machine, which sat poised on two braced legs on which were mounted large narrow tires. I touched the fuselage with the palm of my hands and was jolted by surprise: The plane's skin was made of cloth!

So much for flying. It was evident to me that the only purpose this fragile machine might have would be to splatter my soft body across the nearest wheat field. I wondered what the penalty was for desertion.

"This aircraft is a Curtis JN110," Burger said. "We call it a Jenny. It's powered by an OX-5 six cylinder engine capable of delivering 55 horsepower and a cruising speed of 110 miles an hour in level flight. It has a service ceiling of 13,000 feet above sea level, its fuel tanks hold 36 gallons of gas, giving it an endurance of four-and-a-half hours."

Captain Burger delivered this speech proudly, standing with his hands on his hips with a fierce look of dauntlessness in his eyes.

"This is the airplane we'll train you in. Those of you who can make it perform properly can look forward to an honorable career in the Corps. Those who cannot will be transferred to the cavalry."

Not much of an alternative, considering that I hated horses.

The next morning we were up before the birds. A coolish wind was in the air and a thickening deck of clouds was pushing in from the west. My stomach rose and fell like a bucking ox cart as I walked along with my new instructor, Sergeant Kirkgard, toward a Jenny which was tugging impatiently at its tie-downs in the breeze.

"Hop in front," said Kirkgard, a long-faced lanky fellow who reminded me of an unhappy scarecrow. "We'll try to get in some stick time before the rains arrive."

I clambered up into the front cockpit and lowered myself onto the thinly padded seat. A black metal stick came up between my legs and my feet fell upon two pedals on the floor. A small panel with a sparse cluster of gauges caught my eye. I felt like a beached goldfish. I wondered if I should turn around and inform that good Sergeant that a terrible mistake had been made. I didn't.

For the next fifteen minutes, the instructor checked me out on the cockpit, explaining which devices performed what function. Then a member of the ground crew swung the prop and we were off in a blast of wind and noise. The wind roared into my leather jacket through tiny crevices, chilling me to the bone. My goggles began fogging over. I had never been so steeped in outrageous fear as I was when the Jenny bounced across the field and finally took to the air, rocking its wings in the gusty ground currents and clawing frantically for altitude.

But once aloft and well clear of the ground, the air smoothed and I realized that this strange beast really could fly. The powerful engine sounded lusty and confident. Looking down, I could see the Nebraska countryside clothed in quilted checks of green, brown and black. Fleecy white clouds sailed past in brilliant puffs, through which the sun occasionally showed with golden splashes that enveloped the plane as we soared merrily onward.

For the next hour, I paid great heed to Sergeant Kirkgard who shouted words of wisdom at me through a speaking tube. I was amazed that when I took over the stick and planted my feet upon the rudders, the plane still flew smartly along, as if welcoming me into this grand fraternity of dare-devils.

I thought I was doing splendidly. And it wasn't until after we landed that I learned otherwise. However, my instructor predicted my air work would improve with time.

"I just hope there is enough time," he added.

We continued our training procedure during the days ahead. Unfortunately, my initial nervousness returned and with it, another gremlin: airsickness. I couldn't go up in the air for more than ten minutes without losing my breakfast. Once Kirkgard made me wash down the inside of the cockpit after we landed. My ears turned crimson with embarrassment.

Then came the flight when, like Icarus, my mettle was tested. We were cruising at three-thousand feet, practicing stalls, side-slips and S-turns when Kirkgard rattled my ear with a sudden blast through the speaking tube.

"Let's go home!"

I banked the plane back toward Sanford, feeling a bit nervous since I had barely landed the Jenny more than a dozen times—and usually I had thoroughly botched the job. Oh well, I thought, Kirkgard was alert and ready with his practiced hand to fish me out if I made a muck of things.

I looked back to reassure myself. Holy Christmas! There was Kirkgard, slumped in his seat, his head lolling on his chest.

The truth ripped through me like a dagger: My instructor
was out cold. Furthermore, I would have to get this plane
back down on the ground my myself.

I gulped and pulled back the throttle to lose altitude. The
Jenny put her nose down and I could hear the wind singing a
melancholy song in the wires. In a few minutes, I could see the
bare outline of the field through a thickening fog bank which
had bloomed since our departure less than an hour before. My
throat tightened and my mouth felt as if it were filled with
sand. I had seldom landed properly in decent weather, let alone
in poor visibility.

Over the roar of the prop I heard a moan and I looked
back to the rear cockpit. Kirkgard raised himself up, tried to
speak, then slumped again. Clearly, he had suffered some kind
of attack.

By this time we had descended to about a thousand feet
above ground and I brought the plane around on the first leg of
what I took to be a proper landing pattern. Patches of grey
stratus intermittently covered the field now and I was finding
it difficult to keep the precious landing area in sight. I pulled
the throttle back to idle to begin my final approach. Terrific.
The old OX-5, mistreated by who knows how many student
pilots before me, decided to pack it in. A loud clanging and
pounding ensued and suddenly, the Popsicle stick propeller
was standing stock still a few feet in front of my eyes. I stifled
rising panic and a sudden urge to throw myself over the side.

Now I knew my first landing of the day would be my only

landing. Without power, there could be no chance to try again. I furrowed my brow with concentration and bent to my task. I hadn't lived all these years to give up the helm and deliver some innocent person—even a flight instructor like Kirkgard—to certain death. I would simply have to make this one good.

The Jenny glided down. There was no jockeying the throttle now. It was useless. I managed with what devices I had left—rudder and aileron, straightening the plane out, bringing it down the approach chute straight as an arrow. I squinted to see the ground through the mist. Ah, there it was, the landing area beckoned. The plane soared in over the approach area and I raised the nose slightly to bleed off speed and soften the landing.

I smiled. This was easy. I would be accorded a hero's welcome. Whoops, I had celebrated too soon. The plane bounced off the turf toward the sky, then began bucking like an enraged stallion. The plane lurched sideways in one final burst of delirious momentum and cart-wheeled to a halt, leaving Kirkgard and I suspended ignominiously upside down hanging by our seatbelts. The Jenny had been reduced to splinters and shredded wisps of cotton.

I did receive a few compliments for getting Kirkgard down safely. And Kirkgard, who was rushed off to the hospital, thanked me personally at his bedside where he was recovering from an appendicitis attack. For myself, although I was not pleased with the technical aspects of my performance, I was intensely proud that I had overcome my fears and had not let down my fellow man. Yes, I had busted up an airplane. But I also had saved a life.

Five weeks later, we ran out of time. I received the bad news in the company of eleven other trainees who were also being given their walking papers. Or should I say, riding papers. Within 24 hours of our wash-out, we were miles away in Texas, having a look at our new transportation. I served out the remainder of my enlistment on the backs of a series of hostile nags who made my life as a soldier miserable.

From time to time, while riding tall in the saddle on a decrepit hay-burner, I would hear a familiar muted roar and look to the sky. There amid the clouds, I would see a Jenny, flying fast and free, and I remember the silk-scarved helmeted pilot in the Air Corps poster, arrogant and smiling. Maybe, someday, I would have the opportunity to test my wings again.

Chapter 11

Rogers' cooing admonition that the ordeal I was about to undergo would be in the name of all the peoples, animals and insects of the free world did little to soothe my anxiety as I entered the grounds of the Thorpe Biological Research Institute near Leaburg, Maryland. Thankfully, Allison was at my side, having agreed to accompany me on this journey to the laboratories which were manned by Rogers' tight little group of Methuselah Project scientists.

"Doesn't look like a research place, does it?" she said as we alighted from a car driven by a heavyset Rogers aide-de-camp.

"More like a British country estate," I said, scanning the lush landscape. A broad lawn dappled by stately pines and circular gardens blooming with flowers and neatly trimmed shrubs led up to wide front steps and an impressive columned entrance.

We were greeted at the door by a rotund moon-faced man in a white coat who rubbed his hands together as if launching into a meal of mutton chops.

"I'm Doctor Cannel," he said. The air hung heavy with scents of iodine, alcohol and Clorox, making my nostrils twitch with irritation. A racket of jangling telephones, shouted exchanges and a raspy P.A. system made the lobby seem like the hub of all earthly energies. I introduced myself and Allison, who stood behind me as if I were a shield.

"Mister Rogers has instructed our staff to show you every kindness and consideration," the doctor said. "We hope to have you here for only a few days so we want to use your time as efficiently as possible."

We went into Cannel's office where he explained that Allison would enjoy the comforts of a separate suite and various amenities offered by the building and grounds while he and his colleagues ran various tests on me.

We sat in two leather chairs in front of Cannel's desk. As he talked, I could feel the warm tingle of Allison's hand in mine, bridging the space between us.

"What kind of tests?" I heard myself asking.

"Mostly basic procedures." Cannel beamed with enthusiasm and rubbed his hands together again.

"A complete general physical workup. A good deal of blood

work. Tissue sampling. Mostly painless. A few we'll perform with the assistance of a general anesthetic. Nothing futuristic or extraordinary. Most of what we'll do will not depend so much on the exotic nature of the procedure itself but, rather, the thoroughness and penetration of our methods. As you're probably aware, we have at our disposal a vast array of techniques and tools which will enable us to obtain, document and record visual data down to sub-atomic levels."

"Meaning?"

"Meaning that if there is anything within your physical being that proves or disproves our Methuselah theory, we hope to be able to find it."

"And what if it isn't a 'physical' phenomenon?" Allison asked.

"Oh, I'm quite sure it is," he said. "After all, my dear, no man is immortal, correct?"

"Maybe not," Allison said. "At least not on paper."

She gave my hand a squeeze and looked at me levelly, her eyes telegraphing a message I could not fathom. For some reason, I had the impression that maybe she didn't want me to be just an ordinary mortal.

They started me off easy. While Allison was led off in one direction in the company of a friendly looking woman in white, I was hustled into an elevator and taken up to the eighth floor where I was to make myself at home for the foreseeable future.

My room was comfortable enough, complete with a

framed print of ducks in flight above the single bed that was
straight out of the Holiday Inn Collection of Fine Art. There
was also a television set, a couple of side chairs, bureau and a
small bath. My clothes were stored behind a pair of sliding
glass doors and I was given a light green hospital gown to wear.

Two white-clad technicians arrived. One, a spectacled
brunette woman, withdrew several vials of blood from my veins
while her compatriot, a skeletal brooding man with an unkempt gray beard, jotted down my medical history. Great
pauses of silence bloomed while they tried straight-faced to
digest the centuries-long medical parade of this raving lunatic.
In my tally, I told of my bouts with several varieties of plague,
diphtheria, tuberculosis, yellow, black and red fevers, ptomaine
poisoning, gout, rickets, beriberi, polio, and assorted other
ailments which my system had collected and successfully waged
battle against over the ages.

During the next two days I was ferried about the building
in a wheel chair, usually pushed by Allison, who insisted on
accompanying me to most of my appointments, except for
those exams that required the introduction of various kinds of
stainless steel probes into my body—procedures that merited
privacy. I was thankful that she wasn't around to hear my tearful complaints.

But true to Rogers' word, most of the examinations were
a mere nuisance rather than painful, and I spent much of my
time being wheeled in and out of various laboratories and examination rooms containing electronic devices that buzzed,

whined and winked as they probed the depths of my being in an effort to unlock my secrets.

I was also asked to perform a battery of endurance tests in a make-shift gymnasium, pumping iron and running while technicians frowned at monitors linked to my body by long wires and metal pads taped to my skin. I also submitted to a variety of breathing tests, huffing and puffing through transparent plastic tubes and bellows. And there were nutrient absorption and metabolism tests. I was given minute quantities of various foods by mouth and tube while banks of wise and silent monitors measured my system's processing capabilities.

In a way, if the whole affair hadn't been so disruptive, it would have been rather humorous. Because despite their imposing sleek cabinets filled with electronic wonders and flashing LED's, I knew intuitively that these people would find nothing unusual lurking in my system. Maybe this was my pride, but somehow, I treasured the notion that any answers would be found in metaphysical arenas, rather than in such prosaic environs as test tubes, specimen slides and x-ray films.

On the other hand, what if I were wrong? What if they did flush out some magical answers? I wondered what my reaction would be—if I lost my uniqueness. And if they did find some mysterious something that explained everything, what then? Obviously they would try to pass it on to others—themselves at the head of the line, of course.

I had often wondered what consequences would have occurred had any of my past wives given birth to children. Would my heirs have carried my gift? And, if they did, how long would it be before I occupied a world crowded with my long-lived progeny—and their subsequent children? Indeed, a new master race, far superior to the one that nutty little Austrian corporal used to rave about.

And what of Allison? How I would feel if scientists could pass along my mysterious elixir to her—to become my companion in a life that was forever a summer and where autumn and the end never came? I couldn't believe she would have any part of that. After all, she had already said it: She wished that I could shed my immortality in exchange for a normal life. What more could one ask for?

In fact, could the process, whatever it was, be reversed? Maybe Rogers and his minions could better spend their time figuring that one out. Then again, I didn't especially like the idea of receiving an injection and then suddenly dissolving into a small pile of evil-smelling dust. Such were the questions that filled my senses as I yielded to the probing of my inquisitive hosts.

Whether or not they were succeeding in their mission was not clear until the morning of my third day when Rogers appeared at my room shortly after breakfast. Allison and I had just finished a pillow fight on the bed and we were both a trifle red-faced.

"Well," he said, trying to ignore the tufts of goose down in the air, "it appears that we have completed our examinations, Andrew, and we won't need you around to complete our investigation. I think we have collected enough data to keep us busy for several months."

"What did they find out?" Allison asked, drinking the orange juice from my breakfast tray.

Rogers shrugged. "So far, absolutely nothing of substance. It appears there are no obvious miracle-makers coursing through his blood-stream, although I'm certain that closer examination will reveal more subtle characteristics."

Talk about an anti-climax. "So, I'm free to go now?" I said, knowing that, somehow, this all seemed too easy.

Rogers paused and closely examined his manicured nails. He looked cool and efficient in his usual dark pinstripe, his silver cap of well-groomed hair set off his steely gray eyes which now looked out at me from under nicely furrowed brows. A faint scent of Old Spice wafted toward me.

"Not exactly," he said.

"What exactly then?" I said.

"Well, we would like to have your help on another aspect of our situation." Now he smiled brightly, as if inviting us to participate in a marvelous new parlor game.

"You see," he went on, "we have managed to turn up your friend, Scarlatti."

"Where?"

"It seems he's been lurking nearby, in a manner of speaking, all along."

"In what manner of speaking?" Allison asked. She started to pace the floor.

"Well, it seems as though our Mister Scarlatti is a trusted employee of the United States government."

"You're kidding," I said, heading for the wall locker to retrieve my street clothes.

"Yes, he's associated with the U.S. Army Rocky Flats Chemical Arsenal just Northwest of Denver, Colorado."

"What's the rest of it?" I said.

"Scarlatti is second in command at the arsenal—they manufacture and store nerve gas there, you know."

"Nerve gas?"

"Yes, I should imagine they have enough of the stuff under lock and key to wipe out every living human being on the face of this planet several times over."

Allison's face turned crimson.

"You mean this Scarlatti person, this maniac, is helping run a germ warfare factory? How on earth could this be possible? Don't you investigate creeps like that before you put them in sensitive positions?"

"Oh, he was investigated," Rogers said. "Most assuredly so. Came out good on all counts. Matter of fact, he had an unblemished record—an accomplished scientist, particularly in the area of poisons, etcetera."

"Poisons, etcetera," I repeated.

"Yes, it seems he has been awarded several commendations for his achievements at the Chemical Arsenal and prior to his participation in government work he was highly acclaimed by his scientific peers for the brilliance he displayed in an impressive variety of research endeavors."

"Too bad he's a crackpot," I said.

"In any case, we have good reason to believe he may be somewhere out west at this moment. He hasn't surfaced yet but he apparently is none the worse for that bout with our car."

"How did you trace him?"

"Fingerprints, Andrew, plucked by my men off the front grill of that heroic vehicle. Fortuitous, eh? So now, we at least know who he is and all that remains is to bring him into custody."

"So, how are you going to find him?" Allison demanded.

"That's where Andrew here enters the picture," Rogers said, raising a hand to fend off my objection. "We want you to help us flush Scarlatti, to motivate him to come out into the open again. We have the distinct impression that his desire to examine you personally as we have, coupled with his intense dislike for you may be adequate incentives to achieve this."

"So that's why you wanted to have your people examine me first," I said. "To make sure that if there was anything interesting to find, you'd find it first."

"Something like that," Rogers admitted.

"Well, I'm afraid I'm not the carrot he's interested in," I said. "It's Allison—and she's in danger every minute he's free."

"Well then," Rogers said, "Whichever of you he may prefer to have in his clutches, our basic premise remains: Using you, Allison or both of you to spark Scarlatti's interest and cause him to come out into the open."

"Easy for you to say," Allison said.

"You'll be watched over every step of the way," Rogers said, "I assure you. Of course, we would not entertain the notion of involving either of you in this venture unless it was extremely urgent. But the fact remains, now that we know that Scarlatti may have more scientific capability at his disposal than we originally gave him credit for, we can't waste time. He told you he intends to try to make use of the Methuselah information he has obtained. It is imperative that we retrieve that data and silence Mister Scarlatti. Of course, it's not just the man we're after. We want to locate his private base of operation and put an end to every one and everything associated with his involvement. Time, as they say, is of the essence."

"So, what do you want us to do?" I said.

"I'm going to put you both on a plane tonight for Denver. Scarlatti has shown a knack for finding out where you are. We'll make it easy for him."

Allison shook her head. "Isn't this going to be a bit obvious—us suddenly showing up in Denver singing and dancing on his doorstep? I mean, isn't he going to know that something's up?"

"Oh, he may be suspicious all right," Rogers said. "But we're counting on his obsession to get the better of him. After all, he has assaulted you before—and this last time, he even boasted about his involvement in the Methuselah situation. Very arrogant, I should say."

"He's not dumb," I said.

"No," Rogers admitted. "But then, neither are we."

Judging by the disappointment showing on his face, neither Allison or I looked very convinced.

Although I had read and heard about the famous Rocky Mountains, I wasn't prepared for my first glimpse of that jagged line of towering rock stretching southward to the horizon. Through the window of the U.S. Air Force military air transport jet, I could see the stone escarpments five miles below me rising sharply from the flat brown plains west of the city of Denver. Blotting out light reflections from within the cabin with my cupped hands, I could see snow-speckled precipices marching in single file, their progress halted momentarily by the upward thrust of Pike's Peak, a snow cone matched against the ice blue of the cloudless Colorado sky.

Turbulence marked by standing lenticular clouds downwind of the mountains kicked our jet up and down like a windblown leaf as the pilot throttled back to begin the descent into Stapleton International Airport. The trip was not entirely without merit, I thought, feeling the warm grip of Allison's hand on my arm.

Thinking of her also triggered a ripple of guilt as I thought of the reversals I had thrust into her life since we had met on that day in the New York hospital room. Oh, for those days when my life was my own, independent from the cares and concerns of others. Now, here I was, high in the firmament, sitting next to a girl to whom I was securely shackled by a growing bond that I feared was stronger than any steel chain. I was sure that she was having the same thoughts. The difference was that, in my mind, she was the victim. And a victim could be much more philosophical than a perpetrator.

"Geez, it's awfully bumpy," she said. Her blonde hair was tousled and she looked sweetly vulnerable and in need of my protection.

"Don't worry," I said. "We'll be down in a couple of minutes."

How nice it was to calm the concerns of the fragile maiden, I thought, feeling a surge of confidence and strength welling from within. Unfortunately, after a few additional minutes of teeth-rattling bumps, much more was also welling upward within me and I managed find a handy little sick bag in the seat-back in front of me a split-second before disaster struck.

It is a difficult task to look strong and confident while retching into a bit of plastic wrap. An epoch passed before the plane slammed onto the runway.

"Are you all right?" Allison asked as the jet lumbered to the gate.

"Yes," I gurgled. "I'm fine."

"You look like death warmed over. Ugh."

I had a splitting headache now and I wondered where I

could hide the lukewarm baggie in my hand. An evil odor was beginning to envelope our seating area.

"I'll take that, sir," said a tight-lipped woman in uniform.

"Poor baby," Allison said, patting my arm. She helped me out of my seat and led me down the narrow aisle as one would shepherd an elderly lady up the cathedral aisle to the communion rail.

Once on the tarmac, the crisp Colorado air washed over me and my trauma declined. I straightened my sagging body and untangled myself from Allison who was still gripping my arm, lest I totter and fall.

"I'm all right now," I said brusquely. I thought I detected a slight upturning at the corners of her lips.

Rogers met us inside an empty section of the terminal and after a few minutes of milling around ushered us back outside to a waiting limousine, one of those elongated showboats with dark windows and little jump seats for extra passengers with small behinds.

"Suitably clandestine," I said, as Allison disappeared into the car a step ahead of me. I clambered in after her and was taken aback to see Professor Atkinson ensconced on the spacious seat beside her, along with Rogers.

"Hello, Andrew," Atkinson said. "Don't look so upset."

"Why are we dragging him deeper into this?"

My question was directed at Rogers who sat primly on the seat, leaning slightly forward with his hands capped over his crossed legs.

"In due time, my boy. In due time."

"Seems to me you're just endangering another person."

"Not to worry, Andrew," Rogers replied. "Trust me. After all, security is my business."

I looked at Allison who shrugged and managed a wan smile. Atkinson grinned hugely.

"We are about to have an adventure," he said as the car purred smoothly out of the airport area and streaked down a crowded freeway toward the city.

Twenty minutes later we glided to a halt in front a squat pile of stone called the Brown Palace Hotel in the city's downtown district. From the outside the building looked as if its Palace days were long over but as our sullen knot of humanity swept into the lobby, I could see that enough vestiges of elegance still remained to assure our comfort during our stay.

We bypassed the desk and a couple of Rogers' men showed us to our rooms—three units in a row on the seventh floor, for Allison, Atkinson and myself, in that order.

"Mister Rogers will be up in an hour to meet with you all—try to get some rest," said one man. He turned on his heels and walked away.

Standing in front of her door, Allison turned to me and waved. "Well, see you later," she said. "I'm going to take a shower." She went into her room. I pushed open the door to my own room and went inside. The drapes were drawn and in the semi-darkness, I could see a capacious king-size bed, upon which sat a gigantic piece of luggage. I opened it and found it filled to overflowing with an assortment of men's clothing and toilet items, compliments of our host.

I started to undress and had just begun formulating a plan to coax Allison into my room for a long, languorous evening when the telephone on the night stand jangled.

It was Rogers. "Get to bed early, Andrew, we have a very long day tomorrow. A car will pick you up in front of the building tomorrow morning at six o'clock sharp. Don't keep us waiting."

The receiver clicked loudly in my ear. So much for my long, languorous evening.   Pushing thoughts of love from my mind, I dialed room service and ordered a big New York cut steak, American fries, salad and iced tea. I had just gotten out of the shower, clean but famished, when my feast arrived at the door on a little trolley pushed by an elegantly dressed waiter. An hour later, I was fast asleep, feeling the reassuring pressure of my father's arms, as our rickety four-master approached a rain-swept coastline.

The morning dawned crisp and glorious, with a crackling mountain snap in the air that made Allison and I raise the collars of our jackets as we stood in front of the hotel awaiting the arrival of Rogers' car. An overnight rain had washed the city and it was early enough so that the morning street traffic had not yet wheezed out enough exhaust fumes to dull the icy blue dome of sky over our heads.

I glanced at my watch. One minute to six. Just then a four-door gray metallic Mercedes silently pulled around the corner in front of the Brown Palace awning.

"Classy, huh," said Allison. I smiled in agreement, watching her instead of the car. She looked like Seventeen's idea of a cowhand in her faded denim jacket, jeans and roughout boots—even a checkered red bandana gaily tied about her neck. Whichever lackey did Rogers' shopping certainly had real flair.

We got into the back of the car and the vehicle glided away from the curb. Within minutes, we were rushing westward out of the city toward the foothills. I recognized the driver and another man in the front seat as two of Rogers' muscle types.

"Where is Rogers?" I asked.

"He's already there," came the reply.

"Where is 'there'?"

"Evergreen. A few miles into the hills. Relax and enjoy the view."

It was spectacular. The rising sun behind our backs was painting a gaudy red smear across the face of the rising foothills. The upward sloping sand and scrub, first gradual, then more enthusiastic, was crowned by an upsweep that matched the blaze red against the cobalt western sky. Beyond the crown, the hills swooped downward again before rising again and climbing until, growing a cloak of pines and aspens, they became the upthrusted stone precipices called the Rockies.

Our car swept through the brewery town of Golden then departed the main highway for a two-lane blacktop which threaded its way south and westward up a steep gradient.

The car slowed perceptibly as it maneuvered up the roadway which seemed to narrow as rocky walls on both sides of us increased in height and crept closer to the car.

I hoped I wouldn't get car sick.

"Not too far now," piped the driver to his companion, who nodded absently.

The car crawled around a switch back.

"Careful," said a voice from the front seat. "What's this guy doing anyways?"

I looked between the men in front and saw a panel truck meandering along a wide shoulder toward us, weaving slightly.

Our driver slammed on the brakes.

"Crapola! What gives?"

Almost in answer, the truck streaked over the center line and bashed us square. The force knocked Allison and I against the front seats and to the floor.

"Dammit," yelled one of the men in front as our car ended up on the edge of the road in a swirl of dust. I was dazed and felt warm liquid running down my face but I raised my head and saw two men running toward the car. Oh-oh. Then I heard several sharp cracks, screams and curses, and a gentle blackness closed in upon me.

I awoke to find one of Rogers' men shaking me. I was lying on the back seat of the Mercedes, staring into an intent pair of blue eyes.

"Come on, Merriman, let's get out of here."

A quick glance was all I needed: Allison was nowhere in

sight. Neither was the panel truck. The body of our second muscle man lay sprawled in the gravel by the roadside, collecting flies in the sunshine.

Great. I climbed into the front seat. Rogers' man had considerable difficulty starting the car and maneuvering back onto the roadway. Then I noticed the river of blood inside his jacket.

"What happened back there?" I said, feeling my scalp tenderly to determine where I had punched a hole in it.

"We got schnookered, plain and simple," he said, between spasmodic painful breaths. "Two guys dived out of the truck while we were pinned at the side of the road. Larry pulls his weapon and starts to blast away but takes one in the head. I dive out the other side of the car and take a few pot shots. Meantime, this one guy snatches the girl out of the car. They would have grabbed you, too, except I winged one of them in the leg. He made it to the truck though and they took off."

"My God," I said. "Rogers should have been prepared for something like this. We were like sitting ducks there. Watch the view, you said. I think too many of us were watching the view."

The car, battered doors, fenders and all, was moving at breakneck speed up hill.

"Where to now?" I asked, sopping up the blood on my face with my sleeve.

"Same place," he said, "just two people short."

Allison. What would become of Allison? The frustration

oozed from my pores. Part of me wanted to leap from the car, flee down the roadway and turn the mountains upside down in search of her and the persons who had brought her to grief. But that was madness. I had to get a grip on myself and shut down the adrenalin. My feelings must have been visible on my face.

"Cool it," said the driver. "We're almost there."

The car continued down the road a few miles then lurched onto a dirt lane that led to an old two-story house located on the edge of an isolated mountain settlement.

"A most unfortunate episode, indeed," Rogers said as I burst into the front entry and lunged toward him. One of his stalwarts grabbed me in a hammerlock. Rogers put a linen napkin to his lips and pushed a tray of snacks away.

"Not to worry," I shouted. "Wow, we're not in town for 24 hours before Scarlatti punches holes in your so-called security."

"Let him go, Charles," Rogers said, rising from his chair and rubbing his hands together.

"Now, Andrew," he said. "Don't go off half-cocked."

"What do you expect?" I said, tossing a frown at Charles and rubbing the back of my neck where it had been squeezed in the bodyguard's grip. "You should have had one of these bozos watching our route of travel instead of watching you gobble cookies."

"Yes, I suppose I could have. But we didn't. In any case, we'll retrieve Allison, don't worry. All right?"

No. I was far from all right. I remembered the words in Scarlatti's scrawled message—the one I had tried to hide from Allison. What evil lurks.

"Okay, so what are we going to do about it—sit around and watch you eat Oreos?"

I heard footsteps and looked up to see Professor Atkinson coming down a flight of stairs. "Let us sit down together like civilized gentlemen and discuss this," he said.

"Here," Rogers said, "have a cookie."

I threw myself onto a sofa, my mind drifting beyond the walls. Allison could be dead by now. I slammed my fist onto the arm of the sofa, raging at my own impotence.

Atkinson came over and sat down in a chair across from me. A cozy little party now.

"So sorry about Allison," the little professor said. "This adventure is getting off on a bad foot, I'd say."

"Give me your report, Edward," Rogers said, directing his attention to the wounded muscle man.

We listened attentively as Edward launched through a recitation of events that included a piece of information that jarred us all.

"The one guy could have been Scarlatti himself," said Edward. But the second guy, the guy who did most of the shooting, he was a Taliban-type for sure."

"You're sure?" Rogers gasped.

"I'm sure. He was jabbering like a jaybird, making no effort to hide it. Besides, he was carrying a beat-up AK-47. I saw plenty of them when I worked on Afghanistan assignments."

Rogers shook his head. "Have the doctor look at your wound," Rogers told him, "then please have him come in here and look at Andrew."

I had almost forgotten my own head wound which was starting to throb badly now.

Rogers came over and sat down beside me. I could smell something reminiscent of lavender cologne emanating from him.

"This confirms my worst fears," Rogers said quietly. "Scarlatti is apparently working some deal with Middle-East insurgents and Moscow. They wouldn't be loaning him operatives unless they were in on the deal. I can't imagine the consequences of fanatics gaining access to a workable Methuselah formula."

"It's frightening to contemplate," Atkinson said, clucking his tongue.

"I'm going after Allison," I said. "You gentlemen can sit here and discuss the politics of this from A to Z, but it still comes down to that."

"Don't be hasty," Rogers said, waggling a manicured finger.

"Listen, Rogers," I said, my heat rising. "So far as I'm concerned, you lost your right to chaperone this little field trip when you underestimated Scarlatti."

"Well," Rogers continued unperturbed, "I think Scarlatti has just solved a dilemma for us and handed us a credible scenario for our operation."

Professor Atkinson broke in. "That's absolutely right," he said. "From what both you and Rogers here have told me, Andrew, I think Scarlatti figures he's put himself in the driver's seat now. You don't know where he is, but he knows where we are. So I think it's fair to suggest that you can expect a call from him any time now."

"Why and how?" I said.

"The 'why' of it is that, to Scarlatti, you're a walking laboratory. If he wants to make any more headway in his examination of the Methuselah Project, he needs you, front and center, in person. As for the 'how'—I think if we put a long enough line on you, he has to come around to reel you in."

Rogers broke in. "Now he has something you want, Andrew. And that's Allison. He's not going to hurt her…at least not just yet. He'll use her as the bait to put pressure on you. Of course, now that he has Bin Laden looking over his shoulder, he'll have to proceed with extreme care. He cannot afford any mistakes."

I could see the light. "So we don't have to worry about finding him. He'll find me—and you guys'll find him through me. Is that it?"

"Precisely," Atkinson said. "He will use Allison to best advantage, hoping to lure you into his little web."

The old man looked at Rogers and grinned. "Apparently, he doesn't have much respect at all for you and your little band of merry men. He certainly isn't quaking with fear."

Rogers cleared his throat but said nothing.

"Well, I'm going after her," I said, getting up and pacing the floor. I suddenly became woozy and sat down again, holding my head in my hands.

Rogers got up and left the room, returning in a few minutes with a balding middle-aged man carrying a black bag who examined my wounds.

"I've got to take a few stitches here," he said after a few minutes of probing. "Send him to me when you're finished." Rogers nodded and the man left.

"You think Scarlatti thinks this is some kind of a game?" I said.

"Only to a point," Atkinson said. "But regarding his main objectives—laying hands on you and figuring out what it is that's been holding you together all these years, and then, terminating you—he's deadly serious."

"Remember," Rogers said, "when he had you cornered out in that field, it was Allison he was aiming at, not you. He had some very definite plans for you, Andrew."

"Okay," I said, "what are your objectives?"

"Our objectives are: Bring Miss MacKenzie home safely, terminate Scarlatti and, finally, destroy any remnants of his work that relates in any way to the Methuselah Project—and that includes any antagonists lurking about."

"Can you do that legally—just 'terminate' those people as you say?"

"No, not legally. But quasi-legally—we can and we will."

Rogers smiled at me, a sudden flash of benevolence giving him a warm grandfatherly visage for just an instant.

"These are the kinds of cases that don't reach the courts," he purred.

"Well, when it comes to doing this terminating," I said, "I volunteer."

"No," Rogers said. "That's a bit out of your line—and you should be thankful for that."

"Baloney," I persisted, my head splitting now. "I got Allison into this mess—I'll get her out."

"And how do you propose to do that?" Atkinson said.

"When Scarlatti calls, which I agree he will, I'll go pay him a visit—alone. You give me a transmitter of some sort so you can track me. When it's right, your gang can close down his operation while I personally close him down."

Brave words, I knew. I could hardly believe it was me speaking. But deep down I knew I had learned a thing or two during the past couple of hundred years—and now was the time to bring it all into play.

"Fine," Rogers said. "We've got a transmitter that will fit right in your pocket."

"Not good enough," I said. "Scarlatti will find that in a minute. I need something that's hidden on my person and that's small enough to escape a physical examination."

"We do have a miniaturized model. Fits neatly under the skin—but it requires some minor surgery to put it in place."

"That sounds more like it. Where does it go?"

"Right here," he said, pointing to a spot high on his right thigh.

I didn't exactly relish the idea of anyone putting a knife in that location, but I certainly couldn't think of a better idea. "Let's try it," I said.

"We'll get Doctor Rhoades back in here."

Our meeting broke up a half hour later. I was going to have a little session with the doctor's knife and their resident electronics genius, then relax and await the inevitable phone call. As I left the room with Doctor Rhoades, I turned and met Atkinson's gaze. The old man looked at me solemnly then winked. From my memory came remnants of a phrase that somehow fitted my situation. Something about the inmates guarding the asylum.

The intersection of State Street and Hampton, circa 1927, deep in the heart of Chicago. The city, like an over-dressed tart leaning against a street lamp, was using prohibition to seduce customers into a raucous, new way of living. Everyone knew this giddy escapade couldn't last for long but in the meantime, we were having a hell of a time.

I had been through such times before, when, for one reason or another, a great share of the populace goes crazy. And that was what was happening in Chicago at the time. Gang wars and gun molls. Terrible whiskey and cheap beer. Stuffy backroom bars layered with cigarette and cigar smoke. Godfathers, soldiers, lieutenants. Protection, numbers, vice rackets. Crooked cops and crooked citizenry. All rolled up in a bawdy ball and smashed flat like a roach on the shores of Lake Michigan.

I met Eleanor in one of those backroom joints. She was a cigarette girl. Used to parade around carrying this little tray of smokes, her buns jammed into this tiny little costume.

She had spilled a bourbon and water all over my new double-breasted suit. I was embarrassed because I was the only one in the joint sober enough to be aware of it in the first place—and because I felt sorry for her. As a starving baby-faced string bass player at Woozy's, a speakeasy just a few blocks away on State Street, I knew that jobs were hard to come by—and waitresses had been fired for far less reason than dumping a tumbler of bad scotch on a customer. I tried to downplay the accident but seeing the scowl of her boss, Eleanor broke into tears and ran from the floor.

I saw her again a few days later. I was walking to my gig early in the evening and spotted her on the street. She had just dropped her purse and was stooped over the sidewalk, trying to collect the coins, pins and what-nots that were rolling around the concrete. I shooed some raggedy kids away and helped her put the stuff back into a purse the size of a barracks bag.

She was a doll. Hair done up in a soft brown curls, eyelashes as long as your arm, neat little figure that must have come packed in a candy box, and the prettiest smile that uncovered two rows of perfect teeth. She barely came up to my shoulder.

I talked her into having coffee with me and we found a little spot on Rush Street. The evening mobs hadn't hit the avenue yet so we found a booth right away in this little joint.

I had only been in town less than a year, having matriculated there from New York where my age—or lack of it—had triggered a spate of familiar but unanswerable questions from among my circle of friends and business associates. Again, I had found it necessary to slink off to a new life in a new place to avoid the questioning eyes and muttered references.

Now, I shut up and watched her marvelous face as she chattered on about her life. Poughkeepsie. Secretary first. Fired. No Money. Lucky to be working at Harry's. Wanted something better. Knew she had a lot to offer. Happy. Trusting. Vulnerable. Just my type.

We fell into an easy relationship. I'd pick her up in the wee hours after we both had finished work. We'd go to her flat or over to my boarding house and mess around. There was something special about this girl that made me want to stay in one place, by her side, under her spell. In other words, we were serious. Walks. The zoo. Little presents. Cooking in. Eating out. Tinkling laughter. The works.

In the fall of that year, a new ingredient entered our life. His name was Willard C. Dobb, a small-time hood, trying to big a big-time hood, currently on the string with some big shot named Alphonse Capone.

Dobbs wanted to date her. She did not want to date him. Dobbs insisted. She resisted. One night, I had to work late didn't come by the club as usual. When I finally got home, I called her. No answer. The next day, I went by her place. She wasn't home.

A couple of days later on the way to the office, I spotted a newsstand with a big picture of a girl on the front page of the Sun Times. Her picture. With a story telling how one Willard Dobbs was cooling it in the Cook County Jail pending the filing of a murder charge. My hands with shaking so hard I could hardly read the newsprint, but I saw well enough to know that Dobbs had had one refusal too many from Eleanor. In disgust, he had apparently waited for her outside Harry's place, snatched her when she walked out of the club after her shift, and stuffed her into his car. From there, police said he drove down toward the Lake, where, according to a witness at water's edge, he struck the girl and pushed her off the pier.

They never found her body. Lots of little boats took to the water and men poked the murky depths with long hooked probes. But no Eleanor. After a while, the Chicago Trib dropped the story and the people at Harry's stopped talking about it. Dobbs became one of the few people ever to be convicted of murder without a habeas corpus. They fried him in the electric chair.

For the longest time, I kept waiting for Eleanor to walk back into my life. On certain days, when the sun was high in the sky and the crowds were jamming the sidewalk, I almost expected to see a girl on the street ahead, bending over, trying to shove spilled articles into a huge purse. It felt so real, so possible. But it never happened.

Eventually, I took the 5:45 sleeper out of Chicago and headed back East. As the buildings on the lakeshore faded in the lengthening dusk, I remembered my Eleanor. And it hurt. That's the trouble with falling in love. You end up hurting real bad.

The windows in Rogers' mountain hideaway looked out upon a rich portrait of the muted greens and blue, the skyline created by rising peaks in the distance. In groups and individually, we waited for the ring of the telephone to announce that our adversary was ready to play out the remainder of his little game. I sat by myself mostly, scrunched up in a window box, thinking of what I must do if and when the call finally came.

A tingling sensation high on my thigh reminded me of the dull touch of the doctor's sharp scalpel which lifted a patch of skin to make way for the insertion of a miniature radio transmitter. It was a new digital device, hardly larger than a dime—supposedly possessed of enough power to transmit a clear signal many miles, using my own body as an antenna. According to Rogers, the radio was similar to a GPS navigation system, triangulating off three satellites pinpointing my position in terms of latitude and longitude for Rogers and his men. I had far less faith in this device than they did, and so spent many of the passing hours thinking of contingency plans that might save my buns, should the little tracking device fizzle. After much noodling, I was faced with one simple reality: There were no practical backup remedies. If the tracker failed, there was no way Rogers could track me. I would be on my own. Period.

So now we waited. Rogers looked grumpier as the time passed, walking about the oak-paneled ground floor library with his fists dug deep into the pockets of his nifty maroon smoking jacket. Professor Atkinson sat slouched in an over-stuffed chair, his feet dangling about six inches off the floor, reading a worn copy of O. Several other people, men I didn't recognize, wandered in and out, jackets off, belted shoulder holsters neatly crossing their crisp white shirts.

Evening came. The birds high in the branches of the aspens became quiet. Someone lighted a blaze in the fireplace. I joined my hosts for a dinner of Burger King Whoppers, whisked to our headquarters from God-knows-where.

"Looks like your theory is losing its credibility," I said to Atkinson.

"Give it time, boy."

Rogers nodded in agreement, his head-shaking at odds with the frown on his perspiring face.

Well, I thought, enough of this.

"I'm going to call it a day, guys."

No one objected. I walked upstairs, found an unoccupied

room down a long hallway, and stretched out on the bed. For several intense minutes, my mind boiled with images of Allison and declarations of my own uselessness. But despite my unsettled state, my deeper physiological needs soon lowered me into a deep sleep.

I was awakened by a rough shaking.

"Andrew, it's time."

I squinted in the dim light at Rogers face, grim and tightlipped.

"The telephone, Andrew. It's for you."

I swept the sleep from my senses and stumbled out of bed and out of the room. Downstairs, Atkinson stood by a rough-hewn oak desk, holding the receiver out to me. His smile was saintly.

"Yes, please?" said a muffled voice. Scarlatti, in person.

I hesitated for an instant, like a rookie paratrooper momentarily freezing in the doorway, then plunged ahead.

"Scarlatti," I intoned in my most commanding voice, "this is Andrew Merriman."

"Sorry to disturb you at such a devilish hour but I thought you'd be interested in hearing about the welfare of Miss MacKenzie."

I felt like exploding in a torrent of rage, but I didn't. It would be useless.

"Go ahead," I said. "I'm listening."

"I'll wager you certainly are. Now listen to me closely. And tell your puppeteers to forget any notions about tracing this call. It won't be possible, I can assure you."

Rogers, who was listening with another man on a phone at the other end of the room, grimaced and set his receiver down.

"If you care anything at all about this girl, you'll follow my instructions exactly. Because the only way you're ever going to see her in one piece is by doing precisely as I say, no more, no less. Is that understood?"

"Understood."

"Excellent. Now Andrew, here is my proposition. I want you to make yourself available to me for 48 hours, and after that, I shall release you and Allison."

"Oh sure," I said. "After you've been chasing me down for a couple of centuries, you're just suddenly going to suddenly forget all that, huh?"

"To be quite frank, Andrew, if it were strictly up to me, I would like nothing better than to dispatch you in some hideous fashion like the scum-caked little sewer rat you are. Believe that. But now, other interested parties have become involved, and it isn't just a simple matter of personal vengeance any longer. The fact is, Andrew, we want what you have. And we know the way to get it is through you. So you see, we are at an impasse, even as you are. Understood?"

"Well," I said, "what makes you think I'm in a position to hand over to you whatever it is that I have? I don't even know what it is."

"We believe we know, Andrew. And moreover, we think

we know how to get it. But it'll take your full cooperation—at least for 48 hours."

Dark greying images of Doctor Frankenstein's laboratory flitted across my mind.

"And then Allison and I can go on our merry way, is that it?"

"That's correct."

"I don't believe a word of that."

"You have no choice, Andrew, if you expect to see Miss MacKenzie again. Besides, what do you have to lose?"

"What do you mean?"

"Well, after all, if you're not, shall we say, killable, you have nothing to worry about anyway. And we could certainly dispose of Miss MacKenzie now if we wished."

"Your logic escapes me."

"Well, logical or not, you've heard my proposition. Accept or reject. But do it right now, because you won't get another chance—and, neither will Miss MacKenzie."

I sighed and glanced at Rogers and Atkinson. They were standing less than two feet away with blank eyes and pursed lips, as if they had been sharing a lemon. Well, I hope they were happy now. The truth was unavoidable: If I wanted to see Allison again, I would have to march straight ahead.

"Okay," I said into the receiver. "What do you want me to do?"

"Ah," said the telephone voice, "I relish capitulation.

Now then, that sniveling government operative at your

side—Rogers is his name?—I know he and his bumblers are
hiding in the meadow, waiting to snatch me. Make sure they
understand that if I detect their presence, ever so slightly, at
any step along the way, it's over."

The conversation was now definitely one-sided and it went
on for perhaps a minute or two before the line went dead and
I replaced the receiver in its cradle.

"Perfect," said Rogers, almost clapping his hands and jump-
ing up and down. For a moment, I expected him to grab
Atkinson by the hands and dance ring-around-the-rosy.

"Perfect," I mimicked. "You have a very warped sense of
perfection."

Chapter 12

I followed Scarlatti's instructions to the letter. The early sun was just beginning to burnish the surrounding mountains when I pulled out of the driveway in a conspicuous olive-drab government sedan with a crude penciled map on the seat beside me.

The map would take me part way to my destination. My instructions were to pick up remaining directions in bits and pieces enroute. With the little transmitter under my skin doling out my whereabouts in digital transmissions to home base, I felt that I had a comforting degree of protection. We had tested the device and everyone seemed satisfied that the miniature tattle-tale was capable of keeping a running tab on my movements.

It was a clear, calm morning. From time to time, a deer would materialize at the edge of the woods then prance across the road, which meandered down the mountainside in lazy turns. I made several turn-offs, and stopped twice to pick up additional directions: once in a public camping area, another time taped under a roadside telephone.

As the morning wore on, the temperature rose and dust began to swirl, carried along on a developing mountain breeze. I was becoming hot and sweaty—and hoped the car wouldn't break down. What a fix we'd be in if I failed to meet our agreed upon timetable because of something dumb like a leaky radiator or flat tire.

Shortly after noon and nearly four hours of driving, I pulled into an overlook. Two men were there to meet me. Wordlessly, they motioned me into the large side door of a black van and we took off down the road. Neither man said a word. They looked sorely out of place with swarthy faces, ebony beards, heavy clothing and thick-soled brogues. Fresh from the oasis.

I paid strict attention to our progress as we drove along, thinking the information could come in handy in a clutch. Presently the van lurched off the road and turned onto a trail which led to a broad flat valley ringed by hills. I could see a group of buildings in the distance. Off to the left, a blazing orange windsock buffeted by a strong breeze attested to the presence of an airport. We stopped while one of the men jumped out and swung open a large steel gate. A large sign was posted indicating that hideous retributions would be exacted from any hapless trespassers.

Minutes later we pulled up in a cloud of dust and stopped in front of a brick building, rather new-looking, which was linked to other buildings in a haphazard semi-circle. The men in front hopped out and I followed when the large side door slid open. My new-found companions, grim-faced and sweating in their thick desert garb, ushered me between them up the front steps to the building.

Scarlatti was waiting for us inside in a cavernous empty lobby. He hadn't changed much. Black wet-look hair plastered down on his skull. A powdered pasty face, as if he had just crawled out of a wooden box in a basement. Impressively long-necked and tall, with slender pointy-nailed fingers that you wouldn't want stroking your flesh. He was decked out in a white frock coat decorated in the front by multi-colored stains.

"So nice of you to come," he said. His voice echoed off the bare walls. He turned on his heels and beckoned me to follow. My two escorts stayed behind in the lobby, their silence intact.

I followed Scarlatti into what could have been a conference room borrowed from a Madison Avenue brokerage house. Long mahogany table circled by deep chairs, carpeted floor, wood wainscoting, elegant glass chandelier. Very out of place.

The room was empty except for an obese man oozing forth from one of the chairs. He struggled to his feet and bowed as we approached.

"Andrew, this is Hassan. He is a partner of mine in this enterprise and I hope you'll show him every consideration."

I didn't shake the proffered hand. "You might as well have Al Qaeda written on your forehead," I said.

"As you wish," the man said, turning his chubby palms upward in a mock gesture of supplication. He had a huge bald bullet head, like he was about to be fired from a circus cannon. He also showed a preference for heavy garments.

"Your comments aside," said Scarlatti, "let's have a little meeting. Can we get you anything?"

"You can get me Miss MacKenzie." I could feel my pulse and heartbeat quickening. I felt like flying across the table at him.

"Presently," he said, smiling broadly. "First, let me enlighten you about our schedule. We'll chit-chat a bit, then I want to turn you over to some of my associates. We've arranged some examinations. Nothing exotic. Oh, I know you've been through this before, but please humor me."

"And just what do you hope to accomplish?"

"Mister Merriman," said the Arab. "Doctor Scarlatti and I, with the blessing of Allah, hope to discover just what it is that gives you your remarkable qualities."

"What qualities?" I asked blandly.

"Oh come now. Don't waste our time. Not everyone is blessed with endless time to spare, such as you are. So, let us not dance with each other. Let us be open and frank—and hope that this entire affair will reach a successful conclusion."

He sat back, fat and happy with his little speech.

"What is your idea of a successful conclusion?"

Scarlatti took over. "That we find something in our examination that will enable us to duplicate the wonderful process that your body does so effortlessly, keeping you young, fresh and vibrant—while the rest of society slowly rots and turns fetid. When we have made our inquiries, we will go our way happily. That is all."

"That's a very nice bedtime story," I said, remembering when life was simpler.

"Now," he said, "how many people have followed you here?"

"None."

"Then they're tracking your movements."

"Not that I'm aware of."

"Well, I've made some arrangements which make it advisable that your friends leave us unmolested."

I wouldn't take the bait.

"You might say that we have taken out an insurance policy."

He rose, walked over to a cabinet and returned with a shiny metallic globe and set it carefully on the table in front of me.

"This is what you Americans might call a Weapon of Mass Destruction. It's just a bomb of sorts. Only it doesn't use enough explosive force to cause catastrophic harm. It's more like a trigger, capable of invading the integrity of other containers in its immediate vicinity which in turn will release an extremely toxic gas called TK-11 to be carried over an extremely wide area under favorable conditions."

The globe looked harmless enough. It was about the size

of a basketball, its outer shell a highly polished metal with a smooth seamless surface unbroken by knobs or handles.

"There is a twin to this device," he went on. "It is located in a highly secure area of the Rocky Flats Arsenal, in close proximity to a whole storehouse full of other gaseous odds and ends, thoughtfully developed and stockpiled by my fellow government scientists.

"Should any of your compatriots attempt to disrupt my plans here by any means whatsoever, they will be jeopardizing the lives of many thousands of people. That, my friend, is because the only reason the device at the arsenal has not exploded already is because I keep transmitting signals every thirty minutes on the hour telling it to be patient. Should I somehow become incapacitated, and the device does not receive its soothing little message, it will suddenly become greatly depressed and trigger its own destruction.

"What happens then will be beyond my powers to prevent: Enough gas, of many kinds, will be released from the arsenal to ensure the death of probably everyone living on the eastern and western slopes. Of course, the winds will eventually disperse the gasses and dilute their effect, but not until many innocents have gone to their rewards. I should add that most of these gases are not kind. Death comes slowly, agonizingly—a hideous lingering destruction of bodily tissues and functions that works from the inside out and reduces victims to lumps of viscous pulp."

He paused for effect. "Now then, you wouldn't want that

on your conscious, would you?"

Hassan was licking his lips.

"I've taken the liberty," Scarlatti continued, "of dispatching a notice containing this news to the headquarters of your Mister Rogers. I am sure they will inform him of the situation, post-haste. He will be intrigued, I promise you."

To say the least, I thought. My God, now I knew that any brainless moves on my part would do more than endanger Allison. It would endanger half the population in the country.

"You're not content with holding Allison and myself hostage," I said. "You have to include millions of people."

"Only for a time," he said. "But we will require your complete, enthusiastic cooperation."

The door opened and a woman entered and set a tray of drinks on the table.

"Some refreshments," said the fat man. "Drink up."

It was hot in the room and my throat was parched. I accepted a glass, twirled the ice cubes around a few times with a plastic straw, then drained the contents. Dumb move. Chalk one up for their side.

Scarlatti and Hassan exchanged broad smiles, two skuzzy mice who had just hidden the cheese. And the sun shining through the windows dipped behind a cloud. The room darkened. It was time to sleep. My head fell to my chest. One of my useless arms knocked my empty glass to the carpet. I remember thinking that I wished I had taken a cab on that fateful day long ago in New York. Then I wouldn't have been hit by that car, I wouldn't have been hospitalized, I wouldn't have met Allison, and she'd be somewhere far away now, safe and sound.

∽

I awoke with a bright white light bleaching my eyeballs. I was stretched out on a table, naked. A slight chill raised bumps on my arms, which were at my side, securely immobilized by thick leather straps. My head throbbed and I turned my neck slowly, trying to become acclimated to my surroundings. White walls, lined with cabinets and blinking lights. Stainless steel sinks and tables. Odds and ends of laboratory equipment. Twenty feet away, a row of windows looked out upon distant mountains. I longed to be out there, sitting under a pine on one of those rising slopes.

A couple of attendants came over to me, gazed into my eyes, made minute adjustments on black boxes flanking my body, and returned to other tasks. I tried to speak to them, to find out what was happening, but they ignored me. I strained at my bonds and wished I could remove the needles and tubes which snaked from my body and disappeared beneath the table. All was not good.

And what about Allison? And when were those associates of mine, resplendent in their white hats, coming to my res-cue—answering the claxon call of the tiny spy under my skin? A huge round clock on the wall told me it was four o'clock. In the afternoon, of course. But of what day?

A door opened behind me and two men appeared. Ignoring my exclamations, they disconnected me from the various contraptions, except for the leather restraints, spread a stiff blanket over me and wheeled me out the door. We traveled a short distance down the corridor, took an elevator down one floor, and then rolled down another hall and into a room.

Scarlatti got up from a desk and approached me.

"How are we doing then?"

"Doctor Mengele must have been a relative of yours," I said.

The men left the room and Scarlatti returned to his desk and sat down. I was at a disadvantage, looking sidewise at him while flat on my back.

"Don't look so upset," he said.

"You fink," I yelled. "We made a deal and you copped out. What day is this? How long have I been here?"

"Three days. Just long enough for us to get to know you, physiologically speaking."

"Then it's time to let me get out of here, and take Allison with me. Where is she?"

"Before we talk about that I want to explain a few things to you."

My neck began aching, and I tried to concentrate. Where was Rogers? What had gone wrong?

Scarlatti held up a little object in his hand.

"Recognize this? One of my technicians found this on your person. It seems that technology is more than skin deep."

My right hand shot down to my thigh where a slight soreness marked the spot where they had removed the tiny tracker. So much for that plan.

Scarlatti shook his head, his face expressing mock disappointment.

"I feel sad that you actually believe you could get away with such a ploy. We aren't idiots, you know. We knew you'd be tracked, so it just remained for us to decide how you expected to effectuate it. Child's play, really."

"So are you finished with your examinations?" I asked.

"Virtually."

"You might as well give it up," I said. "You won't find any more than Rogers people did. And I'm sure they were just as thorough."

"On the contrary," Scarlatti said. "Only in a manner of speaking. You see, they were limited because of certain restrictions placed upon their investigations. Restrictions that will not limit our efforts."

"What do you mean?"

"Look at it this way," he said. "Your government scientists were able to probe only a certain distance. It's like that adage about killing the messenger who brings the message, if you get my meaning. They had to impose safeguards on their explorations so that they would not harm their subject."

He paused for effect and smiled triumphantly.

My throat constricted and a lump grew in my stomach as his words began to register.

"Yes," he said. "They were limited because they were dedicated to the proposition of keeping you alive. So they treated you with great care and limited their information-seeking to those areas that could be examined without harming you. Oh, maybe a moment of discomfort here and there, but no more. Here we are bound by no such altruistic parameters, you see. If we don't find what we seek and the patient dies, it is no great tragedy."

"We had a bargain..."

"You can forget that little Eagle Scout agreement," he said, walking around his desk toward me. "You see, I now have it in my power to accomplish two objectives. I can increase the level of our examinations—and remove you from the ranks of the living at the same time. Comprende?"

"You bastard..."

"Yes, it's fitting to call me that, Merriman. After all, it was you who ravaged the Scarlatti family, the midnight rapist who savages women in their beds, slays their loved ones and burns their dwellings to the ground. Better for you had I been a bastard, then we would not be seeing eye to eye today."

He laughed bitterly and his eyes glowed with hate. His face was inches from mine and I had to turn my head to avoid his foul breath.

"Yes, call me anything you like. Because you have reached the end of your long twisted trail. On behalf of every Scarlatti, from the Prince down to myself, I intend to bring your pathetic reign to an end. You cannot die? Ha! I will prove that you can. You are not God-like, but devil-like. And I swear on the graves of my ancestors that my ears will listen to the very last beat of your wretched heart."

Flecks of foam from his lips fell onto my face as he continued his tirade. My God, did the Arabs know they had a complete looney for a partner?

"What about your camel-driving friends," I said. "Don't they have something to say about what happens to me?"

He backed off a few feet and wiped his mouth with the sleeve of his filthy white coat.

"What happens to you is not their concern. Their only interest is information—the precious secret that lies safely locked away inside you."

"And what if you do learn something—what do you intend to do with it?"

"I intend to work closely with my friends so that the information can be used in behalf of believers like myself."

"So you still believe in the tooth fairy."

He shrugged and returned to his desk.

"Joke while you can, my young friend. But let us see if you still feel like making your little jokes when we begin your…how shall we refer to it…your autopsy."

My autopsy. I envisioned paper-thin sections of my tissues being viewed under microscopes. My fluids drained for sampling under slides and spun at high speed in circular cabinets. Various organs lifted from their snug warm, cavities and placed on a shelf in large specimen jars.

"Let Allison go," I said. "She isn't a part of this. You may have some imagined crusade against me. But you have nothing against her."

"She is important to you, is she not?"

He wanted me to beg—so he could laugh in my face. I remained silent.

"Of course she's important to you," he said. "Perhaps the most important thing in your useless little life. For that reason alone, I will personally see to it that she dies in a suitable demeaning fashion."

He was giddy with laughter as the two orderlies reappeared and trundled me back out of the room on the cart.

∽

The prospect of being subdivided by scalpels and pickled on a shelf in a dark room was not very appealing, yet, if I ever wanted to be quit of this life, I'm sure that would do it. And if it were my own self that concerned me, I probably would have layed back passively and prepared myself for my trip into the great beyond.

But no. I was bursting with anxiety about Allison. Where was she now and what was happening to her? Would Scarlatti wait until he had dispatched me before hurting her or was it too late already? The thought of her being harmed made me white-faced and sick. God, when had I last eaten? It must have been three days ago.

And what about Rogers and his so-called crack team? Did they have time to trace my whereabouts before Scarlatti's technicians discovered the implant? That was my only hope—that they were on their way to me at this very moment, ready to blast their way into this joint, free Allison and me, and blast Scarlatti and his gangsters into kingdom come.

Now, I was strapped to a bed in a darkened room, awaiting whatever little surprise Dame Fate held in store for me. There was a window at the other end of the room about 15 feet away and I could see a reflection of moonglow and the dim outline of mountains beyond. The minutes and hours ticked by and I had completely lost track of time. A powerful thirst gripped me and I slipped in and out of consciousness. How long would I have to lie here?

My question was answered with the opening of the door and a click of a light switch that showered me in blinding light. Scarlatti again. He stood there looking down at me, a half-witted grin on his face. In his hand, he held a shiny instrument.

My God, it was a needle. Perhaps the longest needle I had ever seen. He approached me, holding this apparatus out in front of him, squirting a thin test stream of liquid out the end.

"It is time, Merriman. Time for sleep. Consider yourself lucky. If it were up to me we'd conduct the rest of your examination with you fully conscious, just so I could hear your futile child-like screams. But I'm afraid that would be a bit too much for the sensibilities of my staff, so I'm giving you enough sodium pentathol to knock down a fast race horse."

I began squirming mightily, but I was in a weakened condition and held down by restraints. With one hand he gripped me by the arm and with his other hand, in one smooth movement, rammed the needle home.

"Sweet dreams, Andrew."

The room turned over slowly, then dissolved into a hideous kaleidoscope with Scarlatti's rat-faced grin splashed around the edges, red-lipped and drooling. In the deepest recess of my mind, I was dying. I was sure of it. My time had come at last. And with it, the memories of all those years, cascading across a span of time that had left me weak with acceptance of my plight. It wasn't the way I wanted to go, but I went, doe-like and submissive, into the black endless void where there is no time.

Chapter 13

I awoke with a start, faintly embarrassed. It was like saying effusive goodbyes at a party, then forgetting your jacket
and having to return to the house. I had made myself ready for
the glorious journey to the nether world, only to discover that
the bus had left without me.

I was almost disappointed. But my open eyes found faint
traces of light at the window and I could see that dawn was
rushing in upon the mountains. And here I was, stirring in
bed, when I should have been dead. So much for Scarlatti's
knowledge of fast race horses. For whatever reason the pen-
tathlon had not done its job, I was not even curious. Rather, I
felt a buoyant sense of urgency, one that freshened my senses
and renewed my desire to, if not live much longer, at least live
long enough to see to Allison.

Was I too late? I struggled at my bonds and for the first time, really looked at them. My feet were free, but my wrists were encased by thick leather bands. Fortuitously, it seemed that whoever did the binding must have been counting on my weakened condition and drugged state to help matters.

That was a mistake. There was just enough play on my right wrist to allow me to work it back and forth, stressing and stretching the band. After several minutes, I could feel it loosening. I grew impatient. On a table at the bedside was a large container. What was in it—water? Whatever, I knew that liquid—even from a chamber pot, God forbid—would make the leather more pliable. I pitched my body sideways and carefully wedged the pot between my feet then, raising my legs, boosted the container into the air. Straining every muscle, I arched my legs upward until, voila! I dumped the entire contents onto me.

Thankfully, the water gods were smiling upon me. It was not a chamber pot. Now my work went easier. After several more minutes, the leather had stretched to the point where, with great exertion and a burning pain on my right hand, I pulled it loose from the strap. Using my free hand, I loosed the strap on my left wrist.

Free at last. I sat up on the bed, then put my bare feet on the cold tile floor and stood up carefully, knowing that I had no idea of how my body had been weakened. After a moment or two, I tried walking, slowly. I approached the window. After much grunting and groaning, I managed to raise the sash and look out. Drat. I was about 75 feet off the ground, perhaps on the fifth or six floor. Except for a spindly drain pipe traveling up the building about three feet away, the brick face of the building was unbroken. Seeing that a window escape was useless, I turned and walked to the door leading to the hall. It was a metal door. Furthermore, it was locked.

Back to the window. However useless a window escape appeared on first glance, it was obvious, it was the only way. I looked out again. There was no way that drain pipe could hold my weight, even if I could some how lean out and grab on to it. I had never liked heights. The ground below looked hard and unforgiving. I wouldn't stand a chance.

But like it or not, it was my only chance. If I stayed here, Scarlatti or his buddies could be back at any minute. Now, with the sun just ready to appear over the horizon, would be my best time, my only time. Before the rats started stirring in their nests.

I leaned out the window. The morning breeze caressed my face and I could smell the perfume of sweet dew. An outrageously beautiful morning on which to be smashed to a blooded clump of broken bones on the ground below.

Oh well, here goes.

I stretched and reached as far as I could, hanging tightly to the side of the window frame with one free arm and praying I would not lose my balance and simply topple out like a rag doll. My fingers touched the scaling paint of the drain, then got a firm grip. I took a deep breath and paused a moment.

Now I was spread-eagled against the cool brick between the window and the drain. I knew I should not look down.

Teetering on a thin edge of balance, I used my left foot to push myself to the right, then managed to slide the fingertips of my other hand behind the pipe. Eureka! Using every nuance of strength in my right arm, I pulled myself off the ledge toward the pipe and gripped it firmly with both hands, hugging the drain like life itself.

Now, if it would only hold my weight. And in the event it did hold, could I work self slowly downward, without losing my grip? Praying that the gods of drainpipes would be at my side, I began edging downward, hand under hand, gripping the pipe as best I could with my knees and ankles. Whoops— not too fast. Slow is the order of the morning.

As the seconds ticked away, shooting pains began in my overworked, underfed arms and legs. But finally after what seemed like an epoch of agony the ground approached and took me to its bosom. For a moment I lay on the grass panting like an aging hound, waiting for my body to catch up to my spirit. Finally I sat up.

Now what to do? Here I was, outside this building in full view of anyone who passed near, waiting to be easily recaptured. I realized I must be about my business without delay.

First I must find Allison, and then figure out how to get the devil out of there. And so, after fleeing the building, I now must go back inside the building. First, I needed clothes. I was wearing only my briefs. Then I would search as thoroughly as possible and if I didn't find Allison I would have to enter and search other buildings on the grounds.

What a propitious moment for Rogers and his men to have shown up. It was obvious to me that the confounded tracker had failed miserably in its mission. If it had worked at all, Rogers people would have at least traced me to this compound. And they certainly would have mounted a seige of this place after having been alerted by the transmitter's sudden silence when it was removed from my thigh. So much for planning.

I walked around to the front. I wished I had a watch. The sky was cloudless and the sun was just now peeking over the horizon but it seemed I had awakened on the cot hours ago. In any case, I figured it must be about five o'clock. If I searched fast and efficiently, perhaps I could do the bulk of it when few people would be up and about. I walked up the steps to the front door. It was open. Inside, not a soul. I began walking down a corridor, then walked down a flight of stairs to the basement. A door marked LAUNDRY beckoned me inside. Perfect. I snatched a pair of white pants and a doctor's white coat out of a hamper and put them on. A pair of old shoes under a desk in an office area invited me to try them on. Not a perfect fit, but sufficient.

During the next several minutes, I entered every open room in the building without finding a trace of Allison. Several times, I had to duck and hide from hospital workers. But it was obvious that my disappearance had not yet been discovered—

an event I realized could happen at any moment.

A poster reading RESTRICTED AREA caught my attention, as well as what appeared to be an unoccupied guard desk. I scuttled down the corridor, almost holding my breath in anticipation, looking into the rooms through little square security windows in the doors.

No Allison. And time was pitifully short.

Finally, there was one door left at the end of the corridor.

I looked in through the window. No one there. My shoulders drooped in disappointment.

But wait. A faded denim jacket on a chair. That cowgirl styling. My heart idled roughly for several beats and I squelched an urge to scream and beat down the door. Instead, I gripped the door knob. It was the kind you could work from the outside but not from the inside. I turned it. The door opened and, choking with anticipation and fear, I crept inside.

The mustiness of warm stale air hit my nose as I pushed open the door to the dimly-lighted room. I paused just beyond the doorway for an instant, letting my eyes adjust to the light. Then a slight movement made me turn my head toward the half-opened door—a fortuitous move that saved me a major headache inflicted by a blunt object wielded by an attacker.

It was Allison MacKenzie. I jumped aside and grabbed her arm. She looked at me, dazed, then collapsed into my arms. I looked about, wondering if anyone had heard the sound of her weapon when it hit the floor. It was a piece of pipe, resourcefully ripped from God-knows-where.

Carrying Allison to the bed, I tried to coax her into consciousness. What had they done to her? She looked pale and drawn, but otherwise in one piece. And she was still wearing the faded jeans she had on when we were ambushed days before.

She moved her head, and finally opened her eyes. There was no sign of recognition at first, then she began focusing. I let go of her and she sat up, looking about woozily, as if she were coming out of a long deep sleep. Then she looked at me again and threw her arms around my neck.

"Andrew." she said, "I thought I'd never see you again. Those monsters." Her sweet tears trickled down my neck.

"Did they hurt you?"

"No, not really. But they told me they were moving me to another place this morning. What are you doing here?"

In as few words as possible, I described what had happened after her kidnapping and my sojourn as Scarlatti's guest.

"Then you've come to rescue me?"

She made it sound as if I were clad in armor. Not a bad vision, I thought. But there wasn't time to dwell on my magnificence.

"I'm not rescuing anybody unless we get moving now," I said. She put on her shoes and I took her by the hand and led her out into the hallway. We had walked about thirty steps and were just about to open a door marked EXIT when we were challenged.

"Pardon me," said an officious-looking man in white. "Where are you taking this lady?"

I was non-plussed for a second, but then realized he must have thought I was another staff member...a mistake that I knew would rectify itself after he got a closer look at my unshaven face and generally disheveled appearance.

"Doctor Scarlatti's orders," I said in my best I'm-busy-don't-mess-with-me growl. Stroking his heavy dark beard, he looked at me with growing suspicion.

"What's going on here anyway?" He grabbed my arm.

"Don't worry about it," I said, shoving him side and pushing Allison through the door.

"Wait a minute..."

I hate violence, but when I am in danger, I will gladly resort to it. Hence it was with great satisfaction that I felt my right fist sink into his soft paunch, forcing his breath out of his mouth with an explosive gasp and doubling him over. He groaned and stood up just as my toe on one of my janitor's stout black shoes buried itself in his scrotum, dropping him to the polished tile floor in an anguished heap.

I dashed through the exit door after Allison, knowing full well that disabling this one person would buy us only seconds. Sure enough, we had bounded down just two flights of stairs when our ears were jangled by a piercing horn, whose urgent wail reminded me of an air raid during the London blitz.

As we rounded the next landing and pounded down the concrete steps, we heard a babble of voices and the thumping of many feet. I grabbed Allison's hand and together we flew, two steps at a time, stumbling and falling in mad careening flight.

But not fast enough. A door burst open behind us and several people poured out into the stairwell.

"Here they are," shouted one.

"Head them off at the bottom!"

Fortunately, we had already reached the first floor—and a steel fire door that led to the great outdoors. Ignoring the posted plea, DO NOT OPEN EXCEPT IN CASE OF FIRE, we slammed the door open with our shoulders and found ourselves outside the building adjacent a loading dock.

"The truck!" Allison gasped. She was pointing at a small delivery truck backed up to the end of the dock, about thirty yards distance. We could hear its driver gunning the engine.

"C'mon," I yelled, "he's getting ready to go."

With the screams of the crowd at our heels pumping adrenalin into our systems, we ran toward the truck. It was starting to move now, slowly but surely. So close, yet so far. Then the truck paused for a moment as the driver stared at a piece of paper in his hand, then started up again. The delay was just enough. I flung myself off the dock onto the rear bumper, sticking to the moving vehicle like a leech and opening the back door. To my surprise, Allison was right behind me, only she took a giant leap off the dock's edge, flinging herself into the air.

Her aim was perfect. She sailed through the open door and landed with a thump on the floor of the vehicle, gasping for breath and shaking her head. The truck lurched onward, the driver unmindful—or uncaring—of the yelling crowd standing on the dock like stranded cruise passengers.

"God, you can run fast," I said. "That was the most incredible thing I've ever seen."

"Track," she gasped. "I was the Jersey Girls Hurdles Champ."

I grinned back at her, feeling the relief of being safer, even if just for the moment.

"If I hadn't made it, you would have come back for me, wouldn't you?" she asked.

What could I say?

We lay back on the floor of the truck, exhausted, as the vehicle bounced along toward its unknown destination. Finally, our breathing slowed and we sat up. I looked out a side window.

"Where are we going?" Allison asked.

"Not too far, I think. He just drove through the gate to the airport."

Allison walked to the back and looked through the rear window.

"Look at this."

I walked over and looked out, sharing her view of not one

but two cars drawing near in a plume of dust.

"Company," I said. "I knew this was too good to last."

"What'll we do?"

"First time it slows down, we amscray."

"While it's moving?"

"If we wait until it stops, those guys'll be waiting for us."

The truck downshifted and rocked, hauling itself over a steep incline and turning. I looked out the back. The turn had been sharp. We were moving about five or ten miles an hour. Now was our chance.

"Let's go," I said, pushing open the rear door. "You first."

"Thanks a lot," she said, frowning.

I pushed her out the back and watched as she hit the ground running, then rolled into a ball, got up and streaked behind a building. I edged out onto the bumper, neatly shut the door behind me, and jumped to the ground.

Perfect. I ducked behind a couple of ash cans at the roadside as the pursuing cars roared into sight from around the curve. They would have no idea that we were no longer in the truck until the vehicle stopped and they opened it up.

I headed back to find Allison. Sure enough, she was standing by an open hangar, examining her shredded 501's.

"Well, these are shot for sure," she said.

"Don't worry," I said. "It was for a good cause: Your jeans for your life. Are you okay?"

"Just a few bumps. Say," she said, "I always thought the man went first."

"You don't live to be over three hundred years old by going first all the time," I said. I tried to pat some of the road dust off her clothes.

"Now, let's see if we can put some distance between us and this place. As soon as they open the truck and find us gone, they'll backtrack in this direction. And we don't want to be here when they arrive."

We stuck close to the shadows thrown by several large hangars, which contained a variety of aircraft. The place looked deserted, not even a mechanic in sight. Maybe it was too early for the flying day to begin.

We dodged between buildings, getting closer to the runway where I could see several planes out on the flightline, along with a bunch of helicopters.

"There must be a car or something we can borrow," I said. "We can high-tail it out of here, then get back to Rogers."

I looked at my watch. It was just a quarter past seven. I felt as if I had been up for twenty-four hours. My pulse quickened as my ears picked up the dull sound of a car engine coming up behind us. Oh-oh. It was one of the cars that had been chasing the truck. Our friends must have tumbled to the fact that we were footloose and fancy-free again.

We ducked behind a hangar door as the car cruised slowly past. I could feel Allison's heart beating as I held her tightly against me in the dark shadows. Such a body she had.

Good. They had gone. We stepped out into the sunshine and, whoops, there were two men they had dropped off. They stared at us and we stared back.

"Hey you guys," one shouted, running toward us. I grabbed Allison and we were off on a dead run, this time toward the airport runway. Wouldn't you know we were out in the open now and there was absolutely no way to turn back in the direction of the buildings. We were cut off by the two men, who had separated and were converging on us from different angles. Ahead of us were a couple of planes.

"I don't suppose you can fly one of these?" Allison shouted.

Ah fate, thou fickle tormenter of mens souls. We are never entirely free of the past, are we? In a micro-second, even as we ran helpless and breathless onto the grass, my mind replayed all that I remembered of those days, more than seventy years before. Different airplanes, to be sure, but the same grass and the same bold blue sky, beckoning and challenging us newly-uniformed recruits, daring us to break free and soar. My old instructor, probably mouldering under a rock somewhere now—what was his name? Those first tentative flights. My air-sickness. My botched landings and takeoffs. Saving my instructor's skin, but somehow getting us back to earth safely, only for naught. I was washed out anyway—and finishing the war stuffing hay down those ugly crazed nags at the cavalry horse farms. I even remembered my first day at that new and terrible assignment, the sound of the airplane overhead and looking up, making a silent wish that someday I would take to the sky again. And now on this day my chance had come again.

"I said, can you fly one of these things?"

Her face was red and her eyes full of hope, the look people get when they stare a crazy thousand-to-one shot in the face.

"I did once upon a time—a long, long time ago."

She blinked. "You're kidding."

"No, I'm not."

"Then what are we waiting for?"

We ran up to a plane, one of those four-seater types that men haul their families around in.

"How about this one? Try it," she shouted, looking back at the pursuing men over her shoulder.

My God, it was so different than that patchwork of rag and pipe I used to pilot—the ancient Jenny.

We ran around the back and scrambled up on the right wing to the airplane's only door.

"Me first," I said, knowing that in the movies, the pilot always sat in the left seat. I climbed in and pulled her in.

This was clearly impossible, I knew. I had never seen an instrument panel like this one. Think, dum-dum, was there anything among that forest of dials and gadgets that WAS familiar?

"Figure out how to close the door and lock it," I said.

"My God," she said. "You mean you don't even know how to close the door?"

The red knob—mixture. I pushed it in. Labeled toggle switches. A red one that read MASTER. I pushed it. Another labeled FUEL PUMP. On you go. Sweet Jesus, there are ignition keys, just like a car. I turned the key to the detent marked

BOTH. Ah, the prop out front jolted into movement, then abruptly stopped.

What was missing? THROTTLE said the label on the center quadrant by my right knee. I pushed the lever full forward and turned the keys to the right again. The propellor turned—and kept turning.

"Hurry, they're almost here!" Allison shouted. Geez, come on and start! The propellor cranked and cranked. What was I doing wrong? I looked out and one of the men, beet-red and out of breath, was drawing a weapon from his inside coat pocked. He was yelling something.

Then my eye caught a silver knob on the bottom of the panel. PRIMER. Of course! the engine probably hadn't been started in a long time. It needed the help of priming shots of fuel into the carb. Marvelous. I disengaged the knob and pushed it in and out twice, then began cranking the engine again.

Voila! It began sputtering and coughing, setting up a tubercular din that sounded like a Ravel symphony to my ears. I winced as a loud noise erupted next to my head. The man on the ground to my left was firing at me! Yikes. His buddy was on the wing, pounding on the window. I rammed the throttle forward and the engine surged, dragging the plane ahead over the rough ground. The wing walker fell to the ground, got up and started running after us.

"We're doing it! We're doing it!" Allison screamed. She had obviously gone crazy.

The plane slewed to the right and left, begging me to use

the rudder pedals on the floor. This I did—and we began tracking straight ahead. Now the men were running alongside the plane, emptying their trusty pistols at us.

"Get down!" I yelled, knowing full well that there really wasn't any place to duck down into. There was nothing for it but to sit in full view, dodging bullets, hoping against hope that the god of horrible bullet wounds would keep us safe and that flying lead would not puncture any vital systems on the plane. We lurched madly ahead, then bumped up onto a black asphalt taxiway. This was more like it. Now, which way do I go? The two men were now about fifty yards behind us and apparently had run out of ammunition. I breathed more easily and smiled at Allison.

"Not bad, huh?" I said.

"Now, can you get us off the ground?" she demanded. "Here comes that car again."

Sure enough, I could see the car stop to pick up the two men, then come wheeling in our direction. I steered the plane down the taxiway as fast as I could and still keep the wheels firmly attached to the ground. Which way was the wind blowing? I remembered that you always took off with the wind at your tail. Or was it, you always took off into the wind? I looked vainly for that orange windsock, hoping it would impart some mysterious knowledge to me. Now the car reached the taxiway and was roaring toward us.

Well, the devil take the wind. I already had learned a few things about this plane. I knew where the throttle was. And the rudder pedals. What else was there to know?

"Make it FLY," Allison shouted. She was pointing up to the ceiling of the plane with her index finger. Ah—up that way!

I pulled the plane out onto what I hoped was the runway. At least there were painted stripes on it. I pushed the throttle forward and coaxed the plane over to the center line. I could feel the car breathing down our necks as the plane rolled forward, picking up speed.

"Faster!" yelled Allison. "Make it go FASTER!"

Nothing threatens concentration like a panicked maiden. But with the throttle rammed full forward, there was little more I could do now but watch the round instrument labeled AIRSPEED as the little arrow behind the glass window marched clockwise. 40, 50, 60, 65, 70.

Outside, like a thrill driver's show, two men were perched on the front fenders of the speeding car, firing at us. Several round holes were punched in the wide windows. And Allison was beating on the instrument panel, as if flogging a lame racehorse across the finish line.

Ready or not, here we come. I pulled back on the strange steering wheel affair (my Jennie had a STICK, remember?) and a miracle occurred. The plane soared upward, donut tires loosing their grip on the runway, spinning prop pointing toward a ragged line of puffy white clouds. I looked down over my left shoulder and could see the car below, growing smaller and less menacing by the second, little ant-like figures outside it now with flashes of fire coming from their weapons. Allison pounded my shoulder.

"We did it!" she shouted. "I can't believe it—we actually did it!"

Yes, we had done it. But now that we had done it, what do we do with it? Here I was, climbing upwards in this noisy, glorious contraption, but to where?

"Find a map or something," I said, "and see if you can figure out where we are." I needed time to figure out what on earth I was supposed to do now. Ahead loomed a high mountain range. At the rate we were climbing, I doubted we could clear it. I would have to find a canyon and sneak through. Judging by the sun, we were headed east. Okay, so what?

I checked the guages floating in front of my eyes. Thankfully, the little pointers on both fuel guages pointed to "F". Either I had Failed, or we had Full tanks. I looked at the compass over the instrument panel—that was one instrument I remembered how to use. I wished I could say the same for the radios. It looked like there were two of them—a matched set. I twiddled the knobs, hoping to hear the sound of a human voice. In the meantime, I reviewed our predicament.

For one thing, it was about twenty minutes after seven now. That meant that Scarlatti would have to make sure he was in a position to send that radio message to Rocky Flats. If he didn't, the whole chemical arsenal would blow sky-high—and over a million people on the eastern slopes could say their prayers. I wished I could talk to Rogers. However, if he and his gang weren't even competent enough to build a tracker that worked, what good would they be in my present predicament? I felt a tap on my shoulder.

"I think we're about right here."

Allison shoved a map in front of me and, with the plane bucking up and down like a frightened pony, I followed her pointing finger.

"How do you know?" I said.

"Because that must be Aspen down there," she said. "I used to go skiing there with my girlfriends."

I glanced out the window to my left.

"That's the airport," she said. "Aspen Airport. We could land there."

"No we can't," I said. "I could never put this plane down in that teacup." If that was the Aspen Airport, it was out of the question. I could see the narrow runway below, almost lost in the midst of the steeply rising terrain.

"I'll have to find some flat ground."

She shrugged. "Well, I think we're going east. If we keep going this way, we should come through the last line of mountains pretty soon—there'll be flat ground on the other side."

Smart girl, this one.

"And look here," she continued…

"Hold it," I said. "We've got company."

Out my side window I watched as a helicopter drew abreast. It was big, black and mean-looking. And it was very close. We could feel the gutty whop-whop-whop of its huge rotors, smashing down the air upon us. Three men were sitting in the machine—two in front and one in back and one was holding up a large placard for us to see. 122.9 it said. The man holding the sign was Scarlatti.

"Do you see who I see?" I said.

"Can't this thing go any faster?" Allison said, making little giddy-up movements in her seat.

I managed to tune the top radio to 122.9 and removed the beige plastic microphone from its sleeve at the bottom center of the instrument panel.

"Hello," I said. "If anyone is listening on this frequency, I want them to call the FBI in Denver, Colorado and tell them that Andrew Merriman needs help."

"Not very smart," Scarlatti's voice crackled in. "By the time any help arrives for you, your blood will be decorating one of those granite hills down there."

"Why don't you crawl back in your crypt," I said. "And take those ghouls of yours with you."

"Don't toy with me, Andrew. Time grows short—I want to be able to send my little message to our shiny little friend at Rocky Flats. Now either follow us with that airplane, or I'll be forced to terminate your little trip by force. Is that clear? If you agree to return, I'm prepared to live up to our little bargain."

"Some bargain," I said. "You were talking about a damn autopsy—and then getting rid of Allison."

"You must forgive me my little jokes, Andrew. I never had

any intention of going back on my word. After all, my word is my honor."

Allison snatched the mike from my grasp. "Buzz off, pal," she said. "You don't know what honor is."

"Well, that did it," I said to her smiling face.

"I regret to say," Scarlatti said, "that response has exhausted my patience."

The helicopter pulled broadside to our left wing and I could see a couple of long-barreled weapons pointed toward us. I knocked the wheel to the right. We banked sharply and picked up speed. I looked back and the chopper was right on our tail.

I had no idea what stresses this airplane was designed to take but I knew we would be in danger of pushing it beyond its limits.

"Try to raise someone on those radios," I said. "Anyone. Tell them to get a hold of Rogers through the FBI. Maybe they can send up a jet after this guy or something."

I knew our chances were nil but I wanted Allison to keep busy and, who knows, maybe she would get lucky. In the meantime, I would concentrate on flying.

The air became much rougher now as we screamed downward to the lower altitudes. The airspeed needle was pegged in the red area—over 180 knots. I hoped the wings would stay with us. Behind us, the helicopter bobbed and weaved, trying to pull alongside. I hoped that as long as I could dive, we could attain speeds that the helicopter would not be able to hold.

But sooner or later, I knew we had to run out of altitude. I checked the altimeter: 8,800 feet. The pointer on the climb indicator said we were losing altitude at almost a thousand feet per minute.

Below us I could see the entrance to a narrow canyon flanked on the sides by pine-covered rocky precipices. I felt my sphincter tighten as we hurtled toward the gap—the eye of a needle. Allison was too busy gabbing on the radio to see what was happening.

Down we went, the helicopter trying to pull abreast but failing. I heard the pop-pop-pop of gunfire. We must have presented an easy target, like shooting a fat white goose on a pond. But the canyon mouth loomed ahead and, with the sweat of concentration running down my forehead into my eyes, I managed to squeak the plane through the opening unscathed, our slim white wings clearing the rocky sides by a couple of feet at most.

Now my work was really cut out for me. The canyon revealed itself to be very narrow, a mere finger's slice through the rock with no place to make a U-turn. I followed the crease as best I could as our airspeed dwindled in level flight. We were doing 130 knots now, the canyon walls rushing by in a blur of orange and red, interupted by bunches of pines that reached toward us, trying to pluck us into their bosoms.

Ouch—I felt a knock on my left arm. I was hit. Blood began oozing from a wound just below my shoulder. I hoped Allison wouldn't see it—but flecks of blood on the side window told the story.

"You're wounded," she cried.

"Just a flesh wound," I said. "It's nothing." Every man should have the chance to utter that line at least once in his lifetime.

Now I coaxed the plane into a series of roller-coaster climbs and descents, up and down, up and down, hoping the chopper pilot would goof or, failing that, at least interupt their aim. Suddenly the canyon forked, with one turn to the left and another to the right. I headed left—and so did the chopper. Now, an idea popped into my head. I knew we couldn't continue flying like this. It was just a matter of time before one of their bullets punctured our gas tank or our heads—and we'd be heading down for good. But one thing was in my favor: I knew what I was going to do before the pilot behind me did. I could picture him, stressed to the max, ducking threats by Scarlatti who would be screaming for my blood. He had to follow me—and that gave me a whisper-thin edge.

Allison turned up the radio and Scarlatti's high-pitched voice filled the cabin.

"Give up, Andrew. You don't stand a chance. After all, you're no Chuck Yaeger." Hideous laughter, with wild exhortations and chattering bup-bups of gunfire. "You may live through this, but I can promise you, the girl certainly will not!"

Now I waited for another fork in the road—one that would fit my plan. Each time we came to one, I peeled off to the left, with the chopper hugging my tail. Now I could see another fork hoving into view about one thousand yards distance. I pushed the nose down, trying to gain the last ounce of speed from our plane before we reached the turn-off. 130, 140, 160—our airspeed climbed as we rocketed downward. Then, the "Y" in the road filled the windshield. I turned slightly left, held course until my heart almost burst in my chest, then banked sharply right, grazing the rocks on my left with the wingtip.

Allison screamed—and I don't blame her. It was a fool's move. But that's why it worked.

The chopper tried to follow my lead—but it was too late. That pilot was good—too good. Because his reflexes made him bank right to follow me—even though his brain was screaming NO! NO! He was caught in a right turn beyond the "Y"—and splashed his beautiful black machine into the rocks in a hail of flying glass and metal that spewed forth from a crimson-orange burst of flame and smoke.

The radio speaker went silent as the wreckage rained down the canyon walls, broken rotor blades, weapons, bodies—the works.

Allison and I looked out our windows, then at each other. We had done it. Ha—Yaeger couldn't have done any better!

Ahead, the canyon opened upon a broad flat plain and seconds later, the mountains spit us out over the Colorado countryside. The horizon showed storm clouds in the eastern sky, with jagged flecks of lightning. My shoulder throbbed mightily, but I didn't care. We had made it. Scarlatti was a thing of the past. And we had the future.

Wait a minute. If Scarlatti and his pals had become tiny bits of broken bone and seared flesh on the canyon floor, who was going to push the little button that sent the signal to the bomb inside Rocky Flats? The radio crackled into life and Allison picked up the mike.

"If Andrew Merriman is monitoring this frequency, please switch to 119.3."

Allison turned the frequency selector as if she had been doing this all her life.

"Come in," she said.

"Allison, Allison MacKenzie—is that you?" The voice belonged to Rogers.

We looked at each other and she gave me the mike.

"Okay Rogers," I said, "what happened to you guys?"

"Bit of a mix-up, old friend. We had tracked you, up to a point—but your transmitter suddenly went on the fritz. Where are you?"

"We borrowed one of Scarlatti's planes. We're just east of the mountains now, north of Denver. Scarlatti and a couple of his guys just kissed a canyon wall a few miles back. He's dead, I'm sure."

There was a pause. "Then mission accomplished, right?" Rogers said.

"Not quite. I'm afraid there's a complication."

"What kind of complication?"

I explained about Scarlatti and his bomb—and the necessity of the device receiving his radio message to prevent its detonation.

"I would suggest you start evacuating that area," I said. That thing is going to blow, unless we can stop it."

Rogers left the frequency for a few moments, then came back on.

"We're alerting the Civil Defense office," he said. "But in the meantime, there must be a way to prevent that device from going off."

"Not very easily," I said. "Scarlatti told me the whole system is rigged so that any kind of available pressure suits or safety devices won't be able to enter the area where the device is."

"We can't blow up the whole plant," he said.

"No, of course not. Not unless you want to spread several tons of pressurized poisonous gasses over the area."

"Well, let us chew on this, Andrew. We'll come up with something."

"It's too late to chew things over," I said. "We've got less than a half hour before that thing goes off. Besides, I've already figured something out. If anyone goes in there after it, it'll have to be me."

"Andrew!" Allison grabbed my arm but I shrugged her off.

"I'm Superman, remember. If no one can get in close to that device with special protection, then I'm the only one left."

"You're taking an awful lot on, Andrew," Rogers said. "But it does make sense."

"Can you think of something better in the next few minutes?"

"No. Can't say that we can."

"Okay, then it's up to me. I'll try to land near the plant and make it on foot from there. You be close by to take care of Allison. I'll join you if and when I can."

The words sounded vaguely melodramatic and I did not mean them to. It was just that, that's how things were. Period. If more than three hundred years of personal history meant anything, the gas wouldn't harm me. And if it did, what did I really have to lose? I looked over at Allison. She was studying my face.

Who else in history could have found their self in a situation where their actions alone could have saved the lives of thousands, even millions of people? Now, I had that chance. It probably would never come again—nor did I want it to. But if the gods had kept me around all these years for any reason, this must have been it. This was my calling—the goal carved out for me. All else was candy and floss—even Allison. The only thing that counted now was entering the arsenal, finding that damnable device, and disarming it. It didn't matter if I made it beyond that point. I would have accomplished the mission for which I had been kept around these long years. And I would go in peace.

My shoulder was now stinging and my left arm felt slightly weaker, but I could have cared less. What's another wound for a body that had survived a thousand such wounds? An inconvenience.

Tall smoke stacks loomed in the distance, high-lighted by a lineup of deep purple clouds. I could see a curtain of rain wetting the prairie lands a few miles to the east.

"That's the arsenal," Allison said, looking up from her map.

"I'll put this thing down on the flattest piece of ground I can find," I said.

I pulled the throttle back, just as the engine quit. Terrific. I looked at the fuel guages. The little needles were pointing on "E". I knew that didn't stand for Excellent.

"We must have taken some bullets in the tanks," I said. "Well, we were going to land anyway."

Allison smiled grimly. "Talk about timing," she said.

The propellor stood stock still as we descended toward the arsenal. I could see rows of trucks and busses driving away from the long low arsenal building—the result of Rogers' evacuation orders. We were just a few miles north of Denver now, floating downward over the suburbs. Winds off the mountains kicked the plane about as we neared the lower altitudes. I could feel my airsickness cropping up in my throat. I wondered if they kept barf bags in small planes.

Now I banked over the plant, low and slow, trying to figure the best place for my landing. Finally, I spotted a huge parking lot with an open end that led out into the prairie beyond. Perfect. We descended in silence. There was nothing I could do but sit and wait.

"Hold on," I said. The plane neared the ground. I could

see the asphalt parking lot ahead, with a tall stand of cotton-woods at the close end. We had sunk just below the trees. No good. We would impale ourselves in the branches unless I did something. Allison instinctively covered her face with her arms. I hauled back on the wheel. The plane ballooned upward. Nicely done. We cleared the trees by inches, snagging a few branches in our landing gear. Then we resumed our descent, faster now, on the edge of a deadly stall. I pushed the nose down to pick up airspeed, then pulled back on the wheel and flared slightly as we glided over the edge of the parking lot.

One bounce, two bounces, three bounces, careening past parked cars and other vehicles, then out the other end of the parking lot where we plunged over a concrete divider, tearing the nose wheel from the fuselage.

"Make it stay down," Allison yelled.

"I'm trying!"

At last the plane came to a grinding halt, tipped up on its nose like a dying whale. The tips of the propellor blades were curled backwards.

We were down.

"Three landings in one," I noted. "Not bad."

We climbed out the door just as a car drove up. Rogers and a couple of men got out.

"Glad you're safe," he said, walking up to each of us and enclosing our hands in his. For Rogers, a very emotional dis-play.

"Andrew, I hate to see you go ahead alone. Isn't there something I can do?"

"No. I don't think so," I said. I tried to sound cocky and devil-may-care. But who was I kidding?

"If you don't have the gear that will let your men come into the building with me, then it's a solo job. Anyway, when you come to think of it, it's an exercise I'm perfectly suited for."

We talked for a few more minutes, Rogers telling me what he knew about the layout of the arsenal. We discussed my options, which weren't many.

"Here, you'll need these," he said, pressing a ring of keys into my hand.

I looked at Allison. Thank God I had at least gotten her to safety. If nothing else went right that day, I had least done this right. "Just take care of Allison for me. Don't let her out of your sight."

"We won't," Rogers said. He turned to her. "You'd better come with us, young lady. Andrew will be perfectly safe." He definitely did not look too convinced.

She turned and looked at me, obviously reluctant to go.

"Go with them," I said. "I'll join up with you when I can."

I hated goodbyes, and I hated this one most of all. Allison was walking slowly away with Rogers when she turned and ran back to me, tears forming in the corners of her eyes. She through her arms around me and I knew again how much this girl meant to me.

"Andrew, I love you. And I want you to come back to me."

"I will," I said, holding her tightly.

"I don't care if you live forever, I want you with me as long as I can have you."

"Okay," I said. Lame, yes, but what else could I say?

It had started raining now and thunder crackled. She walked away with Rogers and got into a car. A huge clap of thunder split the darkening clouds as I turned and walked toward the arsenal building.

In the abstract, death is almost acceptable, a part of our existence that we are told is a natural and necessary part of the grand concept of total universe, light, and being. But in the specific, death is a sorrow. A stinking sorrow that strikes to the roots of our soul, implacable, unpredictable—an evil whose existence isn't alleviated by assurances about its naturalness or tidy explanations concerning death's place in the intelligent scheme of things.

Who among us has not lost a living treasure and refused to accept the event with equanimity? Those who have not, surely will.

But death is most foul when it cloaks itself in democracy, cutting through masses of humanity like a scythe, sparing neither the innocent or guilty, weak or strong, slow or fast, woman or man, child or adult, Christian, Jew, Muslim or athiest.

And bearing witness to such desecration does not innure one to the effects of it. In my tedious span, I have seen death do its dirty work in vast numbers. A plague in Spain when I was just sixteen that littered the landscape with corpses, sparing not even the cattle, stray cats and dogs. Droughts in Africa that boiled the land and shriveled the peoples in carnages that counted its victims in the millions. Ancient wars across the countries of Europe that killed people by shot, pestilence and starvation. Modern wars spawned by dreary old men, fought by young innocents that netted the deaths of the attackers, the attacked, and those who stood between.

In August of 1945, I bore witness to death of a wholly different kind, borne from a cloud high above the city of Hiroshima in Japan. As an interpreter in the employe of the United States Army, I rode into the city on a dreadfully warm afternoon, seated next to a sweaty, smelling Sergeant who was driving our jeep like a crazy person.

"Don't look too bad from here, kid," he yelled, shielding his eyes from the sun with a huge hand.

I looked at our map. If I was right, we should have been within view of the city core by now, with its office buildings, shops and stores. Maybe around the next turn.

We drove a mile or two farther down the bumpy road, which was clotted with people going in the opposite direction, pushing carts, wagons, a few cars and trucks loaded with odds and ends. Typical bunch of refugees.

We were now in an area of broken buildings and rubble.

"Where's downtown?" I yelled to a soldier at the road-side.

"You're in it," he answered, spreading his arms. "This is all that's left."

I knew there must be a mistake, because we had been told that only one bomb had been dropped. Atomic or not, whatever that was, it couldn't have caused this much destruction.

But it had. And it took a only few brief visits to makeshift shelters and outlying buildings to impress upon me the full extent of the cataclysm that had descended upon the city from the belly of a bird high in the sky.

Again, I was faced with death in the specific. The fresh reality of seared flesh, smells, agony-filled eyes, and high-pitched wails—and fear so radiantly terrifying it erased all heroes and reduced all sufferers to children.

Outside on the broken streets in the sunlight, there were mysteriously few broken bodies lying about. Instead, there were ghostly white shadows holding the images of people who once stood there. On steps, curbs, against walls—wherever innocents dallied and hung about.

The survivors were dazed and uncomprehending. One man, a willowy laborer in his twenties, told me he had been laying brick at the edge of the city when he paused to study the contrails of an airplane flying high above. He knew it was a B-29, he could tell by the familiar growl of the engines. Reconnaissance, he thought, because they usually came over in huge flocks, dropping their greyish steel eggs and igniting great fires.

He watched as the great plane passed over the city then banked sharply and reversed direction. He was just about to turn back to his spade when he saw the mushroom. The towering cloud blossomed over the city like flower from hell, golden white in its magnificence, commanding his attention. Then on the heels of a dull roar came a great wind, that sent him flying back into the deep ditch. His lost footing saved his life, because when he collected his senses and crawled out of the whole, he had been reborne in a new land. Gone were the houses and stores, light poles, trolleys. Gone were the people, to be replaced by screaming parts of people, dotting the cityscape with their ugliness.

Later, when the dust had settled, so, too, settled the radioactivity upon the backs of the unwary who stumbled about in shock, curious about the end of their well-ordered world.

It was these victims who touched me the most, thousands of persons, doomed and dying, duly cared for and yet outcasts because their terminal ills were so unique and final.

Many asked me, "Is the Emperor well?"

"Hirohito was untouched," I assured them. They would nod solemnly, relief spilling out upon their faces.

I was in the Hiroshima region for less than two weeks when I was removed to a staging area a hundred kilometers away. But the distance could not separate me from what I had seen, heard and touched. It was more real and specific than I would ever have it, visited upon thousands—not just a son, daughter, mother or father.

The phenomena of death had been brought home to me again. That it effected me so deeply was costly proof that, although ancient, I was not jaded. I was, for better or worse, still a member of the human race. And I was impressed by the knowledge that I never wanted to see any such holocaust again, no matter how long I might live.

Chapter 14

I wish I could tell you that, as I walked toward my destiny, the stout heart of a patriot beat in my chest. But it wasn't like that at all. I knew better than anyone that I was not cut out to be a hero—now or ever.

But I was also forced to face a couple of truths. First, it had been my actions, a couple of centuries before, that had led directly to the present state of affairs. I felt bad about that. Because if I had not let my foolish quest for romance lead me to that lady's chambers, so much would be different now— and so much pain could have been avoided. If I had not been so intent on wooing the Prince's wife, I would not have been caught in her bedroom. She wouldn't have panicked and toppled out the window to her death. He wouldn't have gone crazy and knocked over the lamp. The house wouldn't have burned to the ground. Several other Scarlatti's wouldn't have died in the inferno. And the Prince wouldn't have been hauled off to some booby hatch, there to plot wild and devious ways to wreak retribution upon me through his surviving son and that son's sons.

So all the events that had transpired since that awful day could be layed upon my doorstep. And now, even with Scarlatti's last descendant smashed to smithereens against the canyon rocks, it was fitting that I would be the only person who could erase the last fruits of his vengeance.

But now it wasn't just my fate that hung in the balance. It was the fate of millions of people on the slopes of the Rockies and westward. Rogers had said the roads leading south and eastward from Denver were clogged with angry evacuees and their families—asking what new government foul-up had transpired that could endanger them so. Of course, they couldn't be told that, if the arsenal was to be blown sky high and deadly gasses released into the atmosphere, they wouldn't stand a wisp of a chance to escape the lethal consequences of windborne vapors.

I imagined the landscape littered with stiffened corpses. Memories from long past flashed into my minds eye. Memories of a Japanese city, crying children, dazed and dying adults— and the rising cloud that evaporated people where they stood and decimated survivors with time-released radioactivity.

Would I want to be responsible for that kind of carnage—

blamed on Scarlatti but really caused by my deeds years before
these generations were even born? The answer made me walk
to the arsenal building, shoulders back and head held high,
looking bold and touchingly manic.

Now, from his lofty perch in the place where the souls of
deceased bad guy's are kept, I could feel the Prince looking
down upon me, laughing in bitter irony.

The Rocky Flats arsenal consisted of a jig-saw pattern of
low grey concrete buildings, windowless and functional—as
befits a warehouse of death. Access doors were limited—a further effort at containment in the event of an accident. As I
neared the building closest to me, I spied a rust-colored steel
door, the only break in the unbroken expanse of concrete. I
took one last look behind me, at the cluster of official vehicles
parked in a circle like Conestoga wagons under siege. Then I
approached the door, opened it and entered the building.

A cold embrace of air-conditioning enveloped me in a
sterile breeze as I closed the door behind me. The crisp efficiency of the scene put me off guard. Instead of being dark and
foreboding as I expected, militant rows of neon blazed high
above me, splashing light across sparkling banks of machinery.
I sniffed the air, like one of their test rabbits housed in early-
warning cages. The floor was painted with a glossy grey paint
which beckoned me to walk along the corridor towards the
center of the building. Except for the faint wheeze of machinery, all was eerily quiet, a place for robots.

I glanced at my watch and quickened my pace, realizing

that now I had a mere thirteen minutes to find Scarlatti's shiny chrome globe, disarm it, and high-tail it out of there. Of course, I knew as much about disarming such a device as I did about nuclear physics. But if I did find it, I might be able to move it to another location within the plant and perhaps minimize its effects.

I moved fast, cruising the corridors, moving from building to building through snakelike tunnels. First stop: Scarlatti's office. I found it easily and conducted a fast but thorough search, emptying drawers and peering into bookcases and filing cabinets. Nothing.

I decided to ignore other office and administrative areas and concentrate on storage areas and adjacent rooms where any bomb-like device would have instant access to surrounding deadly materials. It would also have to be in an area accessible by radio signals. I reasoned that Scarlatti's transmitter could not have penetrated any enclosures that were below ground or encased in metal.

I found what I was looking for in a building that occupied the center-most position in the complex, surrounded on all sides by other look-alike structures. The building's importance was signaled by a perceptible increase in the corridors of live bird, rodent and rabbit cages. Opening a final steel door, I suddenly found myself in the epicenter of the arsenal, a massive doomsday showroom stacked high with bulbous metal containers that looked like those fat little bombs they used to load into the bellies of World War II airplanes.

The carefully-stacked chemical eggs were almost ceiling high, methodically and geometrically precise—arranged with love and concern like newborn babies in a nursery instead of the messengers of death they were. The scene took my breath away. There were thousands of them, all shapes and sizes, their cases coded and marked with orderliness and efficiency. There must have been more than enough there to erase life from several planets in the galaxy.

I opened the door and checked out small rooms lining an aisle at one end of the room. Finally, I came upon an unlocked storage space lined with shelves holding cardboard boxes containing what looked like spare parts. I opened a few boxes, then pulled several more off the shelf and set them on the shiny floor. There on the shelf in plain view was a black plastic box measuring about a foot square. Gingerly, I picked it up and set it down upon the floor. Could it be?

There were two latches. I unfastened one, then the other, and opened it. Presto.

It was the Prince's chrome bowling ball. Nestled into its little square coffin, it looked efficient but friendly, winking little red numbers behind a small window cut into its otherwise unbroken surface. The digits reported present time: six minutes before the hour. If Scarlatti had been right, it would blow its little top unless it had received the correct radio message by the top of the hour, eight o'clock.

Okay, I had found it—now what do I do? Cautiously, I laid my hands against the globe. It felt cool to the touch, smooth and pleasant. I picked it up, hefting it. Weight: approximately seven pounds. Measurements: about the size of a soccer ball. I held it close to my ear and listened. Nothing, not a sound.

From where I stood in the open storeroom, I could see the nearest row of stacked steel-clad gas casings less than twenty feet away. Scarlatti had no doubt crammed this device with enough explosives to shatter the integrity of the first couple rows of gas bombs. If his ravings were based on solid fact (and why not, since he was one of the people who ran the arsenal), then the resulting explosions would start a chain reaction that would wipe out the entire storehouse of gas containers, laying open the arsenal buildings like sardine cans, enabling the gasses to escape into the atmosphere.

I examined my options: Grab the globe and dump it into a bucket of water. Who's kidding? Anyone capable of fabricating something like this certainly knew enough to make it waterproof. How about slamming it hard with a sledge hammer or something, perhaps jangling its interior electronics so as to render it harmless? Brilliant, for sure. I had no assurance that the device could not also be triggered by impact, or some other trauma such as cutting into it with a welder's torch which was well beyond my ability—even if I had a torch.

With the little lighted window merrily blinking time away, there remained just one option. I would have to carry the ball to another area of the building and hope it's effects would be limited when it finally did blow its top. My musings had cost me another valuable minute. With just over two minutes left now, I would have to get a move on right away or wind up with no options at all.

Returning the device to its resting place, I closed the container, picked it up and headed out of the storeroom. Once in the corridor, I made a sharp right. A muted roar of thunder greeted my ears. It must have been storming like the dickens outside and, unaccountably, I could feel the hairs on the back of my neck rising. I could imagine Rogers and his men, sitting in their circle of cars, looking at their trusty government Timex's and squinting at the low profile of the arsenal buildings through the rain.

Their suspense certainly was no greater than my own. For now, as I hustled down a corridor, I felt a vibration coming from the container. It was a subtle sensation at first, but then it grew in intensity until, finally, I stopped and set down the box. Now it was jiggling on its own, fairly hopping a fraction of an inch off the slick tile floor, moving slightly sideways in its dance.

Should I open the box? My watched showed it was now one minute to eight. Wonderful. Oddly, I remembered that in all my past brushes with death, not once had my life flashed before my eyes as tradition demanded. I felt oddly cheated. But maybe this time I would get to see the entire reel.

I snatched up the chest, opened it, and drew forth the ball. It was like holding a kicking baby. The winking light flashed 30 seconds to go. What could I do with it? Where would be the best place to take it? My mind was a complete blank. When was I doing to start thinking like a hero?

Fate intervened. The shiny device, apparently taking its brief future into its own hands, jitterbugged out of my grasp. Hitting the floor with a metallic clang, it bounced out a nearby open door and into a stairwell. I chased it as it caromed off a couple of walls, then started bouncing down the stairs. Bong, bong, bong, bong it went. I slammed my hands over my ears as I chased it down the steps, knowing with every jarring bounce it was going to blow.

My tangled feet tripped on a step and I fell head first all the way to the bottom of one flight. Stunned and barely conscious, I noticed the ball had ricocheted off a closed door and was now spinning around like a top in a corner, a wild dervish that would have mesmerized me had my glance not shifted to my watch and noted that zero-hour had indeed arrived.

Eight o'clock. The jig is up. Please start my movie.

How perceptive was that first person who noted that silence is golden. Because in the silence that followed, a great golden glow transformed the stairwell into a seething blast furnace. My body was slammed by a brutish force that compressed me from all sides like an orange juice squeezer. Plaster painted in sickly government green slid down the concrete walls like pea soup. Bared concrete blocks were scorched, blackened and blown outward in a terrible upheaval that shook the floor upon which I lay. All the while, I heard not a single sound, just a terrible quiet that heralded the end of Andrew Merriman.

But not just yet. There was more. As the fragments of building fell about me in a crumbling pile of superheated dust, choking fumes lanced my lungs. Or was it molten lava running up my nose and down my throat? I rolled over and coughed, spilling liquid upon the floor, my inner life splashing onto the tile. I could see a white cloud hanging a few inches above my face. I reached up and thrust my blackened hands into the vapor and felt millions of hungry teeth nibbling at the burned skin on my fingers.

Even as my mind collected these impressions, another level of my awareness knew that, instead of playing the role of stricken observer, I should have been dying. In fact, I should have been very dead—passing through that famous tunnel leading to the blessed white light that Kubler-Ross interviewees are always rhapsodizing about.

The cloud of vapor diminished as I lay on the floor, waiting for my transference to the nether world. How long I lay, I don't know. And I'm not sure I was conscious the whole time. But after a time, I noted that the air had cleared considerably. I struggled to sit up. Then, with legs shaking in a palsied St. Vitus dance, I stood on my feet. Again, I had risen from the crypt. Cooked like a burger and oozing grease, Lazarus lives.

This realization did not send a surge of joy through my stressed but determined heart. I knew that I had failed. That

Scarlatti's deadly promise had been fulfilled and that, outside, the populace must have been falling like hail as the noxious gasses overtook the countryside.

Under these circumstances, only a very selfish person could have felt relieved. Sad to say, I was, just a bit. For embarrassing though it may be on such occasions, the need to live is so strong that even mass tragedy cannot dim the relief enjoyed by the few who are spared.

I stumbled through the rubble, seeking the outside air, dreading the picture of destruction that was sure to greet my eyes. But reaching the main corridor, I stood stock still with amazement. Although the stairwell itself was a shambles, the rest of the building that I could see looked very much intact. It was obvious that the stairwell had indeed contained the blast. Although the gas within Scarlatti's device had escaped, the explosives had not disturbed thousands of other casings stored within the buildings. The shiny globe with its flashing light and nasty temper had failed to do its job.

I looked up to see gaping holes in the ceilings. Water washed down upon my sooty face. It was rainwater—buckets of wind-driven rain that would keep escaping gasses from drifting into the atmosphere. I made my way into another building and finally reached an outside exit. Pushing it open, I was immediately drenched by a heaven-sent downpour.

What joy! I breathed deeply, letting my tortured body revel in the torrent that soothed my pains. Here I was, battered but alive, confident in the knowledge that my wounds would be healed fast and easily by the miracle within. And the realization that Scarlatti was dead and his plot had missed its mark buoyed my spirits even more. The populace was saved— my haunting memory of Hiroshima would not be reborn. All was well.

Soon I would be reunited with my precious Allison. I would lower my eyes modestly as I received a hero's welcome. Life was good again. Moreover—I could savor as much of it was I wanted, forever, until the very universe shrank into nothingness and all time stopped and God ended his grand game.

I spotted the circle of government cars in the distance, saw figures waving. I began running away from the building. The figures grew larger. The skies brightened perceptibly. It was obvious that, having done its good and glorious work, the storm was passing.

But my relief came too soon. For at that moment, heaven sent another fleet messenger to earth.

From a boiling tumult of rolling clouds that hung over my head like thick wads of cotton batting, a bluish-white thunderbolt flashed downward. A strange smell hit my nostrils in the split second before the lightning fried me. It was frightening, because the strange odor, crisp and clean like ether, had engraved itself upon my senses nearly three-hundred years before—after a storm-crazed bull had flung a small boy high into the air in a dusty village on the Arno.

Now, the lightning had come visiting again, perhaps reasoning that it was time to take care of unfinished business. The bolt struck me in mid-stride, momentarily freezing my body in a running position, like a lighted hood ornament on a post-war Pontiac. The cascade of voltage used my body like a lightning rod, entering my damp head first, coursing downward through shoulders, waist, legs and feet, before entering the wet earth. I was beautifully grounded and my body offered no resistance whatsoever as the voltage surged through me. Thank God, I am immortal, I thought, as a black curtain descended over me.

How comfortable and sublime. I am reminded of that time, ages ago, when I awakened to see the shocked faces of my father and a priest looking down upon me. Except on that occasion, my child's body was layed out in a rough wooden box, placed on a stand in our humble village church. This time it was in a hospital, and the faces belonged to Allison, Rogers and Prescott Atkinson. They were grim but smiling, obviously pleased to see that the stuff of life still surged through my indestructible veins.

I felt weak but I smiled at them.

"Thank God, you're all right," Allison said, bringing her lovely face close to mine. Her freshening tears cooled my cheeks.

Rogers nodded. "It's amazing," he said, "considering what

you've been through. That gas, and then that devilish lightning strike."

Atkinson beamed. "You should be dead and cold as a cod, young man."

In truth, I didn't feel very well at all. I tried to move but jabs of pain racked my body. Allison admonished me for my efforts and I sank back on the bed, weak as a kitten. Various parts of my body were swathed in bandages. The smell of medications and pine-scented Lysol hung heavy in the air.

"The doctor says you may be in here for a spell," Rogers said. He must have seen the unspoken questions in my eyes. "You're in the intensive care ward at the Riverdale Medical Center in Maryland. You've been here three days—we had you flown here from Denver."

Allison squeezed my hand and smiled.

"Of course," Atkinson spoke up, "we haven't told the people here about your unique healing propensities—so your progress may surprise them a bit. But even at that, you've suffered many broken bones, internal injuries and severe burns. You're going to require a great deal of care for a while."

"In the meantime, you just relax and take it easy," Allison said. I felt the reassuring touch of her hand on my arm. "It's all over now."

"Is it?" I asked.

Rogers nodded. "It seems that bomb of Scarlatti's went off in the best possible place. That basement stairwell contained the blast enough to leave the stored gas casings intact. Most of the damage was localized within one building. And the timely rainfall diluted the small amount of gasses that leaked into the outside air. In the meantime, we've shut down Scarlatti's operation and sent his associates back to their Motherland."

"What about Methuselah?" I asked.

"Well, we do intend to pursue it on our own, but I'm not sure we're going to be able to make much headway. I just don't have the funding to keep chasing it."

"What he means to say," Atkinson interjected, "is that so far as the Methuselah Operation is concerned, it's a dead issue, literally."

What a relief. Now my secret, whatever it was, could continue to reside within me only. Localized and safe. It's not that I'm not a sharing person, I thought, but one person on this Earth like me is more than enough.

I looked at Allison. How trusting and hopeful she looked. Suddenly, I was reminded of her mortality. To think, in time, her fresh loveliness would fade, replaced by ever-deepening wrinkles, white hair, missing teeth, bent back, stooped-shoulders, varicose legs and failing internal organs. Finally and irrevocably, I would be called upon to arrange her placement in one of those pretty velvet-lined bronze caskets with fluted handles, nestled inside a thick concrete vault sunk two meters under the sod. A cadre of crawling guests would move in to keep her molding remains company. And I would be alone again. My heart skipped a beat and I tried to swallow.

If only she could join me in my foreverness. What a blissful existence. The two of us. Bound together, never to part. But that was an impossibility. Irrevocably. Utterly.

Suddenly, I was overwhelmed with grief. The thought of having to part with her through her own eventual death was a terrible realization. Of course, it had crossed my mind before. But never with such poignancy, such finality.

Would I want a life without this girl, who loved me and placed such value in me in spite of my sickening arrogance? Without her, would I be alive—or just existing? I knew the answer. For me, it would not be worth living. Yet, unable to find it within me to take my own life by whatever means, I would be imprisoned in my foreverness, doomed to prowl the Earth's cities, set apart, alone—like a different species altogether. The enormity of it all brought a sickening lump to my stomach and I was afraid I might retch. What good was life unending, unloved?

"What's wrong, Andrew?" she asked, squeezing my hand again.

I turned my face to the wall. My heart welled with my love for her. But I could not answer. A short time later, I heard the door to my room close. Turning over, I found that I was alone.

That night I slept fitfully, tossing and turning, my mind filled with contradictions and fears. The question that nagged at me made me feel trapped and vulnerable. And I could see no way out...except to follow a lonely road which my heart truly did not want me to take. At last, soaked in perspiration and entangled in knotted bed sheets, I surrendered to inevitability. It was almost sunrise before I fell into a troubled sleep.

The following day Allison came to visit me. Rogers had put her up in a Marriott near the hospital and she arrived at my bedside looking all flushed and golden. The joy in her eyes made it all the harder for me to tell her what I knew I must.

It was over between us—for the good of both of us. I could not see her again. Ever.

The sunshine in her face disappeared.

"What are you saying?"

"I want you to take up your life where you left it. Go on that trip you were talking about. Meet people. See new places. Do new things. Forget about all of this business." Knives sliced into my heart as I spoke.

"Just like that."

"No, not just like that. But do it. Now. Please."

"You're not feeling well."

"No, I'm not feeling well. But that has nothing to do with it."

"But what about our plans?"

"What plans? We didn't have any plans. We've been too busy being chased and chasing to make any plans."

"Then we'll make plans."

"You make plans. But don't include me."

"What's changed all of a sudden?"

"Me. I've changed. I've reached the point where I can't go on leaving people like you behind. I can't do it any more."

"Isn't that like putting your head in the sand? You'll always have to leave people behind—so long as you are like you are. What else can you do?"

"I don't know."

"Live like a hermit? Is that what you want to do?"

"I can't see you again."

"You said that. I want to know why. Exactly why."

"Because, I don't want to lose you." I could feel tears, damn them, welling up. She should be crying, not me. Man up, Andrew. Stiffen that peach-fuzz on your wimpy upper lip!

"Do you love me?" she asked.

"Yes I love you. Don't you see—that's the problem. Can't you understand?" I wanted to shake her.

"Then just love me, and let the future take care of itself. We'll be together. It's that simple."

"IT'S NOT THAT SIMPLE!"

"Don't shout at me. I come in here, feeling good, knowing that this whole mess is behind us, and you have to start going off the deep end. Pull yourself together, Andrew, do you hear? You're talking dumb stuff and I don't want to hear it any more."

"It's not dumb to me. It's just that you can't see it from

my point of view. I'm the one who's lived my life…every single year of it."

"Wait a darn minute. You've lived all that time, and even though you can't die, you're afraid of death. Isn't that it, Andrew? Isn't that what we're talking about?"

"Not my death," I said. "It's your death that frightens me."

"You let me worry about my death, Andrew. My God, if we can enjoy a couple of years of peace together before I get cancer of the breast or something, isn't that better than no time at all? What you want to do is to avoid the whole thing. You can't do it, Andrew."

"Yes, I can."

"Then you're making a big mistake."

"I know, but I can't help it. It has to be this way."

"Nothing has to be this way. I may be the best thing that ever happened to you, Andrew, and you want to throw me and our future away."

"Better now, than later," I said.

"I'm telling you, Andrew, you're not being logical."

"For me, this is logic."

"But what about the things we've told each other? You told me you wanted to be with me—for whatever time we had together. Don't tell me that was just all talk."

"No, it wasn't just talk. I meant the things I told you. But in the past couple of days, it's dawned on me that I just can't go through this again. I'm sorry, but I just can't. Maybe I'm not thinking normal because I'm not normal, but that's the way I feel, right now, today. I've created nothing but trouble for you since we met, now it's over. Please go back to whatever it was you were doing before you met me."

"You unfeeling, insensitive jerk."

"I'm sorry."

"You're sorry," she repeated. "I'll tell you what you are, Andrew. You're weak. Plain and simple. Afraid to face the facts of life. Afraid to get your little feelings hurt. So you junk my feelings to save your own. I always knew you were arrogant and a bit pompous, but I was prepared to deal with that. But this, this Casper Milquetoast selfishness, that's more than I can take. Go ahead then. Be by yourself. Enjoy that long life of yours. And don't worry about me telling anyone about your precious secret. It's safe with me until the day I—but you don't want me to say that, do you?"

When the door slammed behind her, I felt utterly alone. But I also like a big boulder had been removed from my shoulders. Now I had rid my hands of that problem. Now I needn't fear the specter of my Allison, cold and stiff in a pretty bronze box. She could resume her normal life, meet some decent guy, marry, have children—do all those things that people with normal relationships do. Sooner or later she would realize I had done her a very large favor. Suddenly, life seemed much simpler.

Chapter 15

I had planned to end this journal at this point, with my future prospects unresolved, loose ends dangling like ornaments on a Christmas tree.

What would be the point of prattling on? There was going to be nothing new in my life. Allison would go the way of the rest of my loves. I would continue knocking about, breathing air, taking up space, fleeing from new relationships because I couldn't face the anguish of their eventual termination.

But as I layed my pencil aside, two weeks into my hospital stay, fate intervened with a quiet knock on the door. It was Prescott Atkinson, accompanied by one of the staff doctors, Ralph Harrison, who was smiling and flipping the pages on a chart.

"How are we feeling today?" said the doctor, a thin amiable man in his thirties, looking stern and impressively doctorish: stethoscope draped around neck, big Captain Midnight reflector thingy on his forehead, hands jammed into the pockets of his white lab coat.

"Okay, I guess."

"You're coming along quite nicely," he said. "In just two weeks time, you've progressed from having one foot in the grave to the point where we just have to maintain a watch for recurring infections and the like. In other words, so far, so good."

Prescott was standing at Harrison's side, the somber look on his face not quite in synch with the doctor's happy countenance.

"We should have you out of here in a couple of weeks or so. In the meantime, plenty of bed rest and let nature do it's good work."

Prescott approached my bedside and sat down in a stiff-backed chair as the doctor left the room.

"Tell me something, Andrew," he said. "When the doctor asked you how you felt, what did you mean by 'okay, I guess'?"

"Nothing particular," I said, searching for his meaning. "I just meant, I've certainly felt better."

"And you've been in here for two weeks now, right?"

I said nothing.

"And you still don't feel very well, do you?"

I shook my head.

"Yet, our good mendicant is blissfully at peace with your progress, isn't he?"

"What are you driving at?"

Atkinson sighed with impatience. "Well, Andrew, I'm surprised at you. Don't be so slow. Remember, that doctor doesn't know what we know about you. He thinks you're doing excellent—and you are by ordinary standards. But think a moment: When has it ever taken you, Andrew Merriman, Immortal of the Universe, so long to recover from something?"

His beady little eyes drilled into mine.

"Think back. When you were gored by that little beastie. Stabbed. Beaten. Shot. Broken into little bleeding pieces by that taxi. All the traumas that have been inflicted upon that body of yours for the last three hundred years or so. Has it ever taken you this long to recover?"

I sat bolt upright in the bed.

"Oh yes," he went on, getting up and pacing in front of the bed. "You were taken to the very edge and back again on the day Scarlatti died: Lungs seared by poisonous gasses capable of instantly killing most living things. Battered and burned by explosion. And finally, broiled by lightning—a shock that should have killed you—if you were indeed killable."

"So."

"So, you are recovering, yes. But Andrew, wake up. You're not recovering nearly as fast as Rogers and I thought you would. Or, indeed, as fast as you probably thought you would. Right?"

It was true. There was no denying it. Although I was getting better, it was at a far slower rate than I had many times in the past. Yes, the trauma had been grievous, but I was sure that I should be throwing off its effects by now—days after the injuries."

"What do you think is going on?" I asked.

"I'm not exactly sure," he said. "But it might have something to do with the combination of events that occurred this time around."

Suddenly, I remembered. "The lightning."

"What about the lightning?" He stepped closer to the bed and peered at me closely, as if I were a specimen under a glass slide.

"Long ago, when that bull got to me, I remember there was lightning."

"And that was the first time you noticed anything different about yourself."

I nodded. "A few times since, when electrical storms were about, I felt a bit odd."

He stroked his chin, deep in thought.

"Frankenstein was made by lightning," I noted.

"That was a movie, Andrew." He patted my shoulder. "This is real life."

"But do you think there's a connection?"

"I don't know. It does sound a bit other-worldly. Almost too simple as a matter of fact. But there's no question that all of our examinations and probing turned up no answers.

"So anything is possible."

"Yes, who's to say that perhaps some combination of elements, chemicals or forces within you weren't rearranged when that first bolt struck you when you were a child."

"And maybe the same combination un-rearranged me this time around."

"Perhaps. In any case, I'm almost ready to believe anything now. And I'm sure Rogers and his little squad of scientists are, too."

"So what do we do?"

"We do nothing, Andrew. After all, what is there to do? And why?"

"I don't know, I just thought…"

"I'll tell you what I think. I think there is an extremely good chance that your insides are busy normalizing themselves and throwing off the effects of your most recent injuries. We'll have to wait and see what happens. In the meantime, we'll just let the doctors here proceed with their treatments and see what develops."

Atkinson got a quizzical look on his face. Incidentally," he said, "What's going on with you and Allison? I understand she's moved back to New York. You two have a falling out?"

"Something like that."

He arched an eyebrow. "I'm surprised, Andrew. That relationship was starting to look as indestructible as you are."

∽

How ironic. Because the reign of my indestructibility—
the alter upon which I had been forced to worship for all these
years—was about to come to an end. For that very evening,
my body rose up and flung aside its cloak of invincibility, as if
shouting "Enough is enough—I can absorb no more indigni-
ties!"

I suffered a terrible relapse—the first of my existence. It
was announced by the arrival of a terrible fever that rendered
me unconscious for several days, sucking the last vestiges of
energy from my body and taking me to the brink. Although I
have little memory of what transpired, I recall faint images of
hovering faces, and babbling voices. My consciousness would
ebb and flow, like the flame from a flickering candle. I would
rise to the surface for a few moments, only to be dragged down
into the blackness again by a powerful undertow. All the while,
my mind ceased to operate, composing not a single thought or
observation. I was a dumb spectator at what was undoubtedly
my last grand performance. One day passed. Two days. Three
days. Four, and on. Down through the endless unmarked void
to the new world.

At last, I awakened. It was dark. I could see nothing. My
first waking thought was: I have finally done it. I have given up
the ghost. I flailed my arms wildly to push out the sides of my
casket—but felt only cool cotton sheets and a wool blanket.
Then I understood. I was still in the hospital. The blinds were
closed. A faint perfume of rubbing alcohol prickled my nose. I
wiggled my toes. I was still alive. It felt good.

But I wasn't alone in the room. Seeing me stir, Prescott Atkinson rose from a chair and walked toward me. The thin little man looked weak and tired as though he were the patient. He spoke softly, as if soothing a frightened rabbit caught browsing under a lilac bush.

"You've come back, Andrew. That's good."

"What's happened? How long have I been away?"

"It was ten days ago that we last spoke."

I was incredulous. How could this be? What could have happened?

"You died on us, Andrew, at least a couple of times. But you rallied and returned."

Died. I couldn't believe it. Just the use of that word in regards to me sounded foreign and unnatural. Dying was something that happened to other people, not Andrew Merriman.

"Why didn't they just let me go? Why bring me back?"

He smiled and placed his veined hands over mine. His beady little eyes were bloodshot.

"It's not good form, Andrew. Doctors always try to bring patients back, even after they've crossed the threshold."

"You've been here with me?" I asked.

"As much as I could. I didn't want to miss being a part of history."

He slumped heavily in the chair.

I felt my arm. It was heavily bandaged. "What's this?"

"You cut yourself while you were having a fit," he said. "It's healing poorly."

"Are you sure? That's not possible."

"It's possible now, Andrew." He looked at me, his eyes full of portent.

"What do you mean?"

"I mean, I believe you're one of us now. Whatever it was you had, I don't believe you have it any more. For whatever reason, I sincerely feel it is gone. The magic is missing."

"You mean…"

"I mean you're going to die, Andrew, like all the rest of us. Maybe not today or tomorrow, the next week, month or year. But sometime in the future, your body will throw in the towel for good. In the meantime, you'll live out the remainder of your life, for whatever time fate allows you to have. Then you'll go below. No more immortality. No more infinity. It's over, Andrew. Sooner or later you'll be bug chow."

The lump in my throat was as big as a bull frog.

"You can't be sure," I said.

"Nothing in this life is sure." He studied my face, reading it like a familiar map. "But I believe the signs are there. Your sudden turn for the worse. The terrible extremes to which the doctors had to go to keep your heart pumping blood through your veins. And now, this slow healing. Your body must have given its very last ounce of protection in battling off the wounds you sustained at the arsenal. And now, there isn't much left— at least no more than the rest of us possess. Whatever it was that held you together for all those years, it has evaporated. Gone with the wind. And you'll probably never get it back again."

He looked intently at my stunned face.

"Oh, you probably feel as if you have lost a friend, don't you? That's understandable. Because, in a way, you have lost a friend. Your ace in the hole, your refuge. And I think you'll grieve for yourself for a time, and try to figure out how you can make it in this world with no more prospects than the rest of us ordinary clods. But in time, you'll come to a new appreciation of things mortal. You'll be more sensitive to the sheer beauty and the special symmetry of a finite existence. An existence that has a beginning, a middle, and, most important, an end. You'll discover, as the rest of mankind has discovered, that because your time upon this earth is rationed, you must value each precious moment all the more."

I sat silently for several minutes. Atkinson did not utter a word. Finally, a question loomed in my mind.

"What about Rogers? Does he know about all of this?"

"He knows, yes, but he apparently has no abiding interest in you any more. In the true spirit of government watchdogs, he's chasing down other alleys now. So far as he's concerned, you don't even exist, Andrew. Expunged, I believe, is the word they use."

"And Allison. Does she know I've been sick?"

"No. We have not been in contact with her since she moved back to New York—and she hasn't tried to contact us either."

"So, what is there now?" I said, thinking out loud.

Atkinson smiled. "There is your life, Andrew, the rest of

it, out front of you, waiting to be lived."

He studied me closely. And I knew he could read in my eyes what I was thinking.

"And," he said, "there is Allison."

I found her sitting in a sunbeam on a bench in a small park a few blocks from her home on the Lower East Side. The air was cool and crisp. She was bundled in a heavy blue sweater, watching residents from nearby brownstones taking their morning constitutions. I'd gotten directions to the park from her landlady, a suspicious woman who was certain I was a demented stalker of young ladies until I melted her heart with a wrenching tale about a lovers quarrel.

"What do you want?" Allison challenged, impaling me with a look of exasperation.

I sat down beside her. She moved several inches away, to the very edge of the bench, lest she become contaminated by the leper.

"I want to talk to you."

"What is there to talk about? You made your feelings quite clear when you were raving like a lunatic the other day."

Her arms were crossed and her lower lip jutted in pouty defiance. Such an angel.

"Now you can just take your little speeches somewhere else. I'm in no mood to listen."

"I want to talk about our future."

"We don't have a future, remember? I'm supposed to plan a whole new life. Take trips, meet new people, do new things, remember?"

She drew her legs up onto the bench and encircled her arms around them, chin on knees, eyes staring straight at the grass beyond.

"I don't want you to do any of that now," I said.

"Oh, but what you want is important, isn't it?"

"That's not it at all. I'm thinking differently now. I was thinking crazy in the hospital. Confused. Frightened. All those things. I know that."

"Well, I don't care what you want now, can't you understand that?"

"Don't cry, please."

"I'M NOT CRYING, DARN YOU!"

Tears were streaming down her cheeks. I wanted to take her in my arms, but I was afraid she'd explode in rage. Instead, I got up and began walking away. She called out to me.

"What's the matter with your arm?" It was in a sling under my jacket and I had hoped she wouldn't notice.

"Oh, just some leftovers from my arsenal escapade." Ever the hero.

She rose from the bench and walked toward me. "You mean you haven't made your usual miracle man recovery? Such a nuisance. You must be slipping."

"That's what I've been trying to tell you. I am slipping."

She looked at me blankly, my words not registering.

"Slipping. What do you mean?"

"Just what I said. The doctors are ecstatic about my recovery—but old Professor Atkinson says otherwise."

"What does he say?"

"That I'm going to die."

"DIE?"

"Not today or tomorrow—but in time, like everyone else. He says I hurt myself too badly playing the big hero. Whatever it was that's kept me around so long isn't there any more."

She returned to the bench and sat down, dazed and shaken.

"Why didn't you tell me this before?"

"I tried to, but you weren't in a listening mood."

After a moment, she looked up at me.

"Is this more of your showboating?"

I turned to leave.

"Oh, don't be so touchy. What am I supposed to think? You have the nerve to come over here and tell me that all that guff you gave me about our relationship was a big fat mistake. Do you expect me just to wilt and sigh with gratitude now and believe you didn't mean all of those things?"

"Look," I said, "You called me an insensitive arrogant jerk. And you were right. But what I said then is not the way I feel now, today. Maybe it took a cataclysmic change inside me to change my mind, but it's happened. Now don't you make the same mistake I did."

"What do you mean?"

"I came over here to tell you that I love you. To say that I want us to go ahead and make plans to spend a life together. I know I've hurt you. I don't blame you for being angry and resentful. But don't let some misguided, stupid things I said come between us and our future. If you do, then we're back to ground zero."

Her eyes looked into mine long and hard, measuring my commitment, testing my honesty.

"You really aren't feeling well, are you?" she said.

"Not particularly."

She got up and came over to me. "Come back here and sit with me a minute."

She led me back to the bench, a babysitter taking a damp child to the bathroom.

The park was quiet, except for the singsong chatter of sparrows playing in the treetops. I could smell the freshly cut grass, still wet with dew. It should have been a beautiful morning.

She folded her hands in her lap, then looked up at me. "I'm sorry. I guess I..."

"You don't have anything to apologize for," I said. "I'm the insensitive one here."

I watched her face as she struggled with her feelings, waiting for her to find her way back—for the both of us. At last, the ice melted and the dam broke, washing away the fear and anger. I could see Allison, my Allison, coming back to me. I held my breath as the warmth flooded back into her eyes and color returned to her cheeks. Then she lifted her chin and smiled.

"Well then, I won't waste an apology if it isn't absolutely necessary."

I wrapped my arms tightly around her and she nestled her face against my jacket. We stood like that for a long time, holding each other, rocking back and forth as one. Then I realized she was crying again.

"Hey, what silliness is this..?"

"I'm afraid for you," she sniffled. "What if you're not going to be all right? What'll we do?"

"We're not going to worry about that," I said. "We're going to make our plans, the two of us, and live our lives together for as long as we have. We'll take what comes, when it comes, just the two of us. But no matter what happens, for whatever time we have left, we'll have each other. And we'll love each other. And do you know what?"

"What?"

"We'll never be lonely again. Either of us. Ever. Apart, detached, disconnected—whatever you want to call it. Neither of us will have those feelings again—not while we have each other. End of speech."

She looked up at me with those incredible baby blues, smiled—and squeezed me hard around the waist.

"Forever, Andrew," she said. "Forever."

Oh, that sounded good.

About the Author

Robert Wetherall lives with his wife Ronni and their dog Katie in Shorewood, a lake country village west of Minneapolis, Minnesota. After a creative career as an advertising/promotion writer and broadcast producer, Robert turned to writing novels and screenplays.

His first novel, THE MAKING OF BERNIE TRUMBLE, was published several years ago.

FOREVER ANDREW represents his latest effort, although a third novel is in the pipeline for publication next year.

Wetherall's work views the universe through a unique looking glass—resulting in stories rich in humor and warmth.

FOREVER ANDREW embodies the storytelling power that has delighted readers everywhere.